MOONSHADOWS

Books by Keith Halliday

The MacBride Yukon Kids Series
Aurore of the Yukon
Yukon Secret Agents
Yukon River Ghost
Game on, Yukon!

Other books
The Tar Sands Diplomat

MOONSHADOWS

A Yukon-noir climate thriller

Keith Halliday

Klondike
Samizdat
Press

Published by Klondike Samizdat Press
Whitehorse, Yukon

ISBN 978-1-7382780-0-8

For Yukoners who like a good story
on a long winter's night.

Well it's God's own neon green above
the mountains here tonight

Throwing brittle coloured shadows on the snow

It's four more hours til dawn, and the gas is almost gone

And that bitter Yukon wind begins to blow

Stan Rogers, *Canol Road*

A few years in the future...

Violence Feared at Tonight's Winter Solstice Climate Vigil
The Yukon Sun / Dec. 21 4:00 p.m.
By Winter Slade

Breaking news - updates to follow.

Whitehorse police are bracing for another bout of violence between Greens and the Freedom Movement at the Yukon Climate Collective's annual Winter Solstice Climate Vigil, planned for tonight at the Northern Lights liquefied natural gas facility.

The vigil marks the first anniversary of carbon rationing and the Climate Emergency Act, put in place after last year's unprecedented wildfires and the ongoing climate refugee crisis. Tensions remain high after the recent firebombing of Yukon Climate Collective headquarters.

"As if the Wildfires weren't enough, the fact that climate refugees from places like Guatemala are desperate enough to pay Alaskan people smugglers to drop them off at the border in the middle of nowhere tells us that the Climate Emergency is real," said Yukon Climate Collective campaign lead Brett Schleicher on social media. "Yukoners will not be intimidated. We will keep fighting to stop LNG now."

Freedom Yukon did not respond to requests for comment. According to a Signal group message obtained by the *Sun*, "Tonight is a chance for Yukoners to take back our country from out of touch Green elites who use climate as an excuse to shut down Yukon jobs and freedom while China keeps burning coal."

Police are asking Yukoners to avoid the Northern Lights facility this evening and, if they do attend, to remain peaceful and follow instructions from law enforcement.

1

Chadburn Lake Road

11pm, Winter Solstice - December 21st. -22°C

Frozen gravel rattled loudly off the pickup's floorpan as Winter gunned the truck along Chadburn Lake Road. He gripped the steering wheel tightly through his mitts, squinting into the dark through the frosted windshield. The snow swirled distractingly in the truck's single working headlight.

"Fucking useless electric defrosters," he said to Tarfu. The dog in the passenger seat did not respond. Despite Tarfu's normally uncanny instinct for when his humans were going off piste, he had not yet clued in that this was not the usual ride to the ski trails.

Winter knew he should check the speedometer. But it didn't matter. He already knew he was going way too fast, and it was too risky to take his eyes off the road. Slowing down was no option either. Brett was way ahead of him, and Chaewon's words kept racing through his mind.

He's got something special planned tonight.

What kind of something?

He wouldn't tell me. Something big.

Big enough to explain why there was an empty box from Alaska marked "Caution - Explosive Material" in Brett's office?

Winter's mind raced. Had it been smart to jump into Taiya's pickup and take off after Brett, alone with nothing but skis and a towering personal mushroom cloud of rage?

Probably not. But it was too late for second thoughts. Winter steered the truck up Chadburn hill. Now a scene from high school flashed into his brain: going uphill, too much power to the rear wheels, and into the ditch. His principal joked to the class: "If your parents pick a name like Winter, you should learn to drive on snow."

Winter felt the rear end wobble as the wheels slipped. He steered into the correction and took his foot off the pedal. As the pickup straightened, he slowly reapplied the power.

Fuck you, Mr Arsenault.

The truck crested the summit as the road turned left. The pickup's upward momentum took the weight off the tires. But Winter was ready for this and was already slowing down and steering into the inside, oncoming lane. If someone was driving a real clunker with no headlights, this was going to end now.

But it was Chadburn Lake Road. No one was coming.

Winter felt the truck accelerate on the steep downhill.

About halfway down, he realized this corner might be different.

This time, so did Tarfu. In his peripheral vision, Winter saw the dog -- a husky cross with reddish fur -- tense up and glance nervously his way.

Winter tried to apply the brakes without going into the ditch. The truck's wheels slid on the ice. The right hand turn at the bottom of the hill was getting closer, fast. The pickup's rear end started to slip left.

Option 1: try to take the corner, and probably go sideways into the ditch and roll.

Option 2: give up, and drive straight off the road into the snowbank.

Winter picked option 2.

The truck burst through the snowbank and bounced through the ditch. Winter gripped the steering wheel as everything else in the cab seemed to levitate around him. For a second, the truck cab was like a snow globe. Except instead of flakes of fake snow floating around, it was Taiya's garishly coloured nail polish bottles, dirty old Super Variant masks, a refillable coffee cup containing a brick of frozen coffee, and a startled dog.

Then the truck crashed back into the snow and through a stand of willows that somehow survived the Wildfires. Tarfu and all the formerly floating cab debris crashed into a pile on the floor.

The dog looked up reproachfully at his human. Winter breathed out and relaxed his grip on the wheel. "You're just lucky the Wildfires got rid of the big trees."

Winter jammed his hands into his pockets and pulled out his ski wax.

"Why do I always have the wrong wax? Fuck!"

Winter fired the Swix red onto the pickup's floor. What were the chances Taiya had wax in her pickup? Medium. She was a competitive skier. He glanced at the nail polish bottles. She was also a teenage girl.

He glanced at Tarfu. The dog, normally calm, looked worried. He was channeling his husky ancestors, as if he was wondering if this human outing was going to turn into one of those sled-dog expeditions where they ran out of food and tried to eat the dogs.

"I know, calm down," said Winter. He took three deep breaths, like the podcast guy said.

But not too calm. He still had to catch Brett and stop the madness. And if you needed to beat the crap out of someone, a bit of crazy was handy.

He slipped his headlamp over his toque and clicked it on. Winter picked the rest of the junk out of the console and fired it out of the way piece by piece. A tire pressure gauge. A broken phone charger. An empty box of biathlon ammo, and a *Greta Still Says Blah Blah Blah* wristband.

No wax.

Whatever. This was the bonus of never cleaning your skis, he thought. The wax left over from last time was probably fine. He clicked off the headlamp and pushed the door open into the willows.

Plus Brett is a terrible skier, Winter thought as he grabbed his skis from the pickup box. He skis like a guy from Toronto. Like a guy who didn't spend his childhood shivering in the dark practicing his kick with the Orange Squad kids whose parents all secretly hoped they'd make the Olympics.

Winter clicked on his skis, stuffed his mitts through the straps, and skied away from the truck.

His ski tips sliced through the snow like salmon fins in a shallow creek, but with a sharp hiss. This feels good, he thought, as he got into stride and sucked in the cold air. The fresh snow fell back into the track and covered the tops of his favourite old Rossignols. He quickened his pace.

Tarfu trotted effortlessly behind him, stopping occasionally to sniff yellow snow. Dog, fox, coyote, beer-drinking human. The usual.

The night was mostly clear. Just a few clouds and a few snowflakes, either falling or blowing around in the wind. The Big Dipper was north, over town. The half moon was so bright you didn't need a headlamp. The blackened stumps from the Wildfires and the edges of Winter's ski tracks cast sharp shadows. He curved around some deadfall.

At Minus Twenty, you didn't really need wax anyway.

Winter saw one of the new Volkswagen electric campervans parked near Schwatka Lake. It was in one of those pullouts where it used to be nice to have a barbeque on a summer day. When there was still a forest.

It was hard to tell the colour in the dark, but it was definitely Brett's van. They were so expensive there weren't many in town, and he recognized the bumper stickers. Earth First. Carbon-Free Yukon!

Eaglecrest - Alaska's Best-Kept Ski Secret. Brett didn't just put bumper stickers on this vehicle. He curated them. His van was a rolling Instagram post. There had to be some carefully chosen mountain biking and paddling stickers hidden under the snow. But nothing tacky like an inspirational saying.

How many climate bunnies from Outside had woken up in that creep's van, he wondered, stinking of weed and thinking their Yukon summer adventure was off to a great start?

Somebody's daughters. Like Taiya.

Winter skied up to the van, pulled off his headlamp, and held it against the glass on the driver's window. He clicked it on for a second. Sorel boots. An empty duffle bag. And ripped cardboard packaging for a propane torch. He clicked off the headlamp.

Brett's ski tracks leaving the van were easily visible in the moonlight. They were partly covered by pulk marks.

Winter felt the nervous tension come back to his gut. What could Brett be planning that needed a sled full of stuff and a fucking propane torch? He pushed off with his poles and took off after Brett.

This might get messy. He wished somebody bigger was with him. Like Nestor, and with an ax handle in those giant hands of his. Or, even better, a 12-gauge.

The south wind bit into his left cheek as he glided down the bank onto the frozen lake. Brett's tracks still had sharp edges. He wasn't that far behind. He stepped into Brett's broken trail, and kept going. It was hard work. The snow under the crust was sugary, and his ski sloughed to one side or the other each stride.

Instagram Brett would be wearing his retro three-pin Karhus. They had better flotation on the lake's untracked snow, plus metal edges for cutting through the wind crust. And they were undeniably cooler.

But I'm in better shape than him, thought Winter. I'll just follow in his tracks, catch up, and put a stop to the madness. Right now.

Brett's tracks curved towards the dam. Winter stopped and pulled his toque down over his ears. Could Brett be planning one of his protest theatre stunts at the dam? Climb the tower and unfurl a banner with a snappy slogan? Then why the explosives?

His body fell into its familiar skiing rhythm, while his mind raced ahead.

Did Brett not know how thin the ice would be near the intake?

Going through the ice would be a senseless cheechako move. But it *would* solve the Brett problem once and for all.

But why at night? Why alone when all the protesters were at the Northern Lights LNG plant on the other side of the lake? Why the propane torch?

Brett's tracks began to curve away from the dam. Towards Northern Lights. Where the climate protest was tonight. Where Taiya was going.

But, again, why? Why didn't Brett just park beside Northern Lights? Why park across the lake and approach in the dark, alone? Winter kept up his rhythm, his legs and poles pumping. The steam from his breath pulsed ahead of him, briefly visible in the moonlight before the wind whipped it away.

And why, Winter asked himself, am I doing this? What will I do if I catch him? Other than a few hockey scuffles Winter hadn't been in a fight since Grade 8, and he lost that one. And it was hard to stay angry if you had to ski for 20 minutes first. Even if Brett desperately needed to have the crap beaten out of him.

Winter reminded himself: because of the Molotov cocktail. Because of the money. Because of the booze, drugs and Taiya.

Mainly because of Taiya.

Winter looked in the direction of Brett's tracks and saw a moonlit figure in the distance. It looked like Brett was on the edge of the dam embankment behind the LNG plant.

Winter looked down. Another set of ski tracks crossed underneath Brett's, taking a slightly different angle towards the LNG plant. The pole marks were big and round, which reminded Winter of the old gear in the rafters of the shed at the cabin. The tracks were half full of blown snow.

Winter looked around for dog tracks. Tarfu looked bored. No dog had been around lately. Who would be out skiing alone on the lake in the dark in Minus Twenty?

Winter hurried on. Despite the cold, he could feel the sweat on his forehead under his toque.

Tarfu ran ahead off the lake and up onto the embankment, where he stopped to survey the scene. Winter caught up. Brett's tracks turned off the straightest path to the LNG plant and went right along the embankment. Winter could hear voices, down and to his left.

Two crowds of protesters with headlamps faced each other, waving signs and chanting slogans into the wind. The crowd was surprisingly large and festive for almost midnight at Minus Twenty.

The two lines were lit up by the flashing white, blue and red lights of the cop cars parked in between. It was like the strobes at a rave, if the dancers were wearing parkas and the club was at the base camp of Mount Logan.

Cops stood by their cars watching both groups with their usual mix of boredom and vigilance.

Behind the Greens, the flames of a big Solstice bonfire flickered in the blowing snow. Protesters who had made bad winter clothing choices stood around it, banging their arms and stamping their feet to stay warm.

A protest ditty popped into Winter's mind:

Hey hey! Ho ho!
I'm about to lose my toes.

He looked for Taiya's red camo Team Yukon parka. But half a dozen Arctic Winter Games parkas were visible on the Green side.

Behind the Freedom protest line were a couple of brightly lit flatbed trucks and RVs. How the Freedos loved trolling the Greens, thought Winter. One flatbed had festival speakers and some people standing in snowmobile coveralls around a barbeque. The other had a hot tub on the back. The people in the hot tub were waving at the Greens. Winter could hear a Beach Boys tune through gusts of wind.

But where is Brett, thought Winter? What hare-brained stunt could that guy have in mind to top the Freedo hot tubs? Then he saw Brett in the moonlight along the embankment, kneeling beside his sled. The blue flame of a propane torch stabbed brightly into the night.

Time to get this over with. He turned his skis towards Brett and strode forward.

Then everything stopped.

A bright flash filled the valley, sending angular shadows across the snow at the speed of light.

A split second later Winter flinched as the shock wave pulsed onto his face and ears. A giant hand seemed to squeeze his heart. The boom came next. The valley shook like someone pulled the trigger on a million shotguns at once.

An enormous flame shot into the sky. Jagged shadows danced on the snow.

Winter instinctively held his hand up to shield his eyes from the brightness. He stared in amazement at the flame.

He was snapped out of his trance when a chunk of pipe came crashing down out of the sky twenty feet away, and lay sizzling in the snow.

Tarfu was already long gone.

Down at the LNG plant, the headlamp beams bounced over the snow as protesters fled. But not all of them. Some of the parka-clad figures were lying in the snow with their headlamps shining at odd angles up into the blowing snow, not moving.

Taiya.

Winter didn't even think of Brett as he planted his poles, jump-turned, and launched himself down the embankment.

SUMMER - SIX MONTHS EARLIER

2

Winter's living room, Riverdale

12:10 p.m., June 21st - Summer Solstice. +17°C
2089 days sober

Tarfu snoozed in the sun on the couch in front of Winter's living room window. It was his favourite spot. He could keep an eye out for foxes trespassing in the front yard, see his food bowl in the kitchen and -- most importantly -- watch the side door where Winter kept the bike helmet and bear spray that signalled the possibility of a run.

A husky cross like Tarfu is born to run. They go squirrely if they don't get enough exercise. Much like Tarfu's owner, who at that moment was sitting on a kitchen chair in the middle of the living room wearing shorts and a tattered old Buckwheat Ski Classic t-shirt.

Winter looked like most of the other white, thirty-something guys in Whitehorse, except without the emerging pot belly or questionable mustache. His fit, thin body was erect, his slightly-too-long brown hair cascaded over his closed eyes, and the earbud wires connected to the phone in his right hand indicated he was deep inside his mindfulness app.

He breathed out and removed the earbuds. He opened his eyes and stretched his arms and legs. The sandal tan lines on his feet were getting more distinct, which was the sign of a good summer. Tarfu watched him through half-closed eyes. No movement to the bike helmet, yet. Winter unlocked his phone and opened IAmSober. 2089 days. One more than yesterday. Today's photo was of a moose hunting trip with a much younger Taiya. He went through the ritual: read his commitment to himself, read his commitment to Taiya and scroll through the photos to remind him why. The totaled vehicle. Taiya as a twelve-year-old with her scar vivid in the sunlight. A selfie of Taiya and him after she won her biathlon medal at the Arctic Winter Games.

Then he stood up. His grandmother used to say he was a bit too thin. If she was still alive, she would have said his eyes were a bit too sad.

He walked to the door and stuffed his left foot into a mud-splattered hiking shoe. Before he had tied the laces Tarfu was already standing by the door. The dog didn't want to miss a chance for a run. He didn't know it was Summer Solstice and they'd definitely be going for a long midnight ride that night.

He watched Winter open the garage and choose a bike. Tarfu knew the orange and green bikes meant serious rides. He didn't understand, and wouldn't have cared, that the orange bike had fat tires for snow and the green one sported a carbon frame and full suspension for technical riding.

The dog was disappointed to see Winter choose the white bike, which was for leisurely rides downtown. Winter considered his fixed-up 1992 Rocky Mountain Fusion hardtail expendable. He didn't mind locking it up downtown among the bike thieves with cordless grinders and opioid addicts in need of a few bucks.

Winter jammed earphones into his ears and stuffed the cord into his breast pocket. He never played anything on his earphones while riding. That was how you got killed by a car or a bear. But they worked great to avoid talking to people. It was a small town. The trails would be packed on the way downtown on a Saturday morning.

As Winter mounted his bike, he heard his phone ping in his pocket. It was the tone Taiya had matched to her Signal profile in his phone. He was late. Again.

He pulled out of the driveway and accelerated down the street towards what, before the Wildfires, had been called the greenbelt. Tarfu ran effortlessly beside him, just behind and to the right. Good bike dog.

Tarfu scanned ahead. A human might have remarked on the puffy donut-shaped PowerBlimp hanging in the distance over the blackened stumps along the river. Not Tarfu. He was looking for more immediate and important things. Perhaps a neighbourhood dog. Or a raven picking at a discarded Kentucky Fried Chicken box. Or maybe, like last week, a coyote with a housecat in its mouth.

Being an outdoor cat in Whitehorse was more dangerous than usual. You can't escape up a tree the Wildfires incinerated.

At the end of the street where the houses were being rebuilt after the Wildfires, Winter waved to the builders taking a smoke break by their trucks. Tarfu scanned the group expectantly.

There he was! One of the builders gave a whistle and reached into his construction belt. Tarfu accepted the treat, allowed his neck to be scratched, and sprinted to catch up with Winter.

The clicking of Tarfu's claws on the pavement ended as he splashed through a mud puddle and followed Winter onto the greenbelt trail.

Tarfu scanned the greenbelt for action. Instead, there was just an older couple, walking downtown. A human would have described them as white, older and dressed like retired teachers. Which they were. But to Tarfu, they didn't have a dog, a ball or anything of interest.

But they did have something neither Tarfu nor Winter knew about, although after growing up in a small town Winter should have known. That was a grudge. Winter was a funny guy when he got talking, and had a talent for memorable put downs. They weren't memorable to Winter, who usually forgot them immediately, but the victims tended to remember them once they heard third-hand what Winter had said.

The old woman was Winter's teacher from Grade 3. The old man was her husband, Winter's former principal. Tarfu didn't do email, and couldn't know the retired principal now spent most of his time on conspiracy websites and regularly forwarded items to Winter about the climate illuminati with suggestions on stories to cover. Winter mostly ignored these except by replying "Merry Christmas!" once a year.

The man said hello to Winter and stopped walking as if he wanted to chat. Winter waved, pointed at his earphones, and cruised by.

"Remember his hippie mom at parent teacher interviews?" said Winter's Grade 3 teacher. "She would never believe how much the other boys made fun of that name."

"Hard to believe his dad went for it. Straight up mining engineer."

"Well that's why that marriage was doomed from the start. You could see it."

"Always thought Winter had a lot of potential," said his old principal. "Too bad." He went silent, remembering the time Winter sent him a fake letter from the Minister of Education awarding him the Yukon Principal of the Year award. He had believed it. Even showed up wearing a tie at the Minister of Education's office for the supposed award ceremony.

After that the students and staff referred to him as "Poty" -- Principal of the Year -- for the rest of his career.

You don't ever really forgive that kind of thing.

In one of the backyards that backed onto the former greenbelt, a man was hacking at a stump. He stood up and waved a sooty hand at Winter. Who waved back and, much to Tarfu's satisfaction, kept rolling. Winter didn't have time to talk to the guy about how Tesla lobbyists covered up the carbon emissions from mining lithium. Or about how his wife still expected him to pull stumps out of the backyard, even after she kicked him out for ruining yet another dinner party with her tree-hugging friends.

Tarfu's ears twitched as he saw a dog ahead. It was a Doberman cross. Normally Tarfu would stop and sniff any dog. But this dog was stupid, aggressive and -- how sad -- tied to a baby carriage. Tarfu didn't break his stride.

The two women with the dog ignored them in return. Like Winter, they were BNRs - born and raised Yukoners. They had been in Winter's classes all through high school. They hadn't spoken to him then since they were too cool. They weren't cool anymore. Powerwalking in optimistically sized Lululemon exercise tights wasn't cool. Neither was stalking old friends on Facebook because you were the local rep for a beauty and lifestyle pyramid sales scheme. So the reason they didn't talk to him now was the accident.

"I can't believe he hasn't left town," said SkinTastic, pushing her stroller through a mud puddle. "Or that his daughter still talks to him."

"The scar is still so visible!" exclaimed HealthyChef.

Tarfu was too young to remember, but they were talking about the time Winter rolled his truck. He was blottoed on booze and Oxy. Taiya was in her carseat when Winter rolled the vehicle off a soft shoulder on the Alaska Highway while speeding past the Airport Chalet. The chainsaw bounced up off the car floor. An inch to the left and it would have killed the little girl. But it mostly missed, and just left a jagged bloody cut from her temple past her ear.

Head wounds bleed a lot, and the off duty paramedic who saw the crash and waded through thigh deep snow to the vehicle found Taiya hanging upside down in her carseat with her dad in hysterics pressing a bloody t-shirt onto her wound.

At the hospital, the nurses wouldn't let Winter see Taiya. The cops handcuffed him to his bed, which meant he couldn't get away when his wife Misty burst into the room to beat him with a broom until the nurses dragged her away.

Thanks to Facebook, the whole town knew about the drama about two minutes later.

"Misty never should've married him," said HealthyChef.

"Those sex ed videos were right: A broken condom at the Aftergrad can change your life." They laughed, and not in a nice way.

"But Misty was too young. She should have ended it."

Both thought of SkinTastic's abortion in high school. Neither mentioned it. Neither did they mention how much people had laughed at the Grade 12 New Year's party when Winter said that HealthyChef was so fat it would be like having sex with a waterbed.

"Amber still talks to him."

"That's only because she wants him to put stories about her protests in the paper."

Amber was also in Winter's high-school class. Winter's James-Bond-loving editor at the *Yukon Sun* called her the "Blonde Villain" behind the Freedom protests. She had better political instincts than any of the professional politicians in the Legislature. It turned out that being a hot, popular party organizer in high school had been excellent training for mobilizing the Freedos, the loose movement of anti-vax, anti-carbon-tax and anti-refugee obsessives who Winter spent far more time covering than he liked.

On the other hand, and he would never admit this, he secretly enjoyed watching an esthetician who didn't quite make it through high school run circles around the professional Green activists and comms weasels in the Cabinet Office.

Tarfu heard the noise a second before Winter did. There was a clatter as a biker came fast down the side of Crocus Hill. The rider crouched low over the bike with his weight back as he weaved through trees at speed on a steep downhill.

Winter stopped where the rider's trail would join the main track. It was Nestor Tkachenko. Winter pulled the earphones out of his ears and watched. Lots of guys thought they were technical bikers, but Nestor made them look like Jerrys.

Nestor tilted his handlebars to miss a tree, then steered his front wheel over a root and ran out the final descent before stopping in front of Winter.

Nestor and the bike were splashed with mud, some mangled willow leaves dangled from the front brakes, and Nestor's left leg showed scratches and a few drops of dried blood. On the frame, two mud-free strips indicated he had either needed to use his spare tube or it had been ripped off.

"Living the dream, I see!" said Winter.

"It was okay," replied Nestor with his Ukrainian accent, panting. He squared his massive shoulders and stood up to his full height, well over six feet, and took a squirt of water. Still standing over his bike, he did a hip rotation to stretch out his left leg and looked down at the dried blood on his calf. Which he ignored.

He sprayed some more water on his face which dripped down onto the shirt clinging to his pecs.

This was the kind of thing, thought Winter, that keeps the women in the newsroom talking about Nestor. Winter's editor described him as the perfect man, capable of jumping both you and your truck, and not bothering you with a lot of talk.

"We ride tomorrow? Money Shot?"

"Yep."

"Good. I text you." Tarfu had trotted over to Nestor. The dog had sensed long before that the man was some kind of Alpha human. After Nestor leaned down and rubbed the dog's neck, he gave Winter a two finger salute off his helmet and accelerated away.

Nestor wasn't a BNR. He didn't have a grudge against Winter, because Winter had never thought of anything funny to say about him. And even if he had, Nestor wouldn't have cared.

He'd only been in the Yukon a few years. He was originally from Ukraine. One of the many things he didn't talk about was what he did during the war. But the rumours said he grew up just outside the Chernobyl nuclear disaster zone, and was a coder in Kyiv before the Russian invasion. He had a layer of legend around him that just kept getting thicker. People said he was named after a famous Ukrainian revolutionary. He spent two years on the front line around Kharkiv. He was a sniper with 52 kills. He destroyed a tank with a Molotov cocktail. He crawled into Russian trenches at night and slit the throats of napping sentries with a box cutter.

It bugged the young bikers who grew up in suburban Toronto. Their stories of gnarly jumps or van trips around Alaska didn't impress the girls much when Nestor was sitting around the campfire, and everyone knew he had just solo-biked the North Canol trail or dragged a backcountry skier with a broken femur out from Sharkfin on an improvised sled.

Winter liked his no-bullshit love of skiing and biking. And how he had adapted so enthusiastically to the Yukon. He lived in an offgrid cabin near Annie Lake and helped an aging trapper on his line across the valley. If your snowmobile got stuck, Nestor could just yank it out of the deep snow like a piece of luggage.

And he did all of this with no Instagram, TikTok or Facebook to show it off on. The only way you could reach the guy was through his retro Nokia brick phone, and that only worked when he was in town.

Tarfu followed Winter at a trot as they turned onto the Lewes Boulevard bike path and crossed the bridge to downtown. In the distance, the dog saw Taiya beside the Old Fire Hall holding a bright-pink protest sign. He shot forward.

By the time Winter caught up, Tarfu was already jumping up and down like he'd won the lottery.

"He really loves you," said Winter.

"He loves everyone. He's got no filter." She crouched and let Tarfu lick her face. "Nice kisses, yes."

"Thanks for taking him. I have to cover-" -- he decided not to mention the dead body -- "a story. Pick him up tonight?"

"No problem. He can work with me at YCC," she replied with a smile. Taiya claimed Tarfu was the most popular staff dog at Yukon Climate Collective; the anti-mining guy's labradoodle didn't even come close.

Winter watched her switch to her serious face. "You said you wouldn't ride without your helmet, Dad." She could raise one eyebrow like her mom.

"Thank you for reminding me, daughter. I just forgot."

"You forget a lot."

It felt strange to be lectured by his daughter. But he also liked how it showed she cared about him. That always gave him a sense of surprised well-being. And, as his editor liked to say, somebody had to be the adult in their relationship.

3

Canada Customs, Beaver Creek, Yukon

12:18 p.m., June 21st - Summer Solstice. +21°C

On the straight stretch about two kilometres on the Alaska side of Canada Customs, a little orange electric car pulled out from behind the big Freightliner tractor-trailer and zipped past going thirty over the speed limit.

That's fine, thought the rig's driver. Go ahead and show off your electric motor's fucking torque. I'll drive past as you're sitting around recharging that thing in Beaver Creek.

In the distance, two dots on the highway shoulder grew bigger. Two vehicles with people standing around. A breakdown? There was no traffic for miles, so the truck driver let the rig drift left over the yellow line to give them more space.

The dots grew into a State Trooper cruiser and a van. The trooper was leaning on the hood of his cruiser, arms crossed, watching the people beside the van. The driver recognized the van from the diner parking lot in Tok. An old fifteen passenger cruise ship van, now painted with a giant Alaska flag and a soaring American eagle. And a lot of Alaska First and Sarah Palin stickers.

Behind the van stood a handful of people with luggage. Jesus, Boat People on the road to Beaver Creek. They didn't have backpacks, but suitcases and a blue Ikea shopping bag stuffed with random shit. A guy in a baseball cap and camo t-shirt was pointing at a trail into the bush.

A kid wearing some kind of turban was looking the other way; at the oncoming rig. He was in a t-shirt and flip flops with a Spiderman roller bag. He waved at the rig.

The boy was probably peewee age, about the same as her youngest. Fucking unbelievable. She waved back and pulled the horn. Kids loved the horn.

The boy jumped at the horn blast, then waved again. There was a huge smile on his face as the truck blew past.

She glanced in the rearview mirror. The Pakistanis, or whoever they were, were trudging off the highway towards the trail. The van pulled a u-turn, followed by the State Trooper, and accelerated back towards Tok.

So it was that easy. The governor offered you five hundred bucks to move on from Alaska, and some helpful guys from Alaska First picked you up at the hostel and drove you to the Canadian border. And Customs and the Canadian government just sat there like morons while the Pakistanis walked over the border and signed up for lawyers and welfare.

And if it was that easy smuggling people, no wonder the preppers had no problem getting AR-15s and ammo across.

The truck rounded the last corner before Customs. Get back on task, the driver thought to herself. She did a quick check of the speedometer and the dashboard clock. Just under the speed limit. 12:18 p.m., Yukon time. Perfect.

Canada Customs came into view. She took her foot off the gas and prepared to downshift.

She hadn't driven an 18-speed transmission in years. But it was all coming back from that summer driving truck with her dad. It was like riding a bike.

The key thing to remember was that a forty-foot container with a twenty-thousand litre US Army Mil-Spec bladder full of diesel was way heavier than it looked. She did the mental math: litres to kilos, kilos to pounds, pounds to the weight limit.

A real Customs guy might notice that the truck was sitting much lower than what was listed on the manifest. That's why getting to Customs at least fifteen minutes after shift change was key.

So was having a girl at the wheel. She took off her sunglasses, checked her hair in the mirror and adjusted the push-up bra under her tank top.

She did some more math: start with the difference between what Yukon placer miners would pay for diesel minus the Alaska price. A dozer might have a 900-litre tank, and you didn't haggle much if your mine was about to shut down because you'd used up your carbon ration. Say that was a buck a litre to be conservative. Multiply by twenty-thousand litres.

Not bad for a drive to Tok.

As long as this border thing worked.

She worked the splitter, clutch and range selector: six-hi, six-lo, five-hi, five-lo, all the way down.

She lowered the window and leaned her arm on the sill as she rolled slowly into Customs. Their guy stepped out from the booth. No one else was around. He was wearing sunglasses, a bullet-proof vest and the usual Batman belt of Customs action-man accessories. Like a Chinese gang was about to attack. What a doofus.

But their doofus.

She smiled her biggest, blondest smile. "Hey, how's it goin'?"

After customs, as she rolled through Beaver Creek -- very carefully not speeding; this was no time to get pulled over -- she saw the orange electric vehicle parked beside Beaver Creek's only public charger. The driver was standing beside the charging station, reading the screen with the plug in his hand.

I hope it's fucking broken again, she thought, and you get to spend the day playing pool at Ida's Lounge.

4

Waterfront trail behind the Old Fire Hall

12:30 p.m., June 21st - Summer Solstice. +18°C
2089 days sober

Tarfu was the first to notice someone approaching up the Waterfront Trail from behind Winter and Taiya. He turned in excitement, always ready to make a new best friend. Winter saw that it was Echo, the new CBC reporter from Ontario with the pink hair streaks, sparkly nose stud and distractingly tight shirts.

She squatted and stroked Tarfu's reddish blonde fur. "Aww, cute little freckles on his nose! What kind of dog?"

"He's a rescue dog, from Watson Lake," said Taiya.

"For some reason they only rescue dogs from Watson Lake," said Winter. "The people there are SOL."

Echo laughed nervously; Watson Lake was half indigenous, but it *was* a shithole. She squirmed as Tarfu tried to lick her face. Her low-rise capris stretched down, revealing panties that had definitely not been purchased at Mark's Work Wearhouse and what, had she been male and a hundred pounds heavier, would have been called a plumber's crack.

She was slim and pretty, tended to preface questions with "As an Anishinaabe journalist," and had caused the Minister of Community Services to forget his talking points at her first press conference in Whitehorse. She was in the front row and raised her hand to ask a question, causing her shirt to lift up and reveal a taut midriff with an indigenous tattoo snaking up out of her pants.

Winter's editor, who was several waistline-expanding Yukon winters past wearing crop tops herself, had predicted drama on the co-ed media slowpitch team that summer.

"Part yellow lab?" asked Echo.

"No idea. He's a Yukon special," replied Winter.

"Sit, Tarfu," said Taiya, crouching beside Echo and snapping on Tarfu's leash. Winter saw the scar coming down out of her hairline in front of her ear. It was a constant reminder.

As if he needed one.

Taiya smiled at Echo. "He's definitely a rescue dog, but did my dad rescue him or did he rescue my dad?"

She gave a little wave, first at Winter and then at Echo, and jogged off to her shift at YCC.

"I assume you're also heading down to the scene of the crime?" asked Winter. Echo didn't have a bike, and it would take longer walking, but it was never a bad thing to get to know the new journalists in town.

"Crime? I thought it was a drowning."

Winter shrugged.

"Was that your daughter?" Echo asked as they walked, a hint of incredulity in her voice.

Which part was hard to believe? That Winter was old enough to have a daughter going into Grade 12? Or that he could be the father of such a mature, well-adjusted person?

He increasingly felt like the weird old guy of the newsroom. All the journalists his age now had government comms jobs that paid twice as much. No one else's iPhone listed IAmSober as a Top Five app. When the media went for drinks, he ordered cranberry and soda. When they got to the third round and he felt the urge growing, he just went home. Most of them grew up Outside and considered Whitehorse a temporary adventure to kickstart their careers; he was a BNR. He had a daughter who wasn't much younger than the new J-school grads. And more mature than most of them.

"Oh! I know your daughter," said Echo, finally making the connection. "She does Brett's social media stuff at YCC."

"Brett loves teenage volunteers: digital, and free." Winter hated talking about Brett. Time to change the subject. "What are you working on?"

"Something on the Freedos harassing the refugee hostel. And then the opioid announcement."

"Yeah, Eamon's covering that. I told him his headline should be 'Government announces Year 17 of opioid crisis action plan.'"

Echo walked silently. Everyone clammed up when ex-opioid addicts mentioned opioids. Even his disastrous divorce was considered a more suitable conversation topic. A teenage boy wearing a YCC t-shirt zipped past on an e-scooter. Winter suppressed an urge to straight arm the boy and tell him to get a real bike.

The boy's t-shirt brought Echo's thoughts back to Brett.

"Brett and Chaewon told me they're going to have a huge crowd at their next protest. *Way-y-y* bigger than the Freedos will get out," said

Echo. "They're partnering with First Nation Climate Alliance." Winter eyed her sideways through his sunglasses. Did she want to be liked, or be a good journalist? You couldn't be both in a small town.

Should he tell her it was Brett's job to spin the numbers; too important to delegate to Chaewon, however relentlessly competent she might be? And the First Nation Climate Alliance was a Facebook page and three people, one of whom never showed up.

Echo's question to the Minister had actually been pretty good. He would have stumbled on it even if he wasn't staring at her tattoo.

"I'm betting the crowd will be *way-y-y* smaller than the climate protests after the Wildfires," he replied. "Take a picture and then compare it to the photos online." Winter opened his phone and pulled up a drone photo from one of his old stories. He pointed out how far the crowd spilled up Main Street.

Echo leaned in closer to make a shadow so she could see the screen better. She ran a finger through some stray pink hair to put it behind her ear, then grabbed Winter's hand to tilt the angle and reduce the glare.

Her breast brushed Winter's elbow. He froze and kept his eyes glued to the phone. Don't be the creep who looks down her shirt, he thought. It had been a long time for Winter, and she was delicious and new to town. But she was also barely older than Taiya.

He needed to find someone age appropriate. Someone who was a good role model for Taiya, plus single, cute, funny, athletic and who didn't mind a teenage daughter. Or a cranky ex-wife in a lesbian marriage to a politician on the make. Or a lot of questions about what it was like dating an ex-Oxy addict who didn't drink, smoke or drive. Oh, and she needed good technical mountain biking and backcountry skiing skills too.

"The granolas might think they have smarter chants," continued Winter as they walked. "But Freedo rallies are more fun." He googled "Yukon Freedom hot tub" and found a photo of Amber's husband Zach at the wheel of a flatbed truck with a hot tub, barbecue and giant sound system. This time he handed the phone to Echo.

"I was thinking my angle would be something on the intersectional impacts of climate change. I should be able to get some good quotes from indigenous women and the Two-Spirit Community."

"I was just thinking of reporting what happened. Which I'm guessing will be that the Freedos have a bigger crowd."

"That'll be a depressing story! Racists. Climate change deniers. Evangelicals. Right wing American funding. Basically fascists." The words were like an incantation from Justice Studies 301 at Carleton.

"But that *is* the story," replied Winter. He was beginning to get just a little nervous. How much of this conversation was going to end up on X? "What started as anti-vax wingnuts after COVID-19 has morphed into our biggest political movement. The Greens are so sure they're the angels, they don't even seem to realize they're losing."

"That's depressing, Winter."

"Well, want more bad news? It's not American money and Jedi mind tricks from *Fox News*. It's that all those Canadians who show up at these rallies are really mad about not being allowed to buy gas and seeing politicians on TV acting holier than thou while boatloads of starving people from India beach themselves on Vancouver Island."

"But what about all those climate rallies? They were huge!"

"Not compared to the backlash. The climate crowds were big, but only represented a quarter of the voters. Say you're a worker at Summit Mine who just lost their job. You resent the Greens since they still have their jobs at some foreign-funded NGO or government department."

Winter went on to describe a high-school friend who commuted to a crappy job in a cheap old clunker that used his monthly carbon ration in three weeks. At the end of the month, his mom had to fill the tank. Meanwhile, he saw the Minister of Energy on the front page in her new Tesla and the premier flew to climate summits in Europe. All while Amber was sharing stories on Facebook about how the Chinese are still burning coal.

Echo walked in silence. "So my angle should be?"

"Find some First Nation nutjob in the Freedo crowd and get him to explain why the fuck he's hanging with the white crazies."

5

Bank of the Yukon River, behind Earl's

1:05 p.m., June 21st - Summer Solstice. +19°C
2089 days sober

"Drowned? Opioids?" asked Winter. He recognized the cop from Oldtimers hockey. They had both turned 35 and joined the league the same year. He was from back East, somewhere like Thunder Bay.

The cop eyed Winter warily through his sunglasses. "Off the record?"

Winter nodded. "I'll ask you an official question later." The cop and Winter were standing in six inches of water in the marshy grass beside the Yukon river, behind the Earl's restaurant. The cop had high rubber boots and Winter was wearing urban hikers.

Echo was standing on dry land beside Winter's bike, just out of earshot.

"Not drowned," said the cop flatly. "One of the frequent flyers. She got the living shit kicked out of her. Probably went in the water up by downtown and floated down here."

Winter stepped forward for a better look at the body and felt the bite of cold water moving up his leg.

Winter bit his lip. He recognized the woman, despite the flattened nose and massive welt across her face. She had long black hair in a ponytail, always walking around Main Street, the waterfront or the grocery store parking lot. People remembered her since she always wore the same old lime green Arctic Winter Games jacket whether it was summer time or Forty Below. Usually with a big smile, like she didn't even feel the cold.

Which she probably couldn't half the time, if the ambulance crews knew her well enough to call her a frequent flyer.

Now she was laying in the weeds. Her lime green Arctics jacket was pulled down over her shoulders and held her arms like a straitjacket. She wouldn't have been able to swim even if she was sober. River weeds were tangled in her hair.

"Jesus, what would do that to your face?"

"Anything," said the cop. "Steel-toed boot maybe."

Winter remembered talking to the woman one time in Detox. She was from Pelly Crossing, and said she was born in a wall tent in the bush near Fort Selkirk. A big, messed up family, group homes, some time on Hastings in Vancouver, some time in jail in Whitehorse. Funny when she wasn't wasted, actually. Totally fucked up, but funny. It had been a learning moment for Winter when the nurse told them they were the same age. He had asked himself, do I look that awful?

Now, here she was. It was ironic, or something, that it wasn't the drugs or the booze that got her.

The cop cleared his throat. The rest of the media were showing up. Winter stood beside the cop as the rest of the Whitehorse press corps assembled with dry shoes beside Echo a few feet away. Winter retreated a few steps, pulled out his notebook and prepared for the ritual.

Someone would ask what happened. The cops would reply in that weird kind of passive language they used. A call had been received. A body had been discovered. Signs of life were not apparent. Names would not be released until next of kin had been notified. Were drugs or alcohol involved? Undetermined as yet, but tests would be performed. Was it murder? Nothing had been ruled out. The investigation was continuing. Processes would progress. Further information would be shared when and if appropriate.

The careful listener would pick up the subtext. Stop getting in our way. Stop acting like this is news - this is routine. You and your readers have no idea what really goes on down here on the waterfront.

Winter put up his hand. "Another woman drowned down here six weeks ago. Any connection?"

The cop shot him a look. Winter knew what it meant: don't you dare start a rumour that there is some kind of Highway-of-Tears series of indigenous murders that the police have ignored on the Whitehorse waterfront. No cop wanted to go through a big indigenous cold case review like in Thunder Bay. Or have the police investigated themselves as in Saskatoon, where some officers were convicted of dropping intoxicated First Nations men off for a fatal "starlight tour" at the edge of town when it was Thirty Below.

After a pause, the cop replied, "Indeterminate. Anyone else with a question?"

When it was over, Winter sloshed back through the wet grass. He stepped onto the shore by Echo. The water oozed out of his hikers.

Echo looked surprised. "I thought you were in sandals out there?"

"I wanted a look at the body. It's just water."

He decided to go chat with someone at Legal Aid. They usually knew what was happening on the waterfront. They were going to have a busy year. Any more murders and they'd have to bring up extra lawyers from Vancouver again.

Assuming the cops actually caught someone and charged them. Otherwise, thought Winter, that someone is literally going to get away with murder.

Echo looked up from the puddle oozing out of Winter's shoes. "There was a drowning down here a few weeks ago? I didn't see that in the news."

"A homeless First Nations woman drowning on the waterfront is hardly news in Whitehorse," replied Winter. Echo blinked. Here we go, he thought, she's going to call me a racist.

"What did you just say?"

"We had a tiny piece about it in the City news that day. Ask your boss why they sent you to the airport instead to cover the return of Team Yukon from the Canada Senior Games."

6

Yukon Mud Bog Races

8:15 p.m., June 21st - Summer Solstice. +16°C
2089 days sober

Winter let his bike roll to a stop by the fences around the slo-pitch fields. He pulled out his phone and checked the screenshot of the invitation a friend had sent him: "Friends of Freedom barbeque - 7pm at the Mud Bog Food Trucks. Smokies, pulled pork, drinks and 4x4 mud action!"

In the distance, beside the two mud lanes and the spectators, he could see the announcer standing on a low-boy trailer between speakers. A row of Canadian flags rippled in the light breeze behind him as he channeled his best pro wrestling announcer voice: "Tire class thirty-eight inches and up. The big boys! Finals in fifteen minutes!"

Flag girls, as they called them, scurried along the mud lanes wearing hi-viz vests while they set up the distance and finish-line flags.

Over to the left, Winter could see the rows of jacked up 4x4s as well as the kids' zone and the food trucks. The midnight sun was shining brightly and the crowd had a festive energy. People were clustered together, chatting with drinks in their hands as muddy kids chased each other around the parked trucks.

He locked his bike, before realizing that wouldn't help much if some Freedo hothead recognized him from his photo in the paper and kicked in the spokes. Too late to worry about that. He straightened his old Summit Mining ball cap, put on his sunglasses and began walking as casually as he could towards the food trucks. It reminded him of going to a grad class bush party when he was in Grade 10. Everyone was welcome, in theory, but skinny Grade 10 band kids were wise not to make themselves too obvious to the Grade 12 boys basketball team.

These days, being a member of the lamestream media was the equivalent -- worse, actually -- of being a band kid. Which explained why Winter was trying to blend in with jeans, boots and Summit Mining hat.

Winter had invited Eamon from the newsroom to come along, but he claimed he was busy. Eamon kept describing the Freedos as a "fringe" movement, which Winter thought was just bad journalistic observation. "Extreme" or "Crazy" maybe, thought Winter, but Amber's group chats had way too many recipients for the Freedos to be called "fringe."

Winter was so annoyed with Eamon's repeated failure to observe reality that he had ridden his bike to the Mud Bog Races to have a pulled-pork sandwich and check out how many pillars of the community showed up.

Sandwich in hand, he wandered the crowd making a mental note of the people hanging around Amber's food trucks. Amber was in the middle of the crowd, being her usual life-of-the-party self. She was giving tips on which food truck to try as well as making sure she had everyone's number in her phone.

Coming in person was definitely worth it. A lot of people were cagey about posting their views on social media these days. But here live he could recognize cops, government officials, teachers, business owners and even a retired judge. At the pig-roast pit he took a selfie of himself with the rotating pig, making sure to get an opposition politician talking to Zach in the background.

Then he locked himself out of sight in a Porta Potty and tapped as many names as he could remember into his phone to show Eamon.

After he stepped out of the toilet, he bought a coke and looked around some more. The sound guys were setting up on the music trailer so the band could play after the final races. Now would be a good time to leave, before the band -- advertised as "Grande Prairie's finest" -- started to do Garth Brooks covers.

"Fake news!" shouted someone behind Winter in a loud, accusing voice. Winter cringed and glanced, as naturally as he could, to make sure they weren't shouting at him.

There was a group of people clustered around someone. Mostly older men, but also a few women. Voices were rising and fingers were wagging. "Fake news!" shouted the voice again. It was a sixty-year-old man, pot belly, mesh ball cap wearing jeans with a big belt buckle.

Winter stepped sideways to get a better view.

Echo was in the middle of the circle. She looked terrified.

"I want you to erase those photos right now!" said a tall, bony woman wearing the hi-viz vest of a flag girl. She looked like the scariest Grade 6 teacher ever and punctuated her speech by pointing a finger right between Echo's eyes. "You media aren't allowed to just come in here and take pictures of whatever you want."

"Oh God," muttered Winter. It was as if Echo had gone out of her way to stick out at a Freedom rally: pink hair, a summer dress and leather boots that some designer in Manhattan thought looked rustic. And she was carrying a notepad and pencil.

It was like going backcountry skiing and taking all the precautions, then finding some noob without a beacon who's twisted their ankle in an avalanche chute. The kind of thing that puts the victim and the rescuer both in danger.

"For fuck sakes," said Winter. He took a deep breath and walked straight over to the group. "That's good you found her. She's from guess who? The fucking CBC."

"I thought so," said the man, a hint of triumph in his voice.

"Exactly," replied Winter. He looked straight at the bony-faced woman and held out his coke. "Could you hold my drink for a second? I've got to get her over to Amber."

He reached into the circle, grabbed Echo's arm and pulled her out. "Let's go. The deal was one interview with Amber. Period."

He frogmarched Echo away as quickly as he could. "Keep walking. Don't look back," he hissed.

Echo began walking more quickly. "Thanks Winter. That was … scary. Very scary."

"Don't thank me yet."

Behind him he could hear the voices starting again.

"But Amber's that way!"

"Hey, I don't want your coke."

"Was that Ken Slade's boy?"

They passed the last 4x4 and hustled down the road to the parking. Winter glanced behind. The people who had been shouting at Echo were still watching them. And there were two young men, not smiling, and walking briskly after them.

"Faster," said Winter.

Echo, however, was beginning to feel safer. "But what about media freedom?" she complained.

"Yeah, they're free to hate the media. Where's your truck?"

She pointed at a tiny orange Honda Fit electric vehicle jammed in between two 4x4s. Of course that would be her car, thought Winter.

"Okay Echo," he said, "get your keys out and … run!"

They jumped into the Honda. Echo punched the start button and put the vehicle in reverse. She backed out of the parking spot and turned the wheel. By the time she shifted into drive, one of the men was standing in front of the vehicle.

He stared expressionlessly at Echo, then at Winter. He reached slowly into his pocket and paused. Then he pulled out a can of Kokanee. He popped the top, slurped a slug of beer and then turned the can upside down over the hood of Echo's car.

She watched the beer flow out of the can onto the hood for what seemed like forever.

Then the man crumpled the can and jammed it into the Honda's grill.

"Now get this fucking golf cart out of here," he said before turning and walking away.

7

Ńjür Nàdäk'ą Development Corporation head office, Whitehorse

10:05 a.m., June 22nd. +15˚C
2090 days sober

Karen Felton checked the dashboard clock as she turned her green Nissan Leaf into the Ńjür Nàdäk'ą Development Corporation parking lot. Five minutes late. Good.

The wheels crunched to a halt on the gravel. She picked up the beaded moosehide folder with her speaking notes from the passenger seat. That elder lady in Carmacks had not been shy about the price she charged, but it was a great accessory to remind people of her commitment to reconciliation.

She opened the folder and double-checked that the speaking notes said "Northern Lights project launch" on the top. She wasn't going to get laughed at like her cabinet colleague who took the wrong speech to an event. She took a deep breath, and stepped out of the car.

She smoothed her blazer and made sure her shirt was properly tucked in. The pants were tight. Why did every winter mean tighter pants? She slammed the car door.

The other speakers were standing in the parking lot, chatting.

Smile, stand tall, walk confidently, and don't seem rushed. You have this. Easily.

"Sorry to be late! Meeting with the premier went long," she said with a wave. A power wave, like her presentation coach in Vancouver said, not one of those girl waves with the tiny T-rex arms. She scanned the group as she approached. Jim the mining CEO, check. Alex, CEO of the indigenous devcorp, check. Various ADMs and her own airheaded comms person, whatever.

"Hello, Minister!" chirped her comms person excitedly. She still wore a mask for some reason, a bright yellow one with a happy face printed in the middle.

Karen hated how no one shook hands anymore. Everyone here probably had the new multi-vax, but you never knew.

Without the chance of a firm handshake and bicep squeeze, the best she could do was give an extra nod and some bonus eye contact to the mining CEO. Sitting on a few mining boards would be a great place to land if the next election went badly.

Which it just might if this project blew up. The voters still hadn't forgiven them for the Wildfires clusterfuck.

"Shall we get this party started?" she said, not really asking. Without waiting for the others, she bounded up the steps to the front door and held it open. She smiled as the others dutifully trooped past her into the building.

The media were already in their seats. Even from the backs of their heads, she knew all the journalists. The *Whitehorse Star*'s latest C-student from Carleton J-school. CKRW and CHON-FM radio. New girl from the CBC. Even the Francophone paper had sent their intern. But no one from the *Yukon Sun*.

As the others mingled and dawdled, she moved briskly to the table to take the middle seat. Everyone needed to know their government was working hard to bring jobs and cheap energy to the Yukon and fight climate change at the same time. And that she was in the centre of it.

Except there were name cards and Alex was in the middle. Her comms person had failed to get the event to happen in Yukon Government's media room in the old cafeteria, and had failed to manage the name cards. What I wouldn't give for a competent political staffer like the federal ministers had, she thought.

Karen took her seat, sat up straight and projected a smile at the audience. Align your thoughts with the image you want to present, she remembered. This meeting is going to be positive and interesting! I'm excited to be here to share this incredibly awesome news with you!

The mining CEO sat down.

Then Alex slid into his seat beside her. The reporters stopped chattering among themselves, sat up and prepared their notepads. It was like the teacher had stepped in front of the class. The cool teacher, that everyone had a crush on.

Karen smiled and turned to Alex. It was incredibly frustrating. He was young and good looking. Incredibly good looking actually. You could see his Vuntut Gwichin roots. Something about the men up there, their broad faces and big smiles. Plus he was fit and athletic. No sign of early-thirties beer belly or thinning hair. Everyone just expected him to be sitting in the middle seat at press conferences.

He didn't flaunt his MBA, but wore the same Carhartts and rumpled flannel shirts he had as an HVAC tech out of high school. Somehow this made him look authentic, not unprofessional.

Meanwhile, she seemed to emerge from each winter just a little rounder and out of shape. She could never get her wardrobe just right. Most recently, when she tried khakis, blue shirts and a blazer, she'd heard that Misty's ex-husband Winter had described her outfit as "museum business casual from the 2001 internet bubble."

Winter was a flake, a terrible father and always smelled of sweat after arriving late by bicycle. But he had a flair for devastating one-liners that bounced around town for weeks afterwards. Like the one about museum business casual had, she remembered sourly.

The press conference began. It was already ten minutes late, and they would burn up another ten in · introductions, land acknowledgements and climate acknowledgements.

Finally, it was Karen's turn. She smiled at the audience. "I would like to acknowledge on behalf of the premier, the cabinet and all of us in the Yukon Government that we are honoured and privileged to be holding this conversation on the traditional territories of the Kwanlin Dün First Nation and the Ta'an Kwach'an Council, our First Nations partners who have stewarded this land for countless generations."

She made sure to insert slight pauses in the words "Ta'an" and "Kwach'an". Slight enough to show respect, but not so exaggerated they made fun of you like people who pronounced *Montréal* the French way.

She went on to thank their kind hosts at the Ńjür Nàdäk'ą devcorp, an outstanding example of economic reconciliation in action -- this earned a polite nod from Alex -- and valued partners in this project.

"I would also like to acknowledge our shared biosphere that we all rely on for life and growth, our climate which has been severely impacted by generations of pollution, and those who are fighting to repair it."

She concluded and smiled confidently, ignoring the bored stares of the journalists. "Jim, over to you."

The CEO began his spiel. "You know, every time I get off the plane here I see those videos in the airport. Yukon First Nations and non-First Nations people on the land, working together. You have built something unique and powerful up here. It is a great place to do business and a great place to build the Northern Lights low-carbon power project with our partners."

Which was not what he said when he was chewing loudly on steaks and slurping Oregon pinot at a private table with Karen and the premier. At private meetings, he ranted about unhelpful bureaucrats in one of the half dozen agencies slowing down the project, or the latest out-of-left-field business-case-killing demands from one of the chiefs.

In public, the project was exciting and full of potential. Privately, it was always about to sink under the hurdle rate and never be seen again.

The CEO knew the government needed some kind of win on the economy. During the election, it had been easy to claim they would save the climate and create new green jobs at the same time. But now they needed to show results, which was difficult when the premier kept telling Karen to take the lead but then never made a decision since he was worried about offending all the people who went to him directly behind Karen's back.

She recalled a saying floating around town: "None of this would have happened if the premier was still alive." Also attributed, of course, to that asshole Winter.

Karen took a deep breath to de-stress and looked up at the journalists. Which way would they spin this?

Out the window behind them, she saw a black pickup pull over by the curb. The driver's window was down and she recognized Amber's husband Zach. He tapped something into his phone, then looked up at the N̂jür Nàdäk'ą building.

Oh shit, thought Karen. There was no security at this briefing. The last time Zach and the Freedos showed up at a press conference, a massive, bearded Freedo chased her to her car screaming she was an elitist bitch.

She remembered the last cabinet security briefing. The briefer acted like she was in the CIA, sharing trend analysis from the feds about how Canadian fringe groups were acting more like US militias. Which, if you'd just been chased to your car, you did not need a dedicated social-media security analyst to know.

The anti-vaxxers had never gone away after COVID-19. The next waves, even the one everyone called the Super Variant, just made them more convinced vaccine mandates were a conspiracy. There were too many climate extremists on both sides to keep track of. One of the briefer's PowerPoint slides had been titled "Internal Combustion Engines: ICE is the new fur." Anti-ICErs threw red paint on diesel trucks, and angry anti-ICE-ban Freedom nuts slashed the tires of electric vehicles. Then you had all the anti-immigrant, anti-Indigenous, anti-anti-Indigenous groups and so on.

The threat level bounced randomly between yellow and orange. There was never anything specific enough to be red. But they couldn't move it to green since there was always someone on the internet threatening to do something. That was how the internet worked.

She remembered talking to a political oldtimer. Before the Wildfires, the RCMP swept the cabinet rooms once a year and never found bugs or weird Bluetooth tracker tags. The premier drove alone to town halls, parked with everyone else, and just walked in the front door saying hi to everyone. The worst thing that happened was that some rando brought up a campaign pledge you didn't remember.

A guy pedaling fast on a mountain bike came into view. He braked sharply and stopped beside the pickup. The driver seemed to laugh at a joke and gave a thumbs up.

The biker pushed off and turned into the parking lot.

So it was Misty's ex who was covering the story for the *Yukon Sun*. And Winter was late. As always.

Karen listened to the CEO as she watched Winter lock his bike and then bound up the front stairs to the main entrance. At least he didn't have his stupid dog.

The handle on the wrong door rattled. A second time, louder. A third time, loudly. Finally, the correct door opened with a prolonged hinge squeak. The CEO stopped speaking.

Winter carried a bike helmet, travel coffee cup and notepad, and was out of breath. Karen felt her blood pressure rise. The guy was a mess, although she had to admit he looked more put-together than he had a few years ago. She steeled herself. He acted like he detected bullshit everywhere, and always asked the most off-message questions. Plus he was a BNR with roots back to the Klondike Gold Rush. They all kept score on whose ancestors had been here the longest, and scorned anyone -- like Karen -- who had been here less than 25 years as a cheechako likely to mistake a black lab for a bear.

Winter looked up and their eyes met. Karen stared back blankly. Winter whispered "sorry" to a journalist whose bag was on the last chair in the back row, and slipped into his seat.

Karen's eyes returned to her notes. There are three key messages for you to take away today, she rehearsed mentally. First, the wildfire disaster proved beyond a shadow of a doubt that climate change was real and needed to be dealt with. Second, copper was critical for everything from solar panels to electric vehicles, and building the biggest copper mine in North America gave the Yukon a chance to help solve the global copper shortage that was derailing climate transitions around the world. Third, a mine with carbon-neutral power generated in partnership with First Nations was unique, and offered well-paid jobs and huge economic benefits to the Yukon with no climate downside.

She permitted herself a mental smile. And, fourth, vote for me!

After the CEO, it was finally Karen's turn. She ran crisply through her speaking notes. Maybe a bit too fast, but still professionally. She looked out at the journalists. None of them were writing.

Suppressing a sigh, she said, "Any questions?"

The *Whitehorse Star* guy put up his hand. "Alex, could you show us that diagram again?"

"You betcha." Alex reached over to the computer and flipped the page back to the conceptual diagram he had shared earlier.

The *Whitehorse Star* guy looked more confused than usual. Like he'd moved into a new condo and couldn't figure out how to turn on the dishwasher.

I should jump in and explain it, thought Karen. Stamp my brand on this meeting. But I'd better be right. She started jotting a few bullets.

Then Alex stood up. "Hey, it's complex engineering. But basically, the idea is, well, basic."

He walked over to the screen and pointed at one of the boxes. Karen thought about her presentation coach in Vancouver. Never turn your back on the audience. Don't say the word "basically." Never put your arm into the light of the projector. She had never mentioned a rule about not wearing Carhartts with an oil stain on the leg, but that was just a given in Vancouver.

Alex continued. "In the old days, before the wildfires and climate change and all that, to power something like Jim's big new mine they burned LNG - liquefied natural gas - to make electricity. The smoke and carbon dioxide went up the smokestack and into the sky. Global warming. But now," he paused to emphasize, "we will add more generators plus new carbon-capture equipment attached to the smokestack to capture the carbon dioxide. Then we pump the CO2 over here in a small pipeline, totally safe, can't explode, and inject it five kilometres underground into the Whitehorse Trough geological formation. There's been natural gas trapped down there for millions of years, and the CO2 will end up down there too. For good."

Alex paused. The journalists were busily scribbling in their notebooks.

"So, basically," he went on, "we've solved the problem of how to create mining jobs in the Yukon without causing climate change. And Yukon First Nations own the carbon capture infrastructure and have an equity stake in the power plant, so that helps reconciliation. That's why I think this project is a big deal."

A chair scraped. The CKRW guy crouched and reached forward, grabbed his recorder and clicked it off. "Sorry, one man newsroom, gotta go," he said apologetically, and walked to the exit.

"Awesome, no prob," replied Alex. Karen knew the lunchtime CKRW news would carry Alex's clip and none of her quotes. She felt her molars grinding together and made an effort to unclench her jaw and smile.

The new CBC girl asked a question: "Will Northern Lights be powered by the PowerBlimp?"

Karen glanced over at the CEO. His body language telegraphed his thoughts: there is no such thing as a stupid question, just stupid people.

"No, we don't have a relationship with them," he said in the tone he thought was appropriate for journalists, pets and senile board members.

"But the power from the PowerBlimp goes into the power lines right by Northern Lights, right?"

"Northern Lights will produce power, not consume it. An airborne turbine at that altitude typically only produces ten to twenty kilowatts of power. Enough for a few houses. A fraction of what Northern Lights will produce."

The next question was for Karen, and it was one that even her comms person had predicted. Karen answered it crisply.

Then Winter raised his hand. "The Yukon Climate Collective says this project doesn't capture 100% of the carbon and just encourages the fossil fuel industry to keep producing. They say this project is just greenwashing. What's your response to that?"

Karen was ready for this one too. "This project is a major step forward, in both the Yukon Government's and the mining industry's decarbonization pathways. There is still more work to be done as we move towards Net Zero. But this project, as a partnership between First Nations, the private sector and the Yukon government, is a major milestone."

Winter sat there, pen poised, as if waiting for more. God, he was annoying, thought Karen.

Alex cleared his throat. "95% is less than 100%, but 95% is still way better than 0%. So I think this is a great project. And don't forget it's indigenous owned," he said. "OK, I need a coffee! Let's break."

Karen watched as Winter grabbed one, no two, stale donuts and slipped out the door chatting to the CBC girl. Karen looked around. She needed to grab five minutes with the mining CEO.

8

The wharf at Front and Main

1:15 p.m., June 24th. +24°C
2092 days sober

Winter stood in the shade under the roof of the old train station. It was +24°C; unbearably hot.

How did people survive in India at +45°C?

They probably said the same about us when they saw -45°C temperatures in Alaska on the TV weather map.

Mind you, according to the story Winter was half-heartedly reading on his phone to pass the time, they weren't surviving. Another drought and famine in the North Indian plain. The story said four hundred million people lived in the North Indian plain. A thousand times more people than lived in the Yukon. Or was it ten thousand times more people?

The Indian prime minister didn't seem particularly grateful for the latest Canadian food aid shipment. In fact, he was on WhatsApp saying Canada should get its emissions under control so it wasn't +45°C in the Punjab wheat fields in the first place.

How does a comms weasel in Ottawa spin that one?

Winter checked his watch. It was fifteen minutes after the YCC protest's official start time. The crowd was here, but there was no sign of the organizers.

The Freedos were never late, at least since Amber transferred her attention to the movement from organizing massively successful fundraisers for the rep hockey team. Rolling Freedo convoys of protest floats and lowboy trailers with barbecues -- plus the guy with the speakers and hot tub on his Ford flatbed -- were almost military in precision. Which made sense, since Amber had recruited so many ex-cops and ex-army types.

The Greens, on the other hand, were both flakier in general and had an uber-flake as their leader. Winter knew this because the head of the Yukon Climate Collective, Brett, was his younger half-brother. People were surprised to be told they were half-brothers. And even more surprised to be told, as they usually were if Winter was doing the telling, that Winter and Brett had not met until Brett moved to the Yukon after university.

Winter's parents had split when he was in elementary school. It was an ugly divorce. His father sold his mining company, married the exotic Latin American niece of his Vancouver stock promoter who he'd been having an affair with for years, and moved to Toronto. Winter had stayed in Whitehorse with his artist mother with the gold-rush roots in a small house in Riverdale, taking her last name, getting a job to help pay for gas and repairs to their fifteen-year-old Toyota, and listening to his mom's continuous complaints that she was getting screwed on child support.

There were two much older siblings. A brother who died in a high-school motorcycle crash. And a sister, Brenda. She was named after the amateur midwife who helped mom have an organic natural birth in the living room. Winter's school friends were always weirded out playing Lego on the spot where Brenda had been born, or when Winter's mom told them to be careful playing by the sapling in the backyard since her placenta was buried underneath it.

Meanwhile, Winter was born in the hospital and would have been named Sky or River if the granolas down the street hadn't already taken those names.

Before moving to Vancouver and never visiting the Yukon again, Brenda told Winter he was the result of a parental weekend in Skagway premised on the insane idea that having another baby together would save the marriage.

Brett was born in Toronto a few years later, went to Upper Canada College and got a rowing scholarship to Yale. He was good-looking, charming, and everyone loved him. Except for a string of ex-roommates, ex-girlfriends and other people who became boring or less useful to him.

Winter hadn't spoken to his father in years, other than to call him up and ask why the fuck Brett had a trust fund and Taiya didn't.

Winter was pretty sure he despised Brett on the fundamentals, not just because of the family history.

Winter checked his watch and scrolled through more old stories. It was hard to remember the time when the news had been all about City Council zoning debates and over-budget highway projects. He re-read an old City Council story of his from before the Wildfires; a filler story with a paragraph on each boring item at a particularly boring City Council meeting.

A retired local fire prevention expert managed somehow to get on the City Council agenda. The mayor and councillors struggled to maintain their masks of engaged interest as the expert got deeper into the calculation of the Fire Weather Index and how temperature, humidity, wind and past rainfall factored into it. Winter remembered waiting in vain for something quotable that a normal human could understand.

Of course, later, after half the town burned down, it was pretty clear people should have been paying more attention to the days when the FWI was high.

The FWI usually only went over 35 a couple days each summer. It was 47 in Fort McMurray when they had their big fire. So when it hit 64 in Whitehorse they probably should have done more than just move the arrow on the Fire Risk sign on the Alaska Highway to Extreme.

Or maybe it wasn't so irrational. It had been a once in a lifetime event. Actually, even rarer. In the 130 years since white people showed up in the Yukon and started keeping weather records, nothing like it had ever happened. But that was before climate change.

Winter scrolled through the stories he posted on the day the fire hit. It started south -- upwind -- of town. The cause was still a mystery. No one was admitting to burning their garbage that day. It spread quickly and, pretty soon, strong winds were fanning a crown fire with a wall of flame a kilometre long and a hundred metres high. It was so hot that water bombers had to be careful how low they flew over it.

Winter scrolled to more stories. The fire had moved fast, burning forward at a brisk walking pace and sending embers miles ahead to start new fires.

First the premier told everyone to shelter in place. Then the mayor got interviewed on CBC and breathlessly ordered everyone in the south half of town to evacuate. The mayor and the premier were still mad at Winter for the headline the editor slapped on that story: The Catch-22 Evacuation.

Riverdale looked like a warzone in the photos. Vehicles full of gas caught fire, loose pets ran wildly through the streets, propane tanks vented flames, and burning trees fell across the roads. An accident blocked the bridge to downtown. People abandoned their vehicles and ran past the smashed up cars carrying children and photo albums.

Tarfu had done the smartest thing of all: just hide under the bed in the basement.

9

Inside Brett's powder blue electric van

1:25 p.m., June 24th. +22°C

Finally, twenty-five minutes after the protest's appointed kick off time, a brand-new all-electric powder-blue Volkswagen campervan whirred up Front Street honking. All eyes turned as it pulled into a parking spot beside the wharf.

Brett hopped out and strode energetically toward the crowd. He was tall and athletic, with a hint of his Chilean mother's colouring. His stubble was the fashionable length and longish brown hair flopped over his brow. He was wearing sunglasses, Birckenstocks, shorts and a dark green sustainable cotton t-shirt that said "Greta still says blah, blah, blah."

Brett moved into the mass of people, exchanging smiles and fist bumps, while his lead organizer, Chaewon, swung out of the passenger seat. She glanced at the crowd. A lot smaller than the glory days back in Vancouver.

Brett had given his usual motivational speech before they left HQ. But the smallness of the crowd was obvious to everyone. This was not good for the finance spreadsheet on Chaewon's Macbook. A small crowd was doubly bad. Fewer people to donate and, even worse, even fewer new recruits. Almost everyone at this event had already donated. Brett might have to cut everyone's hours again.

He had also told her to tell the media that 500 people had turned out, and that as a percentage of population this was as if 50,000 showed up at a Vancouver rally. Brett believed in anchoring people on large numbers.

Chaewon felt a knot growing in her stomach. She hated speaking in public. Facing a small crowd did not make it any easier.

She put her weight into sliding the side door open. All her weight was required, since she was 5'2" and 105 pounds. Different people described her 105 pounds differently. Her grandmother in Seoul called her skinny. Her auntie in Teslin called her wiry. And her friend kept telling her to put the word "svelte" on her Tinder profile.

She was in her late twenties and wore a tight tank top with loose olive, German-army-style cargo pants and boots, which was what her old boss Agnethe had always worn to protests in Vancouver. She had straight black, shoulder-length hair in a ponytail poking out the back of a UBC Music baseball cap. Chaewon found it annoying that everyone assumed an Asian woman -- well, half Asian -- would know piano and have overbearing parents obsessed with the instrument; that she was a music major with a piano-obsessed father in Korea made it even more irritating.

And that was when white people didn't just assume she was adopted, since her English was perfect.

As each person clambered out, she gave them a last minute reminder. The videographer was supposed to get some shots of Brett speaking to the crowd, up close and low, framed to make it seem packed. The more kids, youth and indigenous people the better. Ditto for the stills guy. For the banner carriers, make sure they were in front of the procession and had the banner stretched across the front of the march. Chest to knee high. Get lots of people to help hold it up. Brett really wanted the full Yukon Climate Collective brand name visible in the photos.

Two people grabbed armfuls of home-made-looking placards to hand out. The two summer interns from Western University were supposed to be the social media specialists. Their job was to hand out little cards with the hashtags and encourage everyone to post.

They should have been good at it. They were chatty, cute in that sorority girl way, and spent most of their time on their phones.

Unfortunately, this was mostly texting each other. And most of this was about how sad everyone in Whitehorse was. But also, Chaewon knew, about her own unshaven armpits and army pants.

"Remember, split up and work the crowd!" said Chaewon with as much enthusiasm as she could muster.

"Yup," said the two girls in unison before disappearing together into the crowd.

It was too bad that Brett had accidentally scheduled the intern interviews on her day off. She would not have hired Alpha Phi sisters who were more interested in smokejumpers in Carhartts than disappearing glaciers.

She slung the backpack speaker straps over her shoulders, checked her phone in case a text had come in, and headed into the crowd to look for her auntie.

Brett was working the crowd. It was a real god-given talent, Chaewon thought, as she watched people interacting with him. She noticed him spend some extra time with Nigel, the *Whitehorse Star* photographer. That guy attended every event around town, and his photos were good. A big front page photo of this protest would be just what they needed locally.

Brett stood up on a park bench and surveyed the crowd. God I love this energy, he thought to himself. He saw Chaewon looking at Nigel. She should really go talk him into some great pics. He made a mental note to give her some feedback, then hopped off the bench and dived back into the crowd.

He immediately ran straight into Winter, who was talking to a donor. Unavoidable. "Hello, brother," said Brett.

Winter smiled, sort of. "Hello, comrade."

Brett hadn't met the new CBC reporter standing beside Winter yet. He turned and said hi. She was wearing a tight shirt that made her breasts pop, especially with the strap of her camera stretched diagonally between them. He made sure to keep his eyes at eye level. She smiled back and said hello.

Would she end up in the van? On the top bunk with her feet braced on the ceiling?

Maybe. Probably.

But that was for later. He reminded himself not to pay too much attention to the media. It made them think you were desperate for a story.

He smiled and moved on. It was time to begin. He looked around for Chaewon and her auntie from Teslin. Chaewon was standing right beside him.

"Nope," she said.

"Shit."

"It'll have to be me."

"Why doesn't she show up half the time?" asked Brett, not bothering to hide his annoyance.

Chaewon shrugged. The question was too deep to get into right now. She could feel her muscles tightening and her pulse quickening, just like before piano competitions when she was a girl. Her heart was beating so fast she could hear it in her ears. She hated speaking in public, knew she wasn't very good at it, and knew that Brett thought she wasn't very good either.

It was pathetic. A public relations specialist who hated speaking in public.

She also hated when Brett thought she had failed, even when it wasn't her fault. It was even worse than driving home with her dad after she got nervous and flubbed her piano recital.

Even worse was the feeling of not belonging. Chaewon really didn't know why her auntie didn't show up sometimes. Even though her mom was from Teslin and Chaewon really was a Teslin Tlingit citizen, she remembered how Brett, after a few beers, had joked that having a classical pianist who grew up in Korea do the land acknowledgment didn't exactly feel authentic.

Brett put both his hands on her shoulders and leaned in. "You can do this. We can do this. You'll give a kick-ass land acknowledgement, then I'll tell them how important this is, how special they are for coming out, how they can make a real difference."

He looked her in the eyes. She was about to cry.

"And how they can donate to give you a raise," he said, with a wink and a smile. He grabbed her hands, pulled them towards him and twisted them gently outwards. They both looked down at the tattoo winding up her left arm, three brightly coloured eagles in the delicate Korean tattoo style flying along a series of undulating lines. "Eagle Clan, Korean artist," he said. "Be proud."

Chaewon took a deep breath. She knew Brett was faking it. But it still helped somehow. "Thanks Brett," she said, almost tearing up.

She slung the speaker onto the picnic table and turned it on. Grabbing the mic, she stepped up on top of the table. Brett put his finger and thumb to his mouth and gave a sharp whistle, and she began.

"Welcome everyone!" said Chaewon, and there was a huge cheer. She looked out at all the colourful homemade placards, held up her arm and tried to remember the lines Brett had taught her. "I got this tattoo because of my Teslin Tlingit heritage. We're here today because of the future." She knew she was speaking too fast, too loud, not loud enough, too many umms. Did she thank Kwanlin Dün twice? Forget the Ta'an Kwäch'än? But she got through it, handed the mic to Brett and stumbled off the table with relief.

Chaewon didn't even hear what Brett said. The adrenaline didn't wear off until they were already marching along the bike path to the Legislature. But whatever he said, the crowd seemed primed. They waved their placards and chanted enthusiastically.

Then she noticed the social media girls were clumped together, talking to each other. Chaewon moved briskly to remind them to start doing their jobs.

At the Legislature, the plan was to hype up the crowd and do some old-fashioned chants. However, the Green Party candidate for the upcoming election insisted on making a speech. Even Brett had been unable to talk him out of it. Dr. Cameron Dougall was a prominent prof at Yukon University who kept telling you about his research awards and real-estate portfolio. He didn't listen well. Especially to young women, it seemed to Chaewon. You could tell him a million times that a protest was a theatrical event, and he would still go up on stage and talk about the latest IPCC data on atmospheric carbon dioxide concentrations in parts per million.

Chaewon unfolded the step stool, and put the backpack speaker on the ground beside it. The space wasn't ideal: there wasn't much room between the front door of the Legislature and Second Avenue. You could hear the traffic zooming past. She turned up the volume and handed the mic to Dr. Dougall. Her heart sank as he pulled index cards out of his fleece vest pocket and mounted the stepstool.

She squeezed through to the back for a better view of the crowd. Sure enough, Dougall was already putting everyone to sleep by explaining how the PowerBlimp needed ninety percent less material per megawatt-hour compared to a regular wind turbine, since it didn't need a steel tower or deep concrete foundation.

The social media girls were already scrolling their phones.

Chaewon found herself standing behind Nestor and that guy Winter from the *Yukon Sun*, Brett's half-brother who always offended everyone.

"How is saving the climate going?" whispered Winter to Nestor.

"Blyat'," he cursed, blowing out his lips in an exaggerated sigh. "I am not holding breath for these people to make revolution."

"I like listening to Dougall speak. Hearing an aging white heterosexual male in the top 1% tax bracket who knows everything … it reminds me of my childhood."

"I call them clowns. Except clowns are professionals. This is not professional."

Chaewon noticed Karen Felton, minister of economic development, looking down on the scene from a window in the Cabinet Office. Karen was married to the mom of Brett's niece Taiya. Not that this helped Yukon Climate Collective. Brett was protesting Karen's flagship mining jobs project. Taiya's dad Winter had given Karen a nickname she hated -- LDV for Lesbian Darth Vader -- which had gone viral. So Karen, as far as Chaewon could tell, was not very helpful when YCC submitted grant applications.

Today, she just looked bored.

A pickup truck pulled over, just across the sidewalk from the group. This one was big and black, high off the ground with big 4x4 tires, with tinted windows and a diesel engine. It looked new. They must have bought it just before the sales ban on new fossil engines. It looked like it would use your whole carbon ration in one trip.

No one got out, and the engine kept running with a deep, throaty rumble. It had bumper stickers for the Calgary Flames, Klondike Placer Miners' Association and Survival Paintball. There was a Sled Porn decal on the back cab window. And, ominously, another bumper sticker that said "I ♡ DIESEL" and one with a raised middle finger and the words "Ration this!"

She noticed Winter and Nigel looking at the pickup too. Winter had pulled out his iPhone and was snapping a picture. Then Nigel began moving, quickly, in a sort of mini-jog that didn't make the cameras around his neck bounce too much. He dodged between cars on Second Avenue and was headed to a place where he could get the pickup and the crowd in the same shot.

Chaewon felt her heartbeat accelerate again. Was something about to happen?

She would have known the answer to this question if, like Winter and Nigel, she had covered the Freedom convoys. The truck was owned by Amber and her Neanderthal husband Zach. Amber was the one who came up with all their most Instagram-worthy protests, usually involving a low-boy trailer and elaborate accessories. The Classic Rock Rolling Dance Protest. The Hot-Tub Occupation. The mobile oven that baked oatmeal cookies for the cops. And so on.

Meanwhile, Dougall continued to speak, unaware either of the pickup or how boring his speech was.

Suddenly the passenger window on the truck slid down. Chaewon recognized Amber and felt another pulse of anxiety.

Amber was wearing sunglasses and a pink camo baseball hat. She leaned her elbow on the window sill. She was in her late thirties and had long straight blonde hair in a ponytail pulled through the back of her baseball hat. She was still pretty. Her eyebrows and makeup were perfectly estheticized. She watched Dougall intensely. Like a lynx watching a rabbit, if lynx could also smile and chew gum at the same time.

Chaewon could hear hard rock music coming out of the truck. Getting louder. And louder.

Even Dougall had noticed. His speech faltered as he turned to look at the pickup. Amber smiled more broadly.

The stereo got louder. Custom stereo loud. A screeching guitar solo completely drowned out Dougall and the portable speaker. Chaewon could not just hear the bass thumping, she could feel it in her chest.

She glanced over at Brett. He jerked his thumb towards the pickup. Deal with it. Chaewon steeled herself. People like this scared her. When they pulled into a campsite near hers, she usually just packed up her tent and left.

She walked towards the pickup. The pink camo baseball hat said Survival Paintball on the front. Amber smiled and reached down with her left hand. Oh god, thought Chaewon, what if they shoot me with a paintball gun?

Amber's fingers found the stereo and turned it down.

"How's it goin'?" she said easily. Behind her, Zach looked huge. The Caterpillar baseball hat on his shaved head nearly brushed against the roof of the cab, and his black t-shirt stretched tightly over his muscles. He ignored Chaewon, his huge fingers tapping surprisingly nimbly on his phone.

Chaewon tried to smile. She explained the situation and asked if they wouldn't mind turning the stereo down.

Amber considered this. "Actually,' she said finally, still smiling, "we kind of like music. Do you listen to the Wayne Bobalicious show on CHON?"

Chaewon swallowed nervously. Was she being trolled? CHON-FM was the local indigenous radio station. Chaewon never listened to it. It only played rock and country, and the news was mostly local with announcements about First Nations events out in the communities. Everyone she knew who listened to radio tuned in to CBC.

Amber took Chaewon's silence as a no. "Do you know Double Shot Friday? Well, in honour of Wayne, I think," -- she paused and lowered her voice to rock DJ frequency -- "*it's time to plug in the power.*"

Zach laughed, still tapping something into his phone, and Amber continued. "You can choose the double shot. Back in Black? Or Highway to Hell?"

"Maybe later?" pleaded Chaewon.

"Hey, it's a free country." She turned to the driver. "Zach, turn it up. To eleven."

Chaewon turned around and looked for Brett.

Brett was considering the situation. Obviously the pickup assholes weren't going to be helpful. Would it look good if he barged in there and they ignored him? He also had seen the paintball bumper sticker. What if they shot him with a paintball gun?

Then Brett thought about it again. What if they shot him with a paintball gun? In front of photographers?

He immediately stepped forward out of the crowd to help Chaewon.

Unfortunately, Dougall had also decided the pickup people needed a firm talking to. He clambered off the stepstool, wireless mic in hand, and strode over to the pickup.

As Dougall approached the truck, Amber smiled and the music went off.

"Hey you can't-" shouted Dougall, but his next words were drowned out when Zach revved the engine. It let out a huge roar, and a cloud of exhaust poured out of the back of the vehicle. Dougall was completely inaudible. Chaewon was startled by how loud the engine was. It was like an airplane. The crowd began to back away.

Dougall stopped speaking.

Zach took his foot off the gas and the noise stopped.

Dougall moved half a step closer. "What I want to say-" Again, Zach gunned the engine, drowning out Dougall. Dougall's lips kept moving. Amber kept leaning out the pickup window, smiling at Dougall.

Finally, Dougall's lips stopped moving. The driver took his foot off the gas.

There was a brief pause.

As soon as Dougall's lips moved again, the driver revved the engine. Dougall was furious by now. The seconds ticked painfully by as he leaned towards the truck and screamed inaudibly at the woman in the pickup, who just kept smiling.

The cycle happened two more times.

Taiya appeared beside Winter. "Weren't you supposed to have left by now for your job?" he asked.

"We can patch the rafts later. Didn't want to miss Uncle Brett's protest." Winter eyed her. Climate had been more important than school all year. Now work too? He was reminded of it every morning when he put the pea milk she recommended on his muesli instead of 2%. He wanted to say something cutting about the concept of "Uncle Brett," but resisted. He'd never had an uncle and, whatever his half-brother's issues, he had resolved not to take that away from Taiya.

"What's going to happen, now?" asked Taiya pointing at the pickup and Dougall.

"Not sure. At a bare minimum, the smartest guy in the Yukon is being made to look like an idiot by the wiliest bitch in town."

"Is that Zach's truck, your friend from high school?"

"Friends? Let's keep it as 'guys who Minor Hockey kept putting on the same team.'"

Taiya and Winter flinched as a loud grunt came out of a teenage boy behind them. A rock flew over their heads and arced towards the pickup, smashing into the rear cab window. Tinted glass diamonds scattered onto Amber.

"Double damage!" exclaimed the boy, fist-bumping another before sprinting away.

The crowd cheered as Amber shook glass out of her hair. Zach revved the engine and popped the truck into gear. They took off with a squeal of tires, spraying bits of winter road gravel all over the crowd.

One of Nigel's photos made the front page, but not one Chaewon liked. The photo -- with no audio, of course -- showed Amber smiling politely out a pickup window as Dr. Cameron Dougall, candidate for the Green Party, screamed maniacally in her face, with Brett in the background looking at Dougall with a look of puzzled dismay.

10

Schwatka float plane base

11:30 a.m., June 26th. +12°C

The old BNR put on the left turn indicator, then deftly slid the gear shift down into third before putting his right hand protectively across the Kentucky Fried Chicken beside him on the front seat. With the KFC safe from sliding onto the floor, he let out the clutch to slow down. His old black lab, Casca, snapped out of her nap and braced to avoid sliding forward off the seat.

The F-350's transmission was not as smooth as it used to be, he thought. If it goes, that will be one expensive bitch to fix. Maybe they can get a rebuilt one out of Fort St. John.

As he waited for the traffic, he realized the smell of KFC was making his mouth water. It actually is finger-lickin' good, he thought. Not just a saying. That's why, back in the day, you were a hero if you landed in Old Crow or some mining camp with a bucket of warm KFC.

All he had today was a three-piece combo and a root beer. Even that had been hard to order. The kid at the counter was wearing a turban and couldn't even speak English. Fucking foreigners were everywhere. You never see a white kid working at KFC, he thought, let alone a native kid. It was a fucked up world.

There was a break in the traffic -- traffic, in Whitehorse! -- and he gunned the diesel for the left turn at the LNG plant onto Schwatka Lake road. Transmission or no, she still had guts.

He parked across the road from IYY. She was still a beauty, too. Bright red, with her call letters in bold white paint. Old, but still as awesome as the first day he flew her.

He ripped open the KFC. The classic dilemma: start with some fries, or a drumstick? He fed a piece of chicken to Casca.

They don't make planes like that anymore, literally, he thought as he chewed. IYY was a Cessna 180. She was built way back in 1956, but the airframe would last forever. The 180 could carry a good load, four people or a lot of gear or moose meat. More economical than the 185.

They had been late getting IYY off skis and onto floats this year, waiting for some parts for the annual maintenance. He loved the thrill of the first takeoff of the season. It felt wild and dangerous to be sitting in a floatplane, on a trailer behind a pickup racing down the runway until you had enough speed to lift off the trailer and fly to the lake.

Regular people never got to do that.

He put down the KFC. One piece left. He could eat that later. His appetite had never really come back after the chemo. Neither had his strength. Hodgkins fucking lymphoma. Better than brain cancer, though. Mario Lemieux came back from Hodgkins and won the scoring title. He even played against the Flyers on the last day of his last radiation treatment.

It's too bad Mario Lemieux isn't here to help me lug the outboard over to the plane, he thought.

He zipped up his jacket -- a cold, north wind today -- and stepped out of the truck to take a leak. There used to be a tree you could stand behind. But it was gone. He stepped onto the scorched black earth. The old tin shed was gone too. There were a few green shoots, and fireweed was sprouting. Other than that, just burned stumps and firekill as far as you could see.

You had as much privacy as pissing on the moon.

He stood for what seemed like forever. It took a lot longer to get the piss going these days.

The PowerBlimp hung in the distance. Its rotor turned slowly in the slack wind. God, that was a stupid idea, he thought. And near a floatplane base!

Still waiting. He tried to think of waterfalls.

He remembered the day the fire had come through. It moved so fast. He barely got to IYY in time. He'd been dropped off a hundred yards away, and had felt the heat on his face as he ran to the plane. The wind was dropping cinders on the road and into the lake all around the plane. Visibility had been terrible with the smoke.

Getting airborne had been a relief. He had circled for a while, high enough to be out of the way of the water bombers, watching in amazement as the bright line of fire moved north with the wind. It burned over the Chadburn ski trails and headed straight for Riverdale.

They said it was climate change. Bullshit. There had always been forest fires. More like the government agreeing to send all our smokejumpers to BC to help with their fires.

He reached over the tailgate for the big flat edge screwdriver. I should really get this fixed sometime, he thought, as he levered it into the latch. But who knew how much a replacement tailgate would cost. The tailgate fell with a thud.

He untied the outboard, dragged it to the edge of the tailgate, and turned it so the skeg under the propeller would hit the ground. Best way for one guy to do it. Keep it upright, drag it a foot at a time.

He checked for traffic and started dragging. One foot at a time. Don't hurt your back. The sweat trickled down onto his glasses. Keep going. He was almost across the road.

Suddenly, voices. He looked up. A bunch of young guys on mountain bikes came around the corner. The first biker saw him and pulled into the middle of the road. One of those expensive bikes, probably worth more than the pickup. The others were sitting up, not paying attention, no hands, squirting water bottles into their mouths like they'd finished a ride.

"Hey!" he shouted. But it was too late. They flashed by him, some swerving, some not. Close. Too close. Distracted for a second, he felt the outboard motor begin to tip. He strained, but it was too much and he let go.

It crashed heavily into the asphalt. Fuck.

The last biker turned around and laughed. "Watch where you're going old man!"

A flattened beer can was lying in the middle of the road beside the outboard. He kicked it violently into the ditch. Bastards!

It was no use complaining. He took off his baseball hat, wiped his forehead, and put the hat back on. He spun the engine around so the propeller was pointing at the plane. He bent his knees and put a hand on each corner of the cowling. Lift with your knees, not your back. He began straining.

"Do you need any help?" said a voice out of nowhere. He stood up.

It was a teenage girl with a dog. The dog stepped forward to smell him. "Tarfu! Sit!" said the girl. Her voice was calm, but firm. Tarfu sat immediately and watched him, panting but alert and friendly. He noticed the girl was wearing an Arctic Winter Games biathlon shirt and running clothes.

"Nice dog,' he said. "Well trained."

"He's a goof," said the girl with a smile. The man put out his hand, and let the dog sniff it. Without asking she looped the dog's leash around the ball hitch on the pickup and ran back. "Well, we both take a side and lift it onto the prop end?"

"Sure," said the old man, startled by both the offer and her apparent comfort with outboard motors.

The skeg dragged on the asphalt and then over the gravel and dandelions beside the road. They moved it up the plank, across the floating dock, said "one-two-three" together and heaved it into the plane.

"Thanks!" he said.

"No problem."

The man felt a sudden need to prolong the conversation. "Any chance you're related to Winter Slade?"

"My dad! Do you know him?"

The old BNR's face creased into a smile. "Tell him you met the guy who gave him a case of Old Style when he turned nineteen."

Taiya gave him the thumbs up, and ran off to untie her dog. He watched her for a minute as she loped into the distance. A girl who could shoot and lift outboards. Winter must be doing something right.

Then he turned to tie down the motor. You didn't want something like that sliding around on takeoff.

11

Miles Canyon bridge, east bank

12:30 p.m., June 29th. +22°C

"It's not just bears and bad planning that can kill you in the Yukon," said Taiya with a smile to Chaewon and the tour group. "We also have our share of poisonous plants."

It was the YCC's guided nature hike, and it was one of those warm and sunny Yukon summer days that made the winter worthwhile. The group stood with the roar of Miles Canyon in the background. "First is wolf's bane, also known as monkshood. It's a beautiful little purple flower, but highly poisonous. First Nations knew that, and the ancient Romans even used it to execute people. Some people say it protects you from werewolves."

A teenage boy in baggy cargo shorts and a hoodie looked up from his phone at the mention of werewolves and poison. "Didn't that nomad guy in Alaska die from eating that?"

Taiya smiled the smile of the tolerant tour guide. Someone always brought up Chris McCandless and the Magic Bus near Denali. "The book *Into the Wild* talked about how he might have starved because he ate alpine sweetvetch, and a toxin in it caused his digestive system to shut down. But a prof at the University of Alaska disproved that. He might have just starved to death. He's become a kind of romantic hero on the internet, but most Alaskans and Yukoners think he was just irresponsible to go alone into the wild without a map."

Taiya closed her binder. "Nature is not your friend," she added before turning up the trail.

She was a good tour guide, Chaewon thought. Even if Brett only hired her because he wanted to be the cool uncle who could hand out jobs and presents.

Taiya got the tours a lot of five-star reviews on TripAdvisor, far more than the sorority girls Brett hired from Western. They spent most of their time posing for save-the-planet selfies with Brett or leaving early to party with the smokejumpers. As a feminist it pained Chaewon to admit it: eco-bunnies was a terrible, misogynistic term, but people would keep using it as long as such dumb girls pretended to be environmentalists.

The tourists particularly loved Taiya's story about her great-great-grandfather. His scheme to get rich during the gold rush had been to be the first to get a herd of cattle to Dawson City, and sell the steak for twenty times what the cattle cost in Seattle. Racing another guy with the same idea, he successfully drove his herd over the White Pass trail, built a scow and floated his forty cows to Miles Canyon.

Where he had a choice: take a day or two and coax the cows out of the scow and walk them around the rapids, or take a risk and run the rapids. Keeping in mind that the second guy to get steak to the goldfields would make a lot less money.

Taiya always asked the group to vote on what they would do. The boy in the hoodie voted to walk the cows around, while his grandmother remarked, "You gotta risk it for the biscuit."

Taiya's great-great-grandfather had decided to run the canyon. His scow smashed into the canyon walls and goldseekers in Whitehorse gorged on free drowned steak.

Now, thought Chaewon, if only Taiya's dad would show up when he promised to. Winter had promised his daughter he would snap some photos with his good camera for the YCC website.

Chaewon noted that Taiya had changed the tour without asking, adding more flora and fauna and taking out some of the less interesting blah blah about the settlers and the Klondike Gold Rush. That was good. The cow story was all you really needed to understand that whole ridiculous event.

The version in the binder at the office went on and on about Sam Steele and how he ordered everyone to have a professional pilot for Miles Canyon. It was one of those examples Canadians loved because it showed that the gold rush was more civilized on their side of the border.

Of course, the regular text didn't mention that Sam Steele was the head of a paramilitary force whose job was to take the Yukon away from the indigenous people. Or that he was a misogynist. He let the pimps carry on sex trafficking pretty much openly in Dawson. Or that he would give a "blue ticket" to anyone he thought was a troublemaker; an order to just leave the Yukon, no reason needed, no appeal possible.

Even worse, Miles Canyon was named after a war criminal - the general whose troops committed the Wounded Knee atrocity against the Sioux. So much for Reconciliation.

An idea struck Chaewon. Taiya had a wildlife camera she put on trails around Riverdale. Maybe she could work a few photos of animals into her talk. Including how climate change was threatening them. Brett always said charismatic megafauna were good for fundraising.

Brett would suggest grizzly bear cubs starving to death after warm weather woke their mother from hibernation early. Or a story from the Wildfires about finding a den of roasted fox cubs.

She tapped a reminder into her phone to talk to Taiya.

She heard a camera bag unzip. Winter had arrived.

"The guide's dad. The Oxy guy I was telling you about," whispered one woman, not quietly enough, to her out-of-town guests.

From the back of the group, Chaewon could hear the teenage boy talking to his brother. Both were wearing cheap tourist hoodies from the cruise-passenger shops in Skagway. One had a mock dictionary definition on top of crossed rifles: "Vegetarian - An Alaskan too lazy to hunt."

They were arguing, increasingly loudly, about the latest controversy in Washington, DC. "No, you moron," hissed one brother, "a false flag operation is when you attack yourself and blame the other side to make them look guilty. You heard Joe Rogan. There's no way Ivanka's fans would do something that stupid!"

The argument was beginning to distract Taiya.

Out of the corner of her eye, Chaewon watched Winter sidle over to the boys. "You should be quiet. You're disrespecting the tour guide," he said softly.

The oldest boy silently gave him the finger.

Winter leaned a bit closer. "I'd be careful. She's a biathlon champion. Know what a White Stocking is?"

The boys looked blank.

"Ukrainian biathlon girls. They sniped Russians at night. Usually aimed for the balls." Winter had their attention now. "Google it and shut up."

12

The *Yukon Sun* newsroom, Third and Main

11:15 a.m., July 6th. +18°C
2104 days sober

The editor of the *Yukon Sun* -- crutches in one hand and railing in the other -- jumped up the stairs two at a time and burst into the office. Artemis waved a crutch accusingly at the newsroom. Everyone looked up from their screens. "Why the fuck, if I may use the local vernacular," she said, pausing to pant from the stairs, "don't we know the Freedos are blockading YESAB?"

YESAB was the environmental assessment agency, and the Freedos believed it was the centre of the Green plot to shut down the mining industry and make everyone work on low-carbon kale farms.

"I was just on their Facebook page," said Eamon, the *Sun*'s junior reporter. "They're still raging on the socials about Amber's truck window. There's nothing about YESAB."

"Of course there isn't," responded Artemis sharply. While everyone tried to like Eamon, he slipped too easily into the role of the guy who was always one step behind. The crutch moved from a general accusation against the newsroom to pointing specifically at Eamon. "Not even my grandmother uses Facebook any more. They're all on Signal. Or Telegram. Or Dis-fucking-cord!"

"Right," stuttered Eamon, reddening.

"YESAB is only a couple blocks away. Even a cripple-" -- she paused to point at her missing leg for emphasis -- "could walk that far in two minutes."

The editor turned her crutch to Winter.

"News to me, boss." He had been focused on his Alaska diesel smuggling story. Which everyone knew was happening but wouldn't talk about on record. "I think Amber found out who was forwarding me their group chats and cut me off."

"Can you go cover it?"

Winter shook his head. "I have to-"

"I know," interrupted Artemis wearily. "You have a family entanglement involving your daughter at the airport." Winter guessed she wanted to add, "and your daughter is more important than the news." This was a catchphrase he used whenever someone suggested something completely unacceptable, like cover City Council instead of helping Taiya pack for an Outdoor Ed trip.

Artemis supported Winter in principle, and did a pretty good job hiding her frustration when it interfered with her ambition to run a smart and professional local paper. This frustration usually only bubbled to the surface when she had to rely on Eamon. Like now.

All eyes turned to Eamon, who stared back for a second before he realized everyone expected him to stand up and leave to cover the blockade. He stood up and grabbed the coat off the back of his chair.

Artemis put her hand on the sports guy's shoulder. "I think this requires a trusty sidekick with a camera. In case Eamon ends up duct-taped to a chair in Amber's RV."

After Eamon and the sports guy had left, the editor sat down beside Winter.

"Remember how the preppers reacted when Eamon tried to ask them how much food and ammo they had stored at their compound?" asked Winter. "Maybe we should get him a police escort."

"Police? Nestor would be better. If we could find him. He's still not on Tinder you know." The women in the office had a running joke about what Nestor's Tinder profile would say: fit, exotic accent, looks good in Carhartts pulling your truck single handedly out of a ditch.

"He's not on any of the platforms. Just that Nokia brick phone."

"How does he make a living?"

"I think he codes. Outside clients. He's got one of those Elon Musk satellite dishes on his cabin roof."

"I heard he looted a hockey bag of cash from a Russian convoy."

Artemis sighed and looked out the window.

"It's great to be here with you," said Winter.

Artemis laughed sardonically. "Fuck. 'Here' is getting fatter, more out of shape and more single every winter, while the news gets more and more depressing," she said. To emphasize her point, she leaned back and wedged a thumb into the waistband of her tights, pulled it out and let it snap back into place.

She was almost ten years younger than Winter, and was indeed a few sizes larger than she had been as a rookie reporter. She was short, with dark, active eyes and curly black hair that exploded into a static electrical storm whenever she took off her toque. Her colouring was vaguely Mediterranean or Middle Eastern. Eamon — who had a terrified kind of boss crush on her – had once described her as "racially ambidextrous."

She usually told people she was originally from Ottawa, just to keep it simple, but this wasn't really true. Her father had been in the Foreign Service and her mother was from Delhi. She grew up as a dip brat moving every few years from one African capital to another. She spoke English, European-accented French, pretty good Swahili and a little Hindi, and was a competitive swimmer at the American School in Addis Ababa before a drunk Swedish diplomat and his Volvo removed her left leg.

She was named Artemis because her father was obsessed with ancient Greece. In university she had tried switching to her middle name, Shilka after her grandmother in Delhi, but a girl named Shilka Henderson who spoke Swahili just confused everyone even more.

Her father didn't hide his disappointment that she hadn't followed him into the Foreign Service. Once she graduated, she got a job at the *Yukon Sun*, which just happened to be the newspaper that was farthest from Ottawa while still being in Canada.

Winter picked up his coffee and silently took a sip. Even with women who were friends, you had to be careful what you said after they referred to their waistlines.

Artemis broke the silence. "What I can't figure out is this: what should we do about the Freedos?" she asked. "They are infinitely frustrating to cover effectively."

Artemis and Winter had a good relationship. He really didn't mind that the publisher had made her editor instead of him when the previous editor had gone on vacation to Thailand and never come back. She was good at it. And he enjoyed the flair with which she terrorized the government officials supposedly in charge of accessible entrances and snow-free sidewalks.

They had talked about the Freedos many times before. Despite the fact that Amber seemed to run the whole thing, they didn't have an official leader. They didn't put out press releases, never used their public Facebook pages and wouldn't talk to lamestream media. Half the time they tried to keep the *Yukon Sun* out of their events. If you showed up, you had to be ready to be followed around, shouted at, and sometimes worse.

"It's kind of our fault," she went on. "We had so much fun with the crazy Facebook posts in the anti-vaxxer trials that everyone's paranoid now."

Winter pulled out his phone. "There are so many trolls and weirdos out there that even the normals are on Signal." He showed her the mom chat group for Taiya's Outdoor Ed class that he was a member of.

"Quite so," agreed Artemis. "Now, if you're organizing any kind of protest, swapping porn or just sharing a few thoughts with a former cellmate on the new guy entertaining your ex-girlfriend, you want end-to-end encryption and everything stored on some server in Switzerland."

Artemis pulled out her phone and scrolled through her chats. "Meanwhile, the Greens actually want us to cover them. They send me a ceaseless stream of news opportunities. Including from your daughter. She appears to be the ringleader on at least two of their groups."

"She runs the Instagram account for their wildlife camera." That account was aimed at aging animal lovers who might donate. "Also some youth chat for the kids at school who want to save the planet."

"The chat equivalent of gateway drugs," replied Artemis. "That's probably how Amber got started."

Winter tapped his watch, stood up and grabbed his bike seat and helmet. "Text me if I have to cover a double hostage taking."

"They'll be fine. Probably. Get out of the office and talk to some regular people," she said with a wink. "Some good advice someone gave me when I was a rookie reporter."

13

The Black Street Stairs

11:45 a.m., July 6th. +19°C
2104 days sober

Despite how everyone thought biking to the airport was nuts, Winter kind of liked the route. It was 3.5 kilometres and you got a 60-metre thigh burn on the Black Street Stairs in the middle. The last bit was a flat bike path beside the Alaska Highway, and you could just put your head down and pedal on pavement that was so new it didn't have any frost heaves yet. This also beat biking on the highway itself, since there was no chance a cranky trucker headed to Alaska would share his thoughts on carbon taxes and bike lanes with an accidentally-on-purpose close pass.

As he reached the highway, Winter saw a figure standing on the shoulder waiting to jaywalk. He recognized the stance, olive drab jacket and spiky black hair. It was Henry Crossfox.

Henry and Winter had known each other since Grade 3. Their grandmothers had known each other too. Winter's grandmother told a story from her school time about the day the first Indian girl, as she described it, had been allowed in their class. In Grade 6, Henry beat Winter in the Yukon stage of a national science fiction writing contest. Winter's story featured everyone in the future having a cellphone that was connected to the central world computer that told everyone what to do. In Henry's story, everyone and their dog, literally, had brain implants that were networked so you could get thought messages from others or see what they were seeing in a computer window that opened in your head. The trapper who rescued the crashed Chinese astronauts controlled his dog team with his brain, not by shouting "Gee!" or "Haw!".

Some of the kids said Henry only won because he was indigenous. Winter thought Henry's story was just better, and said so. This earned him a pat on the shoulder from the principal. This sparked a vague, unformed thought in Winter's young brain that it was kind of fucked up that the smart white kid should be congratulated for just admitting what was obviously true.

Henry made it to Grade 12, but not quite to graduation. After that, Winter ran into him only occasionally on the trails or in the supermarket. He knew vaguely that Henry had a couple kids he didn't get to see that often. He'd also lost a finger in some work accident, and spent some time in jail. Winter was unclear exactly why – you didn't ask – but he knew it was some combination of the usual: break-and-enter, drunken fighting and drug possession.

Winter didn't really re-connect with Henry until they'd both been in Detox together. After the time the summer students at MacBride Museum came to work in the morning to open for tourists and found Winter passed out on the lawn. One of those waves of shame that struck periodically swept over him. One of Taiya's best friends was working at the museum's front desk that morning and called it in to 9-1-1.

Winter pedaled towards Henry. At that moment, a vehicle on the highway suddenly decelerated. Henry tensed and looked up as a pickup cruised past at half highway speed. "Why don't you steal a bike?" shouted a young man's voice. A Tim Horton's Iced Cappucino cup arced through the air, spraying its contents as its lid came off.

Henry ducked and the cup flew over his head, but he couldn't escape the spray. The truck sped away.

"Fucking assholes," said Henry angrily.

"Fucking racist assholes," said Winter.

"Goes without saying." Henry shrugged, brushing a lump of brownish slush off his jacket. "They could use some new material too. That Indian-with-a-bike joke is fucking antique."

Winter had heard it a hundred times too. In fact, one of his first news stories had featured it. A First Nations family had taken the kids for a Sunday-afternoon ride on the waterfront trolley, and had been amazed to hear the volunteer driver asking tourists what they called an Indian with a new bike. The trolley manager had fired the driver, and Winter got his first experience of how deranged the comments under one of his stories could be.

"That joke is like a brain virus that keeps spreading," said Winter.

Henry considered this for a minute. "That's a good one. A brain virus … without a vaccine. Once you hear it, you can't unhear it. You're infected."

Winter noticed Henry was now also missing a front tooth. He tried not to stare.

They shot the shit for a few minutes, catching up on Taiya, Henry's kids, and their various ex-wife issues. They didn't talk about Detox, and Winter didn't ask why Henry was trudging along the highway in the middle of the day.

Winter's phone alarm went off. "Shit, I gotta go. Picking up someone for my daughter at the airport."

"On a bike? It'll be a helluva double if they've got luggage," laughed Henry

Henry reached out for a high hand clasp. Winter grabbed his hand and leaned awkwardly off his bike for a quick man hug. Then Henry continued on his way. Winter noticed he stepped down off the paved shoulder and walked along the ditch to be out of beer-can range.

14

Erik Nielsen International Airport

12:15 p.m., July 6th. +20°C
2104 days sober

Winter glanced at his watch. Taiya had told him three times -- the last time with her eyebrow fully raised -- not to be late picking up the VIP clients who missed their flight. He increased his cadence.

Taiya's main gig that summer was as a junior guide on rafting expeditions in Kluane National Park.

She had applied there without telling any of her parents, which caused a worse-than-usual spat with Misty and LDV. It was risky work. Both the Alsek and the Tatshenshini had lots of big water. Turnback Canyon had that name for a reason.

Winter said it would be a good experience for Taiya. He told them the company had a strong reputation for safety and that steering a raft full of gear was more about judgment and skill with the oars than brute strength.

That just made both women accuse him of mansplaining. After that, they acted like it had all been Winter's idea, and that if he hadn't killed her rolling his truck he was going to get her drowned on the Alsek River.

Taiya excelled at the job. She learned fast and didn't complain, even about the shit jobs the junior guides had to do. And some of them were literal shit jobs. Park rules meant they had to carry out the toilet waste, and the way they did it was have the clients shit into ex-army ammo cases lined with hazmat bags. Taiya's job was to seal them up each morning.

It made Winter proud to see her earn the respect of her bosses. In her drysuit and sunglasses, she looked like a professional as she lashed ropes, pulled the oars and politely but firmly told bank executives from Toronto to sit down and start paddling.

It was also grizzly country. Neither Taiya nor Winter told Misty that most trips carried a pistol-grip short-barrel 12-gauge loaded with bear slugs, and that Taiya knew how to use it.

Taiya's crew and the rest of the clients were already at the put-in assembling the rafts. Winter's job was to meet the bigwigs who had missed their flight, double check they had the right equipment and get them into a rental car headed in the right direction.

Every trip, one of the clients didn't believe the kit list and they had to squeeze a shivering fat rich lady into Taiya's emergency base layers.

He turned his mountain bike off the Alaska Highway, pedaled through the parking lot, and -- dodging a taxi with a texting driver -- hopped his wheels onto the sidewalk in front of the terminal.

Fortunately, the flight was late. The giant video screen showed a continuous loop from the Department of Tourism. Happy white people who seemed never to sweat or be bothered by mosquitoes grinned at him from mountain tops and canoes.

It seemed a bit late to be advertising to tourists who had already arrived. Maybe the point was to reassure them that they hadn't made a terrible vacation mistake; previous tourists had survived and even enjoyed their trip to the Yukon.

Misty did comms at the Department of Tourism now. How she would have ripped into this crap when they were younger, he thought. Before she gave up on theatre and got a government job.

He sat down and pulled out his phone. He did his daily check in with IAmSober. Today's photo was him paddling with Taiya on Tarfu Lake. A favourite lake, a favourite dog named after it. And appropriate for him, since the lake was named after an old army saying: Things Are Really Fucked Up. He tapped to recommit to his pledge. 2104 days sober. That was a lot. But don't think about the race. Just the next stride.

Time for a mindfulness podcast? No, he decided, and started flipping through the competition's stories.

Brett was in the news again. Last year, every journalist in town seemed to love him. A freelancer even did a profile about him for the Walrus in Toronto. But lately the headlines weren't "Inspirational young environmental leader battles to save the Arctic." They were the passive aggressive kind editors used when they had a knife they wanted to twist. "Questions raised as foreign-funded activists target carbon-neutral First Nation project."

Brett's uptight sidekick Chaewon denied it, but Winter thought Brett's most recent protests had attracted noticeably fewer and less enthusiastic participants.

The first passenger appeared through the glass. It was Alex, CEO of Ńjür Nàdäk'a. In business class with no luggage, probably just a day trip to Northern Lights meetings in Vancouver. He walked up the hallway with the fast, easy stride of a hiker.

Winter spotted one of the clients immediately. She came off the plane right after Alex. Probably beside him in business class. Around forty, athletic build, tall and assured, and dressed in the full Patagonia. She carried a camera bag and a sleek laptop satchel. Unlike the locals walking behind her, she sported no duct tape patches on her jacket or crumpled fleece jackets in colours Mountain Equipment Co-op had discontinued fifteen years before.

Winter held up a crumpled piece of paper from his recycling bin with the word "Anna + Greg" scrawled in sharpie.

"Just Anna," she said as she approached. "Greg had to cancel at the last minute. And sorry to be late. They cancelled my flight out of Seatac." She spoke with a smile and the kind of fake friendliness you showed low-level helper folk.

"No problem. If you'd flown Air North, they would've given you a warm cookie."

"Oh? I don't eat sugar."

The Patagonia jacket didn't look totally brand new. Maybe she actually used it for more than going to the mall. Winter noticed it was co-branded with Clima Foundation on the shoulder. The dots began to connect. That was the big American foundation that funded Brett's projects. Clima featured prominently in the conspiracy rants Winter's former principal pasted into the comments box under his stories.

Winter knew what Taiya would say: no jokes about climate activists flying jet planes to the Yukon wearing Gore-Tex made from petrochemicals.

As they waited for the luggage, Winter opened Taiya's checklist on his phone. "Toque slash ski hat?"

Anna pulled up the same list on her phone and showed it to Winter. "Got it all."

They stood silently beside the luggage carousel as Anna sent a few texts. Winter eyed the dark blue Berkeley alum sweatshirt visible under her jacket, trying not to stare too obviously at her breasts. Which were hard not to notice.

She looked up from her phone and eyed him doubtfully.

"Is that cotton?" he asked.

"Huh?"

"Your sweatshirt. If you're counting that as one of your warm layers, we'll need to get you a thick fleece."

"Really?"

"Yeah, cotton is a fake friend. Gets wet and stays wet. Just waiting to turn a wet day into a hypothermia rescue. Plus, it's probably grown by labour camp inmates beside a dried up river in Xinjiang."

She turned and looked more carefully at Winter, as if she had discovered her Uber driver had a PhD in climate modeling. She pulled the collar of her sweatshirt around and felt for the tag.

"I can't see it," she said, flipping the collar over with her thumbs and showing it to Winter.

Winter put his hand on her shoulder and leaned in on his tiptoes. She was wearing some kind of scent – not husky dog with a whiff of diesel like the last woman Winter had been with -- and he saw the silver chain of her necklace disappear over the strap of a sports bra and down a muscular shoulder.

Suddenly, Winter heard Brett's voice: "Anna! Welcome!"

Winter and Anna both started and took a step back like they'd been caught necking behind an ore truck in the Kopper King tavern parking lot.

"Brett! Hi!" Anna's smile looked a bit brittle. Winter recognized the look. Since the accident, it was the one that came across the faces of the girls he knew from high school when you ran into them at Canadian Tire.

"Brother," said Brett to Winter.

"Comrade," Winter replied flatly.

Winter smiled politely as they exchanged the usual greetings. Anna's plane was late. Brett just got her text and zipped over to say hi. Anna had no idea people lived just five minutes from the airport in Whitehorse, how lucky it worked out! They both looked forward to a meeting next week. The weather for the Alsek looked good, but you never knew with the Alsek.

Winter hated airport conversations.

Anna seemed as relieved as he was when the bags finally came. Matching North Face waterproof duffle bags. Winter figured Anna's luggage was worth more than his bike. He hefted one of the bags onto his shoulder and, before Anna could grab the other, Brett picked it up and began carrying it out of the terminal.

"Hang on," said Winter. "We still have to get Anna's rental car."

"Rental car?" asked Brett. "Aren't you driving her to Haines Junction?"

"I don't drive, remember?"

The gears in Brett's brain clicked forward. He turned to Anna. "I could drive you out there. No problem."

Anna was already ahead of him. "That would be great, but I have some errands to do first. Probably best if I have my own car."

"But won't your car spend most of the week just sitting at the put-in?" asked Brett.

"Thanks but I got a good deal and it's already paid for," said Anna.

Brett smiled as graciously as he could, wished Anna good luck on her trip and said his goodbyes. As Anna completed her paperwork at the rental car kiosk, Winter tried to calculate how much money Anna was spending to rent a car for a week to avoid a two-hour drive to Haines Junction with Brett.

They went to the parking lot and tried to stuff Anna's bags into the tiny trunk of her Korean electric car.

"The tag says that sweatshirt is made in China, one hundred percent cotton," said Winter as they got into the car and Anna tried to figure out how to start it. "You should ask yourself why Berkeley is trying to kill you."

"I suppose there are shops here, within a five-minute drive of the airport?"

"Yep, I could take you shopping. Or if you're never going to use it again, I could lend you some of my daughter's gear. Her winter camping stuff is at my place."

"Let's do that. Avoid needless consumption," replied Anna, and steered the car onto the road. "How did you get to the airport, anyway?"

"Bike. I can pick it up later."

"Why don't you drive? Carbon emissions?"

Winter considered this. He looked at Anna's hands on the steering wheel. She was wearing a wedding ring. What the hell. "Well, since you already let me look down your shirt, I'll be honest. Because I was buzzed out of my head on vodka and Oxy and drove my truck off the road with my daughter in the backseat. You'll see Taiya's scar."

"Wow, so you don't drive at all?"

"Or drink. Or take painkillers. I promised Taiya."

"You're basically an outdoor education monk."

"Yeah, the fun never stops. First stop is my ex-wife's to get a drysuit gasket you have to take to my daughter."

To Winter's relief, Misty and LDV did that thing where they put the package for Taiya in the mailbox and pretended not to be home.

On the way to his house, Winter pointed out the unauthorized tourist highlights. The Marwell area, where they used to make indigenous people live when they weren't allowed to own land inside the old city limits. The toxic sludge pits beside the World War Twoera oil refinery that the government had been planning to clean up for as long as Winter could remember. The blackened skeleton of the SS Klondike sternwheeler and the line of old houses and big trees showing how far the Wildfires got.

"Does the Tourism department pay you extra for this?" Winter glanced at her. She seemed to be enjoying herself.

Winter lived in the tiny old one-and-a-half government house he grew up in and then inherited from his mother when her cancer came back; she had lived to see Taiya born but not -- and this was fortunate, the neighbours all agreed -- the accident. Two bedrooms upstairs, living room and bathroom on the main floor, and a big unfinished basement. Winter jumped up the stairs, opened the front door.

Tarfu went nuts, running between Winter and Anna.

He pointed Anna to the bathroom. "Long drive ahead."

"You don't even lock the front door?"

"Nothing worth stealing in the house. The garage is locked. That's where the bikes are."

Winter went down the stairs to look for Taiya's winter gear box. A few minutes later, he heard the toilet pipes rattle above his head, followed by the sound of Anna's boots on the stairs. Tarfu's claws clicked on the stairs right behind her.

"So this is the monk's lair!" said Anna, running her hand over the kayak gear and skis racked along the wall. This trip was already working, she thought. It was good to get out of her usual bubble where everyone knew Greg and, apparently, that he'd been having an affair for months. Her eyes lingered on the guest bed in the corner of the basement, covered with sleeping bags and bike parts. Maybe even some vacation sex. Her new friend was fit and funny. Despite the Oxy and alcoholism, he seemed more balanced than the VC bro who just asked her out in Seattle.

She turned back to Winter. "Talk about conspicuous consumption," she added. "Do you really need twenty pairs of skis?"

"Half of them are Taiya's. We got rid of the ones we don't need." He ran through the list: cross-country skis for groomed trails, skate skis for biathlon, rock skis for shoulder season, some old metal edged telemark skis they mostly used for long-distance touring, alpine touring for turns in the passes, and some alpine skis and rock skis for afternoons on Mount Sima.

Winter found a thick sweater of Taiya's and a midweight layer which looked like they would fit Anna.

He walked her to the car, explaining the directions to Haines Junction and how she would be out of service for half the drive. He texted her the What3Words link showing the exact location of the parking spot where the guides were assembling the rafts.

"You better get going," he said. "If you're late, you'll get hit by afternoon headwinds and have to drag the rafts through the shallows."

"That's not in the brochure."

"Bonus character building. Give the sweaters to Taiya, or text me when you get back."

"If I want to not have a drink."

"Something like that."

15

A rafting camp near Lowell Glacier

2:37 a.m., July 9th. +6°C

The noise started Taiya out of a deep sleep. Her eyes popped open. It was pitch black and there was a roaring noise in her ears.

It took a second to remember where she was: guiding a rafting trip on the Alsek. The noise was the wind. The same wind that had held them at Lowell Glacier for an extra day.

She pushed her eye shades up onto her toque. The gust had the tent almost flat. The fly flapped wildly just inches above her face. The midnight sun glowed faintly through the fly. It was darker than usual. That would be the clouds dropping the rain that the wind was hammering into the tent.

The wind abated for a few seconds and the tent poles pushed themselves back upright. Hopefully the client tents were properly pegged and no poles broke. She really didn't feel like running around in horizontal rain fixing poles.

She looked over at her tentmate. The other guide's hand appeared out of the mummy bag, found a missing foam earplug and jammed it back in. "Fucking wind," he said before readjusting his eye shades and rolling over.

Taiya looked at her watch: 2:37 a.m. Four more hours of listening to the wind before she got up to make coffee. And the clients would need their coffee today. They would be sluggish and bleary eyed, and wondering why they hadn't chosen a rafting trip with luxury lodges in Colorado.

She stretched in her sleeping bag. Her shoulder muscles screamed. She slowly flexed her hands, which seemed to be frozen in the shape of the oar handles.

And when the clients rolled groggily out of their tents and squinted apprehensively into the wind, it would be her job to be cheerful. A good guide fed the group positive energy. She knew she was good at this. It was her job at home too. Mom's doom loops after a couple glasses of wine. Karen's frowny face. If mom wasn't in a doom loop, there would be something political. And dad. Well, he had a lot to think about.

Thoughts rolled through Taiya's mind as she tried unsuccessfully to get back to sleep. The biathlon race where she was in the lead but shot zero out of five on the last lap. Leaving Karen's birthday cake where Tarfu could reach it. Not getting invited to Julia's party.

Her mind wandered to the time she drove out to the family cabin at Marsh Lake for a solo study weekend before final exams. The musty cabin smell and the light flooding in as she opened the bear shutters. Tarfu jumping up into his favourite spot on the couch to nap. Sitting on the moose rug by the woodstove, like she used to do when she was a kid.

Mom called the cabin the "time capsule." Before Gramma died, she had covered a wall with photos. The cabin being built when dad was a kid. Boats and floatplanes on the beach with Grampa and his friends either smiling with beers or holding lake trout for the camera. Dad making his valedictorian speech at high school. Dad getting his journalism award. Photos of Taiya at the cabin each summer, until Gramma couldn't go out any more.

How could everyone look so happy in the photos and be so mad at each other in real life?

Which had led her away from Biology and down an internet rabbit hole in the *Yukon Sun* archives. Stories about the accident. Gramma's obituary. Dad's first story after starting at the paper. Dad's hockey team in high school. Grampa as a young man speaking at a memorial for an exploration buddy. Grampa smiling proudly at his mine's first gold pour. Grampa selling the company and moving Outside.

Another gust flattened the tent. Over the wind, she heard shouts from a client tent.

She felt an elbow from her tent-mate: "Your turn," said a muffled voice from deep inside the mummy bag.

Taiya sat up and reached for her rain jacket. "Fucking wind."

16

Z-Dog Placer Mining, Whitehorse yard

2:10 a.m, July 9th, +7°C
2017 days sober

Winter crouched by the chain link fence. It was like high school. The problem with sneaking around the Yukon in the summer was that even at two in the morning it wasn't really dark.

To the north, the pink shades of the sunset bounced off layers of cloud. It was like a Ted Harrison painting. But that was for tourists with insomnia. Back to work.

He could see the gray shapes of shipping containers scattered around the Z-Dog compound.

Zee-dog. Only Zach would think of such a stupid name for his company. And he was undoubtedly proud of it.

The Whitehorse end of Zach's placer mining operation had exactly the kind of random junk you'd expect: barrels, crates, pipes and beat-up equipment. It was hard to tell what was new and headed to Dawson, or damaged and heading the other way. Dandelions growing through the tracks of one cat suggested some gear came in and just never left.

Was this a bad idea? Probably. If Artemis knew about it, she would insist the camera was planted outside Zach's property line.

However, if she kept talking about how the paper needed to do less press-release chasing and more investigative journalism, she was going to have to be okay with some investigating.

He felt the bear spray on his belt. Doberman spray, in this situation.

There were no signs of humans or guard dogs. He stepped out of the willows, put his fingers and the tip of his right shoe into the fence, and started climbing the eight feet.

Good thing Zach had cheaped out and not bought the barbed wire accessories for the top of his fence. He rolled his body over the top, being careful not to catch clothing on the wire ends, and dropped onto the gravel on the other side.

As he moved into the yard, the junk took on more definite shapes: a small office trailer, an excavator missing a track, a half dozen bulldozer blades and a variety of bent metal pipes and sluice box gear.

There was only one fuel tank visible. A red thousand-litre unit for the back of a pickup. That was too small. Winter's Oldtimers line mate said you could buy thousands of litres at a time from Zach.

He must keep it in one of the containers.

Winter set up the wildlife camera in a pile of junk with a view of three shipping containers. It was one of Taiya's older cameras, but had good settings for distance and field of vision. He set the motion detection to low. He was looking for trucks not chipmunks.

The cops were profoundly uninterested in fuel smuggling or carbon rationing violations. The Greens complained they got arrested at protests but the Freedos never did. Winter suspected this was as much personal as principle. The Greens were annoyingly smug and, unlike Amber, never handed out fresh-baked cookies to the cops working a protest.

He activated the camera and scaled the fence. He stumbled through the willows back to the trail, then biked back to the Miles Canyon bridge.

17

Robert Service Way Snow Dump

10:00 a.m, July 9th, +12°C
2107 days sober

The old black F-350 slowed as it passed the LNG plant and pulled up to the stop sign on Robert Service Way. The oldtimer noticed a bunch of vehicles parked in the city snow dump across the road. In the summer? He slipped the vehicle into neutral and let out the clutch. Were they bringing back the monster truck event they used to hold there?

The City had refused to renew the lease unless they switched to electric monster trucks. How stupid was that?

His distance eyesight was still excellent. He saw the crowd of people and the Yukon Government portable press conference backdrop.

"More fucking bullshit," he muttered to himself. There had to be at least twenty vehicles in the parking lot. How many bureaucrats did it take to put in a lightbulb these days? They were too busy arguing over whether they were male or female to get anything done. It was getting out of control.

He remembered the kid on the Millenium Trail who heard him calling Casca, and told him he shouldn't name his dog that without getting permission from the First Nation.

What the fuck, I mean really, he thought, feeling his blood pressure rise. That kind of thing made you mad. Really mad.

He saw Alex's truck with the Ńjür Nàdäk'a Devcorp logo. A big, white, brand-new pickup. Whatever was happening, he thought, it would mean more handouts for the Indians.

He turned to his dog, who was napping on the seat beside him, and rubbed the dog's neck. "It's one giant clusterfuck performance, Casca. Like those fags at the Guild Theatre, except we all have to pay for it."

He saw the granolas protesting off to one side. There were only six of them. What a joke.

These were the people who went to the old Capital Hotel bar and paid ten bucks for a fruit beer from Vancouver. They didn't even carry Yukon Gold there. When he'd asked for a Reuben the waitress seemed to not even know what that was. He wasn't paying twenty-five fucking dollars for a fucking veggie burger. Jesus.

He shook his head. Maybe we should do what the Russians do, and just arrest the environmentalists and send them to work up north. At least the East Indians at KFC did something useful.

Thinking of Dirty Bird, maybe he would treat himself to KFC for lunch. He put the vehicle into gear and turned right onto Robert Service Way.

As he shifted up to second, he saw a biker coming towards him. The biker seemed to recognize the truck and waved. It was Kendrick's boy, Winter.

Not a bad kid. Too bad he picked such a useless job. And biking around town? Did he think he was in Europe? The oldtimer waved back and accelerated into third gear.

Winter turned off Robert Service Way. His mood wasn't much less sour than the oldtimer's.

Did LDV's comms woman really think they'd get a better story if they made the media get in their cars -- or on their bikes, in his case -- and come out to a litter-strewn gravel pit to hear the usual suspects read the same talking points they could have just emailed with the press release?

Plus, where was he supposed to lock his bike in a gravel pit surrounded by burnt-out stumps. He pulled his notepad and recorder out of his bag, put his helmet inside and slipped his lock around the frame and back wheel. Then, lacking any better ideas, he laid the bike down on a patch of dandelions near where everyone else had parked.

He heard boots crunching on the gravel and looked up. It was Echo. The wind was making her pink hair fly around.

It was also pressing her shirt tight against her body. The boots were leather city boots with heels, and she wore tight elasticized khakis. God, she dripped sex, thought Winter.

Winter couldn't help but see how tall and thin she was. As usual, her shoulders were slightly hunched. It was like the weight of the air over her head was about to crush her slender body. If you took her to the Chilkoot Trail and put a forty-pound pack on her, she would snap like a twig.

"Hey Winter!" she said cheerily. "Where are you going to take your photos? Where the carbon pipeline is supposed to go? Or maybe the minister with the LNG plant and Grey Mountain in the background?"

"That's what they want us to do. The only time it's interesting to take pictures at the snow dump is in the spring, when the snow pile melts and all the mangled bikes and frozen missing pets appear."

Echo suppressed a laugh. Oh god, thought Winter, she's going to put that one in her blog.

Another gleaming white pickup pulled up and parked beside Brett's campervan and a beat up Mazda with an "LNG is LNG" bumper sticker. The pickup had an orange light on the roof, safety whip-flags and the mining company logo on the side. Winter recognized the CEO, Jim something, as he got out of his truck.

"Is that the best they can do?" said Jim dismissively, gesturing at the bumper sticker. "Of course it's LNG. That's a feature not a bug. We can capture the carbon."

The spinning had begun already. "But not all of it," Winter replied, making sure to smile.

"Sure, sure. We'll just buy a few offsets for the extra," replied the CEO confidently. "I think people are over this fixation on LNG. Look at the" - he made air quotes with his fingers - "protesters. More public relations people here than protesters. Makes the chess club at my high school look like a mass movement."

Echo was making a note in her notebook. Winter sighed inwardly.

But the CEO wasn't wrong about the number of protesters. It was so embarrassing Amber wasn't even bothering to counterprotest.

The CEO leaned closer to the Mazda and ran his finger over the bumper sticker. "It's not even a real bumper sticker," he said derisively. "They just printed it out on label paper. As soon as it rains, this protest is over!" Ignoring Winter and Echo, he turned and strode towards the press conference.

Again, Winter had to admit he wasn't wrong about the bumper sticker. Which was puzzling. Usually there was no limit to what Brett would spend for his campaigns to look professional.

Mind you, Taiya had said something about budget cuts at YCC. Apparently Brett's co-pilot Chaewon, who Winter thought was sometimes vaguely hot in a kind of fit-Korean-granola-with-tattoos-and-leg-hair kind of way, had been given a few weeks of unpaid vacation.

Winter and Echo turned and followed the CEO. He kept talking, whether they showed any interest or not, about the project and showed them the route the eventual carbon pipeline would take.

Winter decided maybe he would take a photo. One taken from ground level, with some dandelions and snow-dump litter in the foreground and LDV out of focus doing one of her arm-wave things in the background.

18

In a Short-Take-Off-and-Landing Cessna over the Alsek River

4:30 p.m., July 16th, 14°C
2114 days sober

Music crackled into Anna's headphones over the roar of the engine.

"Fly me to the moon
Let me play among the stars
Let me see what spring is like on
Jupiter and Mars
In other words, hold my hand
In other words, baby, kiss me…"

The pilot's cheerful voice came in over the music. "A bit of a bumpy ride today. Maybe some classic Sinatra will smooth things out."

Fuck, thought Anna. Get me out of here.

She gripped the door handle as the plane lurched again. With her other hand, she pulled out her phone. Maybe they were in coverage. Two days in a tent waiting for the wind to let up enough to fly out had given her a lot of time to think. Her wedding ring was in the arm pocket of her Goretex jacket. She'd taken it off when her fingers started to swell from all the paddling. But there was no point in putting it back on. She had decided. She couldn't go back this time. Greg would always find another cute, smart junior associate at his firm.

Her mind turned to that guy she met in Whitehorse. She had spent a lot of time in her sleeping bag -- unable to sleep as the wind battered the tent -- thinking about him too.

She turned on her phone and stared at the apple on the start-up screen. Suddenly the plane dropped, with her stomach seeming to follow one roller coaster car behind. The corner of a vomit bag poking out of the seat pocket in front reminded her that reading in motion might be a terrible idea. She swallowed, looked at the horizon and tried to listen to the music.

She looked over at Taiya, who smiled. Taiya leaned in and shouted, "If he flies you on the way in, he plays the helicopter music from *Apocalypse Now*."

The pilot, like everyone in the Yukon, thought he was a character. Mostly, they were just nuts.

The plane approached the runway. Anna craned her neck to look out the front window. It didn't look like they were lined up with the runway. She glanced over at Taiya, who was smiling and humming to the music.

The runway got closer. They definitely weren't headed for it.

She gripped Taiya's arm and leaned over to shout, "We aren't headed for the runway!"

Taiya leaned in and shouted. "That's right. He hates landing his tundra tires on asphalt. He'll land on the grass beside the runway."

Anna stared straight ahead and gripped her seat.

After they had landed, loaded all the gear into the vehicles and said their goodbyes, Anna got into her rental car. She just sat in the driver seat for a minute and took a deep breath. Then she took her phone off airplane mode.

Over 1000 unread emails and dozens of Signal, iMessage and Telegram conversations.

She found Winter's last Signal with the directions. She hadn't dated since Greg and wondered what people texted each other on Tinder. She tapped out a reply: "Back in town tonight. Still up for that drink?"

Her thumb paused over Send. She remembered the alcohol and drugs. She changed it to "Still up to connect?"

No, too corporate. "Still free to meet up?" She hit send.

She watched her phone to see if he replied. This is so high school, she thought to herself. But then the symbol showing Winter was typing popped up. "Yep. How about a ride and then dinner?"

Whoa. Hang on, cowgirl, she said to herself. A ride was exactly what she had been thinking about. But that was direct. And before dinner?

Another Signal came in: "I have a bike that will fit you."

Was he that clueless? He just might be. She started tapping a reply, then stopped and hit the call button. She glanced in the rearview mirror. There was a twig in her hair. Better stay audio only.

"Hey," said Winter.

"Hey," replied Anna. "Maybe something more lowkey and civilized? Like dinner? As you know, I've been going to the washroom in a World War Two ammo box for a week."

"It's Whitehorse so I can't promise civilized. But definitely indoors."

They agreed to meet at her hotel when she got back to Whitehorse and had cleaned up.

Two hours later, she let herself into her hotel room and headed immediately for the shower. It was amazing how good it felt. Infinite hot water, whenever you wanted it, just coming out of a pipe in the wall. She scrubbed the sweat and dirt off every inch of her body.

She stepped out of the shower and looked at herself in the mirror. The sunglasses tan was terrible. But maybe she'd lost a few pounds. She flexed her arms in the mirror. Maybe even gained some muscle tone. It felt like it, anyway.

She picked up her wet paddling clothes and slipped them into a plastic bag like toxic waste. Then she got dressed and put on her makeup. Smart casual. She put on her sunglasses and headed to the lobby to meet Winter.

The elevator door opened and she stepped out. She could feel the teenage boy at the Check In counter watch her cross the lobby. He hadn't done that when she was wearing Goretex and had leaves in her hair.

Winter was leaning against a pillar by the entrance. "Welcome to the big city!" he said, putting away his phone. "What kind of food do you feel like?"

"Doesn't matter. Somewhere off the beaten path."

"Still emotionally exhausted from the Alsek?"

"No, it was great. Your daughter was great. I just have meetings all day tomorrow and don't need to run into anyone tonight."

Winter appeared to consider this. Did he realize it was Brett she was avoiding? "The Airport Chalet," he said. "Got your car keys?"

Winter sat in the passenger seat and gave Anna directions up Robert Service Way.

"Want to stop and visit your PowerBlimp?" asked Winter.

Anna laughed. "That's okay. Our finance department keeps me up to date."

"Taiya runs its Instagram account. The problem with blimps is they don't do anything. Once you've done three 'blimp at sunset' photos, there's not much else."

The Airport Chalet parking lot was gravel, with giant mud puddles in the middle and 18-wheelers parked around the edges. Her electric rental car felt tiny in comparison. She steered it slowly around the puddles and potholes, only to see a mud-spattered Chevy Bolt charge straight through the puddles, spraying water in all directions, and take the parking spot she had been heading for.

Instead, she steered the car in beside an 18-wheeler.

The long, flat building appeared to be a classic 1960s Alaska Highway lodge, low, flat, with dark-brown wood siding. The deck was decorated with planters full of half-dead flowers, and covered with worn, green indoor-outdoor carpeting. As their eyes adjusted to the darkness, an old Super Variant poster with "not!!!" scrawled in Sharpie between "Masks" and "Required" came into focus on the dark fake-wood paneling.

They got a table between the big stone fireplace and the windows facing the airport. Anna pointed at the bushplane photos on the walls. "I was hoping not to see one of those things again."

"Those are all the planes that people have puked up Airport Chalet dinners in," replied Winter. Anna stared at him for a second. "Old joke," he said. "Sorry. Food's good actually."

The waitress came by. She was chewing gum vigorously. Winter ordered a cranberry and soda. Anna took off her sunglasses, looked up at the waitress, and asked for a pinot grigio.

Anna noticed the waitress's jaw pause for just a second as she looked at Anna's raccoon tan. "We got white and red," she said finally. "I'll check the box on what it is."

When she left, Anna turned to Winter. "Is it that bad?"

"Full raccoon," admitted Winter with a smile. "I'd consider it a badge of honour."

Greg would have pretended her disastrous tan lines didn't exist.

Anna felt a strange yearning for red meat and fries. But Winter ordered the Alaskan halibut -- Taiya was boycotting beef -- so Anna did too.

They talked about the rafting trip. Winter had a hard time hiding how proud he was when Anna told him how professionally Taiya carried herself.

"She said you're a journalist," said Anna. "You didn't tell me that when we met."

Winter shrugged. "It's the *Yukon Sun*, not the BBC."

"What do people around here say about Clima Foundation?"

"No one knows who you are, except my old principal. Who has lost his nut. He keeps writing letters to the editor saying you're the climate Illuminati pulling all the strings."

"What else does he say?"

"Other than that I had a lot of potential? That all the money for Brett's protests comes from you."

"What do people say about Brett?" Winter looked up at her sharply. She suddenly felt like she'd ruined a fun dinner. "Sorry. I shouldn't have asked that. He's your brother. Let's change the subject."

"No, it's okay. He's my half-brother. And we're not close. He grew up Outside after my parents split up. He got the trust fund from dad and I got-" -- he waved his arm at the view across the valley -- "all this."

"And, if you don't mind, what do people say about him?"

"Half the people love him and his dedication to the climate. Half the people think he's a rich, arrogant prick who's more interested in being famous and shagging eco-bunnies than saving the planet. And all the people think he's crossed a big red line by going after the First Nations and their Northern Lights project."

"That's what some of my board members think too. We're getting a bunch of blowback on the socials."

"Yeah, I checked out your website. Lots of new projects about indigenous economic empowerment in the Brazilian rainforest."

"What do you really think about Northern Lights?"

Winter looked at Anna's glass of bad wine. He pushed it out of his mind and concentrated on swirling the ice in his cranberry and soda. "I won't admit to this quote, but underneath all the PR bullshit I think Alex has a good project. Cheap power, most of the carbon underground and all that. And it actually is the kind of big First Nations business project people have been talking about forever."

Anna knew it was time to change the subject. Any more, and he might get a hint of what she was going to tell Brett the next day. "Let's talk about your daughter," she said.

"You have to ask about my dog Tarfu too," Winter laughed. "I have photos."

As they drove back to her hotel, Anna made some connections. Taiya was taking care of Tarfu tonight. Which meant she probably knew they were out for dinner. It *was* like high school.

But would Winter make the next move? He seemed to be enjoying himself, but he hadn't really followed up on her hints. She might have to throw herself at him, she decided.

When they got to the hotel, they got awkwardly out of the car.

"That was a lot of fun," said Winter. He picked up his bike seat and helmet from the back seat.

"Oh, I forgot," lied Anna. "Come on upstairs. I have to give you the sweater I borrowed from Taiya." She felt herself blushing. Of course, she had thought of giving Taiya her sweater earlier but had forgotten on purpose.

When the elevator doors closed, Winter started telling a story about when Prince Charles stayed in the hotel. Anna turned to him, looped a finger inside his belt, and pulled him closer. He didn't pull away. She kissed him.

The elevator doors opened. The hotel only had three floors. She put her boot across the door, and pulled out her room key.

"I … I don't have any protection," stuttered Winter. She looked at him. "I didn't think I had a chance. You know, booze and oxy problems with a scarred daughter. It's not a great dating profile."

"Don't worry about that. I bought the last box at the gas station in Haines Junction, just in case," said Anna, tugging on Winter's belt. "All they had was blue raspberry flavour."

1982 - JUNE

1982-1

Unnamed mountain near Big Kalzas Lake

Noon, June 22nd, 1982. +21°C

Shawn grabbed a willow and pulled himself up off the loose scree and onto a solid rocky outcrop. He ignored the stray rocks clattering downhill from his last step. Salty, stinging sweat dripped into his eyes. He sat on the outcrop and panted, looking at the rock cuts on his hands. He glanced uphill. Where the fuck were those guys?

The mosquitoes buzzed around his head. He didn't care. He shrugged off his pack, pulled the front of his t-shirt up and rubbed the fabric across his face like a towel. He looked down at the upside down Rush world-tour logo. Now the girl in the panties was covered with mud, sweat and a spot of blood from a flattened mosquito.

It had been a great show. And a wild weekend in Vancouver.

You needed big bucks to live like that.

Which reminded Shawn why he was halfway up some mountain in the middle of nowhere, trying to keep up with Kendrick and that Native guy, Wayne.

His pack was mostly empty. A squashed baloney sandwich, a quarter-full canteen and an Oh Henry bar wrapper. Plus some of Kendrick's geologist stuff and, in case of bear trouble, a sawed-off pistol-grip 12-gauge. By the time they filled the pack with mineral samples, the way back to the plane would be even worse. He could see the plane pulled up on the beach, far below and in the distance. At least it would be downhill. Mostly.

God it would feel good to stagger out of the bush onto the beach, strip off, and jump in the lake.

Shawn knew he shouldn't get too far behind. He squirted some more DEET onto his hand and rubbed it all over his face and neck. Then he stood up, shouldered his pack, and started climbing. They were headed up to the ridge, so he couldn't go wrong if he just kept climbing. It was kind of amazing to think of how much money Kendrick was spending just because some old Indians told Wayne they saw something here. Kendrick called it a "showing." Shawn couldn't remember the description, but the shape and colours had got Kendrick all excited. He'd been hiking the mountains around here for two years and, who knew, this could be the one.

Well, I get paid whether they find anything or not, thought Shawn.

Shawn kept climbing. He was strong, but six inches shorter than Kendrick and had what his sister called love handles. Unlike Kendrick, he hated jogging and preferred hockey and a few beers to cross-country skiing. You could tell that, when his thirties hit, his love handles would merge into a beer belly.

He went slowly but steadily. It was steep. The last dwarf spruce were far below and he was almost out of the buckbrush. He was learning to follow the game trails when he could, and which rocks to trust for a foothold.

Finally, he saw Kendrick and Wayne up and far to his left. He began sidehilling on a slight upwards diagonal towards them.

They were standing where a huge jagged outcrop jutted out of the mountain. The slope was super steep, and long runs of rock debris fell away to the left. It was as if this outcrop was one of the mountain's ribs, protruding from its protective mossy skin.

Shawn noticed how excited Kendrick was. These rocks were a UBC geologist's wet dream, apparently. Kendrick was soon collecting samples, taking photos, making notes. Wayne seemed to have caught the spirit, and was following Kendrick around with his bag.

Shawn sat down to catch his breath. They'd give him a bag of rocks to carry soon enough. In the meantime, Kendrick produced a long tape measure, more maps and a geologist's field guide full of colour pictures.

Finally, Kendrick came over to Shawn and slapped him on the shoulder. "Copper-gold porphyry, possibly enormous! I'm guessing lots of moly too." He went on describing how porphyry deposits were formed miles underground millions of years ago. Shawn listened politely as phrases like "porphyritic intrusive rocks" flew past him.

Kendrick started describing how many claims they would stake and where they would drill. Shawn looked back down the mountain, calculating where he would put a cat trail to get the gear up here from the lake.

Kendrick was still elated. He reached into his pack and pulled out three stubby bottles of Old Style, each in a protective wool sock. "I had a lucky feeling," he said with a big grin. He popped the tops with the opener on his keychain and handed a beer to each guy.

"Ken, I'm gonna be the next Skookum Jim!" said Wayne, beaming.

"You betcha, brother!" agreed Kendrick.

"50-50," said Wayne, still beaming.

"Mmm, hmmm," replied Kendrick. Shawn noticed a bit less enthusiasm. Share half of it with an Indian, just because the guy's uncles told some story about coloured rocks they saw on a hunting trip? That was stupid, thought Shawn. Sure, Skookum Jim got rich during the gold rush. But he actually found the gold in the first place. He wasn't just tagging along with a guy with a PhD in geology from UBC.

Wayne as a mine owner? Maybe waitresses from the KK would drive the cats too.

Kendrick went on describing the future. It would be the whole package. Maybe underground *and* open pit. A mill and power plant closer to the lake. The camp over there. The airstrip beside it. Stock on the Vancouver Stock Exchange. Cigars and Crown Royal all around.

Shawn drained the last of his beer and stood up. Far below him, a marmot was sunning itself on a rock. Shawn leaned back and threw the beer bottle. He watched as it arced silently through the air, hurtling down towards the unsuspecting critter. It was a good throw. The beer bottle smashed only a foot away from the marmot, who chirped in alarm and scrambled for cover.

"Fucking A," said Shawn. "Let's get back to the plane."

1982-2

The Vancouver Club

5:00 p.m., Friday, July 9th, 1982. +25°C

Kendrick strode confidently along West Hastings, looking for the Vancouver Club. He was pretty sure it was between Burrard and Hornby, but had never been there. He hadn't been the kind of UBC student who got invited to the Vancouver Club.

That had now changed.

He was wearing a new suit he had picked up earlier that afternoon at Eaton's. It fit well and needed only a few quick alterations. He wore it with old shoes and his favourite tie. He had rumpled the suit up a bit in his hotel room as he changed. He didn't want to seem like the kind of guy who needed to buy a new suit because the only other suit he had ever owned had a cigarette hole in the sleeve from the Yukon Geological Survey Christmas booze up.

He had flown down from Whitehorse on the CP Air noon flight -- just one stop, thank God, not the milk run through Watson Lake and Fort St. John -- wearing jeans and a t-shirt. Just one drink on the plane and then the bus downtown to meet his fictional great aunt for tea on her birthday. He knew half the people on the flight and didn't want to be one of those geologists who started rumours by flying to Vancouver in a suit to meet bankers and lawyers.

Which was exactly what he was doing.

He knew he needed a Vancouver mining lawyer. He couldn't use anyone in Whitehorse, since word would immediately get out. He didn't want to go to the Kopper King and have the barmaid congratulate him on the latest assay results.

Plus, his wife's cousin was a lawyer in Whitehorse. If Kendrick didn't use him, it would be an insult. If Kendrick did use him, his wife would know the details. And that, plus the usual cocktails, would result in half the wives in town knowing.

There might also be some awkward questions about why his wife had zero shares in the company.

It was better to have the lawyer in Vancouver, the wife and her vodka slimes in Whitehorse, and the kids in the basement either beaning each other with lego or watching Gilligan's Island.

Plus, if things went well, he would need someone in Vancouver who could connect him to the Howe Street guys he would need to list the company on the Vancouver Stock Exchange. If this recession ever ended. It wasn't exactly great timing to be starting a Yukon mining company with the Faro mine threatening to go under.

Then again, maybe that's why a Vancouver mining lawyer had enough spare time to invite him to the Vancouver Club.

But, as Kendrick strolled down West Hastings and enjoyed the hustle and bustle of the big city, he realized the best thing about having a lawyer in Vancouver: a perfect excuse to get out of Whitehorse.

It was too bad he had booked himself a return flight the next day.

The evening's plan was simple. Meet the lawyer at the Vancouver Club bar. Have a drink and finalize a few details. Then upstairs to sign a few documents, and back to the restaurant for dinner. The lawyer was bringing his wife to celebrate.

Kendrick wondered if many mining companies were born in the Captain's Bar at the Vancouver Club, or if his lawyer just needed to spend a minimum amount at the Club each month.

He hopped up the Club stairs two at a time, checked in, and was shown to the Captain's Bar on the third floor.

Everything was as he had hoped and expected. The Captain's Bar oozed privilege and exclusivity. His lawyer was grey-haired, portly, in a nice three-piece suit and eminently respectable-looking. He seemed to know half the people in the bar, who in turn all seemed to be mining executives or stock brokers, and Kendrick enjoyed being introduced as a "hotshot geologist from up North."

The only surprise was when the lawyer spoke Spanish to the bartender. It turned out he'd worked for Anaconda Copper in Chile in the 1970s.

The Captain's Bar's legendary personal private liquor lockers also existed. Kendrick was expecting Black Label, but instead his lawyer produced a bottle of eighteen-year-old Glenfiddich with an elaborate backstory involving a cousin in Glasgow. Kendrick had never heard of single-malt scotch, or drinking it straight, but it seemed to be part of the show.

The business didn't take long.

"Most of your investors are from back East," noted the lawyer.

"Friends and family, mostly Toronto," replied Kendrick. It had not been easy getting seed money out of the family, or even explaining what seed money was to some of them. His share was from maxing out the mortgage on the house. If the wife ever bothered opening a bank statement, there would be trouble.

"No Yukon shareholders, I see," said the lawyer. "I thought there was an Indian fellow you co-discovered it with."

Kendrick lifted the scotch to his lips and took a sip. "I paid him out in cash," he replied. The lawyer's eyebrow lifted. "He signed a receipt," added Kendrick.

The lawyer seemed mollified.

"Wise not to have local investors. It'll be easier for you to run a tight ship. I could tell you about a gang of buddies who found a deposit near Williams Lake. Sued each other silly." He gestured with his cigarette around the bar. "Good for the lawyers, though."

The two men headed downstairs and chatted about Latin America as they waited at the women's entrance for the lawyer's wife before going to dinner. Two ladies arrived, and Kendrick immediately lost interest in his lawyer's Chilean mining stories. Both women were tall with long black hair, stylishly dressed and with striking Latin looks. The first looked older, but had aged well. The younger was in her mid twenties and was absolutely spectacular.

They just don't have women like that in the Yukon, thought Kendrick.

"Ah, my wife!" enthused the lawyer. "And her niece Cristina too. Visiting for the summer from Santiago."

Kendrick smiled, and the introductions were made.

"Do you visit Vancouver for a long time?" asked Cristina. Kendrick loved the soft Spanish accent and slightly garbled English.

He smiled. "My great aunt's birthday lunch is tomorrow. So I don't go back North until Sunday night."

FALL

21

Yukon Sun newsroom, Third and Main

8:54am, September 5th. +8°C
2165 days sober

Winter scrolled through wildlife cameras on Amazon. The one at Zach's yard was so old and clunky. He thought he'd set it to only capture large objects, but when he retrieved the SIM card it had 10,000 photos of fireweed swaying in the wind. Plus one very fucking annoying squirrel. And dead batteries.

He had double checked the settings when he put in new batteries. But now he'd have to risk sneaking into Zach's yard -- again -- to retrieve it.

Artemis crutched over to Winter's desk and took a sip from her insulated Yeti water bottle as she waited for Winter to look up.

"Did you read the comments on your Northern Lights article?"

"If my old principal wants me to read his stuff, he should write for Backcountry magazine."

Winter made a point of not reading the comments about his stories on the paper's Facebook page.

But Artemis did. It was part of the editor's job to make sure not too many references to Hitler made it through the filters.

"Commentland actually likes Northern Lights," she said, leaning her hip on Winter's desk. The project seemed to have something for everyone: jobs, clean power, First Nations ownership. "The normals seem to love carbon pipelines, and the nutbars are breaking three to one in favour too. It's amazing. Amber and your ex's robo-wife actually agree on something."

"But Brett doesn't. How's he doing?"

"Losing. Badly. I thought he had this town wrapped around his little finger. But not this time. Even Clima's X feed has gone totally silent on the Yukon." She popped open the Yeti's straw again and hydrated herself. "I hear YCC is out of money. Any Clima bigwigs coming to bail them out?"

Winter looked at his phone. In his Signal app was a message from Anna suggesting a weekend in Seattle. "Not that I know of," he replied.

Artemis shrugged and wandered off to explain the concept of dangling modifiers to the intern.

Winter logged onto the system and checked out the stories for the next edition. He clicked on "Stock Option Bonanza." Maybe, for once, the business columnist was onto something interesting.

He waved Artemis over again and pointed at the screen.

"The stock options for the mining CEO involved with Northern Lights. Are these numbers right?"

"The English is right, or, rather, it is now," she said, with an eye roll. "English-for-Economists would be a welcome innovation at Canadian universities."

"Yeah, but the math. I mean, these numbers are huge."

"Under which rock have you been hiding? Of course mining bosses make prodigious sums."

"But, I mean, this is *huge*. This says if the share price goes from a buck to ten bucks-"

"Which is the kind of thing that happens when a junior mining company actually makes it." Artemis leaned in to read the numbers on the screen.

"Yeah, then the CEO will make a couple of million. At least. That's like ten times what I make, all at once!"

Artemis glanced sideways at Winter. "Ten times? I guess *you* didn't take Math-for-Journalists. There's a calculator on your phone."

Winter tapped the numbers into his phone. "Holy shit!"

"That number's so big only because you keep refusing, I suppose because you love working with me, to apply for a better paying comms job at the gov."

Winter whistled. "I guess I knew they got paid a lot. But I didn't realize it paid off like a slot machine if you actually got it approved and up and running."

"Plus the CFO and all the other top dogs also get big bucks. Not to mention steak dinners and board seats for people like LDV." She patted Winter on the shoulder and turned to walk away. "It's a feel-good story, really. Something to warm the hearts of Greenies and everyone at Summit Mining whose job got vaporized by the carbon tax."

Winter returned to his computer. His 9:00 am reminder to call a source popped up, as did a new email at the top of his inbox. It was from "Yukon Freedom Front" and the subject line was "Yukon

Climate Collective." The publisher insisted all their email addresses be on their stories. Which occasionally delivered an interesting lead, but more often just batches of hate mail. But Yukon Freedom Front wasn't Amber. It was a new one, and the subject line wasn't obviously deranged. He sighed and double clicked.

It was an anonymous ProtonMail address. Could be anyone, anywhere, with any axe to grind. With ProtonMail, it probably meant they were slightly more paranoid than the usual anonymous gmailer. He began reading:

"YUKONERS NEED TO FIGHT BACK AGAINST BIG FOREIGN MONEY USING FAKE CLIMATE SCIENCE TO UNDEMOCRATICALLY ATTACK THE YUKON WAY OF LIFE. BANNING PICKUPS AND BLOCKING NORTHERN LIGHTS MAKES NO SENSE AS LONG AS CHINA CONTINUES TO BURN COAL.

"YUKON FREEDOM FRONT TAKES RESPONSIBILITY FOR THE ATTACK ON YCC HEADQUARTERS LAST NIGHT."

Attack?

Holy shit.

This was actual news. He checked the email addresses. He had been bcc'd, and couldn't see who else had been copied. Presumably all the other reporters in town.

The message went on to rant about YCC and Clima Foundation, how hard-working Yukon families couldn't afford fancy new electric cars and heating systems, and so on. The usual stuff. He shouted at Artemis, pointed at his screen and then grabbed his notebook and ran for the stairs.

YCC headquarters was just a few blocks North of Main Street in an old Whitehorse house. Not too far from the homeless shelter on Fourth Avenue, whose neighbours Winter was supposed to interview for yet another story about noise and property values.

The YCC house was painted bright green and covered with colourful climate murals and slogans. It had a big wooden sign in the front yard, as well as a picnic table, organic vegetable garden and bird feeders. Brett's powder-blue campervan and a bunch of aging Subarus with kayak racks were usually parked out front.

He was glad he knew Taiya was studying at his place the night before. She spent a lot of time at YCC headquarters.

Winter rounded the corner. Brett was already out front, being interviewed by Echo from CBC. How did she get there so fast? Winter had actually seen the email come into his inbox.

The front window was smashed and the house was covered with obscene graffiti in black and orange spray paint: Fuck you, Fake Science, Freedom Fighters, Blah Blah Bullshit. There were even a few swastikas.

Brett's lead organizer, Chaewon, was standing on the lawn looking at the swastikas. She wore loose cargo pants and a tight, almost military, tanktop. She was visibly upset. Winter could see the muscles flex under the Korean-Tlingit tattoos on her arm as she pushed her fingers repeatedly through her hair. "Do they even know what that really means?" she asked nobody in particular, before turning and looking for someone to answer the question. Winter felt the intensity of her stare. "Well?"

"I knew we had assholes," he replied, returning his gaze to the graffiti. "But not Nazis. It must be revenge for the rock through Amber's pickup window." Winter clicked on his recorder and held it in front of her. "How do you feel about the attack?"

Chaewon almost said something, then stopped. "What kind of question is that? How do you feel about Nazis attacking your office? Hmm. I feel like you should talk to Brett," she said, before walking angrily away.

The cop Winter knew from the Oldtimers league was writing in his notebook, looking profoundly bored.

Brett meanwhile was in fine form. "YCC's mission is too important to future generations," he said into Echo's mic. "We won't let extremists silence our movement. Already we're getting floods of support, calls, volunteers and donations to continue the struggle to save our planet."

Winter made a mental note to point out to Echo that Brett couldn't possibly already be flooded with volunteers and donations; the attack had just happened.

The rest of the media was arriving, including the TV camera from CBC. Brett was going on Northbeat across all three territories at six, and maybe the National.

Brett saw the camera crew, looked behind, and moved to the left so that more swastikas were in the background. "All good?" he asked.

The CBC camera guy gave him the thumbs up.

"Are you scared about future attacks?" asked Echo. "I mean, you could have been in there, or they could have attacked, you know, your van?"

"We are not afraid to stand up for the future of this planet," replied Brett, looking just above and to one side of the camera. "We won't back down no matter what they throw at us. Yukon Climate Collective programs will continue as planned."

Winter was struck by Brett's defiant tone. For a guy who's so worried about his hair, Winter thought, he doesn't seem too concerned about running into a few Freedom Fighters in a dark parking lot.

22

Yukon Independent Grocer

10:30am, September 6th. +12°C
2166 days sober

It was Saturday morning and Winter was in the grocery store. The aisle was crowded, so he pulled his grocery cart all the way over and re-read Taiya's grocery list. She was in Outdoor Education this semester and was organizing her group's food for the Haines bike trip.

Do not screw this up, he reminded himself.

The list was not one Taiya's Sourdough ancestors would have recognized. Eight packs of her favourite Korean ramen, a mix of spicy and normal flavours. Sesame seeds. Dried seaweed. Dried mushrooms. Dried soy protein. Plus dried fish to put on top.

And that was just breakfast.

It was quality carbs and protein, Winter had to admit. The ancestors would have liked how light it all was. And quick. Taiya just had to boil water in her ultralight stove, and the ramen cooked in your insulated cup.

But he wondered what Great-Grampa Slade would have thought about the Korean part. No one's family histories mentioned whose Gold Rush forebears organized the posse that ran the Chinese arrivals out of town in 1902. But from the story in the *Whitehorse Star* archives, it seemed like the entire chamber of commerce had been involved.

Was great-grampa racist?

Was anyone not racist in those days?

He had been thinking about doing a story about it. But he hadn't yet. Partly, he had to admit, because he didn't want to cause conniptions among his mother's cousins and their friends.

He pushed his cart around the corner, coming head to head with another. He looked up. It was Misty and LDV. LDV pointed at the arrows on the floor. "You're going the wrong way."

This was why he usually avoided grocery shopping on Saturdays.

Meanwhile, Misty was looking in his cart. "Ramen?"

"I'm shopping for Taiya's bike trip."

"Ramen? She really needs something healthier." Winter smiled wanly as Misty lectured him on the importance of nutritious breakfasts for teenage girls. There was no point in telling them about the quality protein and carbs in Taiya's ramen breakfasts. Taiya had actually researched the quality of the noodles in this brand. But they hated mansplaining, especially when it was right. He made a mental note to tell Taiya to tell them.

LDV cleared her throat. Oh god, thought Winter, there's more.

"We were talking last night," said LDV, exchanging looks with Misty. "We need to have a conversation about risk. You've been encouraging a lot of activities that may not be appropriate for Taiya."

They always acted like Winter was trying to talk Taiya into climbing Mount Logan in flip flops with nothing but a Mars bar in her back pocket. Didn't they understand that Taiya was driving this truck? It hadn't been his idea for her to become a whitewater guide although, he had to admit, he much preferred it to LDV's idea that Taiya apply to be a summer intern in Policy Branch.

Winter cocked his head, put his serious listening look on, and thought about blue raspberry condoms and moving to Seattle.

LDV's lips stopped moving.

"I totally agree," said Winter. "We should have that conversation. Let's find a time with Taiya." He smiled and moved to turn his cart around.

"I think it should just be the three of us," said LDV.

Winter raised an eyebrow. "She's in Grade 12. I think a strong female leader like Taiya should be involved in conversations about her choices."

Misty and LDV both pressed their lips together and stared back unhappily at him.

Winter waved and rolled his cart away. He knew he would pay for that one, some day.

Winter remembered when lesbians seemed kind of exotic in Whitehorse. Now they were just people who complained about property taxes and how the neighbours couldn't control their dog.

He wheeled his cart quickly away and, seeing the arrow was going the right way, turned quickly into the snacks aisle.

A woman he'd known since Grade 4 was coming against the arrows with her teenage daughter in tow. As usual, she blanked Winter and stared straight ahead as she steered her cart past him.

"Hello!" chirped the girl. She was an acquaintance of Taiya's.

"C'mon, we're late," said the woman, pulling her daughter's arm as if the girl was exchanging phone numbers with a homeless man.

The shame came sweeping back over Winter. That woman might be a merciless bitch, but she hadn't rolled a truck with her daughter in the back seat. What Winter didn't remember, but the woman did, was how she got that hurtful nickname the boys used back in high school. It started after a party where Winter remarked a bit too loudly that if her mustache got any thicker they'd have to start calling her Adolf.

"But it's Taiya's dad…" muttered the girl.

"Late!" replied Adolf through clenched teeth.

"See you later, Nancy," said Winter loudly. "And bye for now, Sierra. I'll tell Taiya I ran into you."

Winter renewed his vow to never shop on Saturdays again. This couldn't get any worse.

He cruised past the potato chips when a huge man in a Skidoo windbreaker and a backwards black baseball hat turned into the aisle. Also going the wrong way.

"Fuckin' A … a new kind of Doritos!" said the man. It was Zach. Winter froze. Now would be a good time to remember you forgot something in Aisle 4. He started to turn his cart around.

"Hey, Winter!" called Zach.

"Oh, hey!" said Winter, feigning surprise.

Zach appeared to be even bigger than before. He'd been tall in high school, but in recent years had turned into a gym rat. The collar of his Alaska Iron Dog snowmobile race t-shirt strained against his neck muscles. He was wearing his Chamber of Mines ball cap backwards. The letters on the back rim of the cap, "Before It's Yours, It's Mined," ran in an embroidered row just above his eyebrows.

Meanwhile, Amber hadn't put on any weight since high school. She had expanded her esthetician business into fitness and pilates. She was undoubtedly somewhere in the store, fully made up with her blonde ponytail through the back of her baseball hat, rocking some black Lululemon tights and a Sled Porn top that showed off her rack and how toned her upper arms were.

The way she casually referred to Zach as her "sex toy" amazed Winter, and gave his editor fits of uncontrollable laughter.

"How's it hangin'?" greeted Zach enthusiastically. He feigned a boxer's stance and landed a few playful punches on Winter's arm. "Zach attack!"

Winter had a flashback to high school. Zach wasn't going to put him in a headlock and give him nuggies, was he? "Surviving. How 'bout you?"

"Well, I'd rather be riding my Italian model for sure! But, you know, the fucking rain." In addition to "Zach attack," one of Zach's go-to jokes was the "Italian model." He thought this was a clever play on sex and his Ducati Diavel, the ridiculously overpowered Italian motorbike he seemed to love more than his kids.

It was a mystery to many, including Winter, how Zach's placer mining crew could put up spending an entire summer with him out on the creeks.

Zach reached into Winter's cart. "Korean ramen? Get some real food, buddy!" he laughed, tossing the packet dismissively back into the cart.

Zach thought it was entertaining social banter to critique everything about you, and simply didn't care about social cues.

Now, he was asking about the battered used electric pickup Winter had bought for Taiya. Also a rich seam of humour. Winter decided to ignore the question. "That was pretty funny what you did to Cameron Dougall at that protest." Zach looked blank. "His lips moving but all you could hear was you revving your engine." Still blank. Winter raised his hand and flapped his fingers and thumbs together like a silent puppet while making a "vroom" sound.

"Oh right!" remembered Zach. "That was hi-fucking-larious. What a doofus that guy is. How do you pass professor school if you're so boneheaded you think how much gas the Yukon uses makes any difference at all? We're just a mosquito fart at a giant Chinese bean-eating contest."

Zach also had views on the vandalization of Brett's headquarters. "Listening to CBC made me want to puke. More than usual. Brett spray paints for Greenie protests and gets treated like a hero. Now he gets some paint back, and he gets sympathy like a cancer victim."

Amber appeared and dumped a load of steaks into the cart. She was indeed all put together for an appearance at the grocery store. If you did a reality TV show on the hot wives and girlfriends of professional snowmobile racers, you would want the women to dress like Amber.

Except that Amber wasn't stupid. People always underestimated her since she was a blonde, good-looking hockey mom. But, as the girls from high school knew, she had claws. She liked to be the centre of attention. If she were a grizzly, she'd be the kind of bear who was attracted to rifle shots rather than scared off.

Amber jumped into the conversation immediately: "Yeah, spray paint the Greenies, it's like a Nazi war crime. The rink down the street from our place is covered in graffiti and the CBC doesn't give a shit."

Winter had no sympathy with the people who complained the media were biased just because they didn't like the news. But the CBC did increasingly seem like the official radio station of the Greens. Winter also found himself listening more to Wayne Bobalicious's drive-time show on CHON-FM. A daily dose of AC/DC, Led Zeppelin and Rush. Guaranteed. No bullshit. No unlistenable crap by singer-songwriters you'd never heard of trying to connect with the spirit of the boreal forest.

Amber was ranting about Brett now. Whoever had spray-painted Brett's office, they had a fan in Amber and Zach. Which was a weird thing to bring up, since half the town assumed Zach had done it.

Winter felt his urge to flee die away. It was good to talk to different people about politics. Eamon only talked to other journalists. For him, spending a snowmobile weekend at the Pass with Zach and his friends would be like parachuting into an undiscovered tribe in the Amazon.

Amber's political philosophy was clear. A lot clearer, actually, than he had ever been able to extract from the conceptual ramblings of Dr. Cameron Dougall.

Politicians were useless, said Amber. Not just the Liberals and NDP and the Greens, but the Yukon Party too. All the same bullshit, just different colour lawn signs.

The mania about climate change was a joke. What was the point of making regular Yukoners pay thousands to switch out their furnaces when the Saudis were pumping more oil than ever. It was just an excuse for what the Greenies had always wanted: ban the snowmobile, make everyone eat granola and bike to work in Forty Below.

Someone needed to do something. Like have a government that actually listened to regular Yukoners. All those deputy ministers and environmentalists should spend a winter working a real job -- an open pit mine would be the place -- before they were allowed to boss us around.

A twelve-year-old boy in a Mustangs rep hockey jacket appeared at the end of the aisle. "Zee-Dog!" barked the boy. "Praaaaah....ctice!" he said with a pre-teen eye roll, then turned on his heels and headed for the exit.

"Well, gotta go. Gotta get the rugrats to the rink." Zach slapped Winter again on the shoulder, then gestured at the Ramen. "And get some steak!"

Amber reached out and put her hand on Winter's bicep and gave a slight squeeze. "CBC's a joke. We need you to keep the coverage fair."

The pair pushed their cart down the aisle.

A disturbing feeling began to spread in Winter's stomach. If Amber ever ran for office, she would probably win.

23

Chaewon's trailer, on the corner of Brett's property

8:00pm, Friday night, September 8th. +13°C

Chaewon stood in her underwear in front of the tiny mirror in the tiny trailer bathroom. She was in good shape after a summer of hiking and biking, she decided, and the tatts looked good. She put on some lip gloss and checked her hair.

Friday night in the Yukon. She stripped off her sports bra and quick-dry hiking panties and put on her nicer ones. Even if you're wearing jeans and a down jacket, she felt sexier with her Pinks underneath.

In the back of her mind, she knew Will wouldn't notice. And, after drinking a six pack of oversize overstrength IPAs, would probably make the night just a little bit less special with one of his "trailer sex" jokes.

She pulled on her jeans, straightened her shirt and checked her hair one more time. She reached for the mosquito repellent. Yukon perfume, Brett called it.

Actually, it was September and it was already getting cold. There probably wouldn't be many bugs. She grabbed her down sweater instead.

It would be chilly in the trailer tonight. They couldn't stay in a summer trailer on Brett's property too much longer.

She opened her phone and checked Signal. No news from Will. "ETA?" she typed.

Will was her boyfriend, or maybe it was partner by now, and was supposed to be getting their food for the barbeque. Brett always threw a good party. The rally earlier that afternoon had gone super well. A big, enthusiastic crowd for a spontaneous event outside the vandalized HQ. Loads of sympathy for YCC and Brett. It felt like a step to getting their mojo back.

She was hungry. She grabbed a handful of trail mix from her hiking pack. Will wasn't great at remembering things.

Chaewon saw the little dots in the chat indicating Will was typing. He typed for a few seconds. Then the dots disappeared. No text arrived.

Actually, he wasn't that great as a boyfriend either.

Her mind went back to some advice she'd received at her mountain-biking friend's book club a few nights before: never break up just before the snow flies. You'll end up spending the winter alone, getting desperate enough to settle for Tinder and bad basement-suite sex with some guy with a Freedom baseball cap on backwards.

The Indian-Canadian woman with the missing leg -- Artemis? -- had suggested waiting till Spring and then trading up to a better model.

When they found out that she knew Nestor because he volunteered at YCC -- and it seemed like it wasn't the first time Nestor had come up at book club -- the women changed their advice: trade up now.

Artemis actually knew the historical guy Nestor was named after. So did the skinny lawyer. Those women were so well educated. Chaewon had heard of anarchists and the Russian Revolution, but these people talked about it like everyone was expected to know that kind of thing. Chaewon made a mental note to spend some time on Wikipedia reading about Nestor Makhno.

It was hard to believe she had actually discussed Will with a group of strangers, especially lawyers and geology PhDs who were supposed to be reading a novel retelling the Trojan War from a feminist perspective. Mind you, the gin and tonics were so strong she had to walk her bike home.

She smiled to herself. It was a guilty pleasure to think of trading Will in like a car you were bored with.

She saw Brett walk by with Echo from the CBC. He was giving her his personal tour of his cabin, the organic garden, the sauna and so on. An image flashed into her mind of Echo in the office, oohing and aahing over Brett's selfie with Greta or the piles of research for his Cambridge Masters thesis.

One thing she didn't dare tell the book club about was Brett. It was definitely not cool to have a high-school crush on your boss.

That was never going to happen, anyway. At the moment, it looked like Brett had his eye on Echo. Not everyone got the tour. How had she been the first journalist at the vandalization? Brett must have texted just her. Classic Brett. It made a journalist feel special so you got a better story. And it gave him a chance to lay on the charm.

What was Brett's joke? Get two birds stoned at once.

She checked the time on her phone. Not only did her boyfriend no longer bother to lay on the charm, he couldn't even provide basic necessities like food. She opened the trailer fridge, grabbed a beer and a vegan pepperoni stick, and walked over to the campfire by Brett's cabin.

By 10:30, it was starting to actually get dark. Summer is over, and maybe we'll even see stars tonight, thought Chaewon.

Will eventually arrived with the food. But the veggie burgers were frozen solid, and he got the kind that didn't stick together very well. So dinner was the fragments of veggie burger that didn't fall off the grill into the fire, some burnt and some still cold on the inside, on buns with salad out of a plastic bag.

The Tinder option was starting to look better.

But the party was fun. Everyone was clustered around the fire in the Fall chill. Music, laughter, drinks. There was no wind, and the smell of weed hung pleasantly in the air.

Everyone had been wearing shorts and t-shirts at the protest, but by now people were huddled around the fire with layers of fleece, down sweaters and toques. Especially the women.

In fact, that was one of Chaewon's jobs. She remembered Brett's directions. Stay sober. Work the crowd. Make sure everyone has fun. Have spare fleeces and toques handy in case any key supporters get cold. He didn't want anyone leaving early just because they forgot it got cold in the Yukon on September nights.

On the other side of the fire was Brett's niece Taiya and a couple of her friends. When they first arrived, they were self-consciously sipping their White Claws and talking quietly among themselves, like kids who had snuck into an adult party.

Now they were chatting comfortably, even too comfortably.

All of them seemed to be drinking. Who was their designated driver?

Someone bumped into Chaewon from behind, spilling her drink.

"Sorry! Tripped on a root," said a woman's voice. Chaewon turned.

The man standing beside the woman reached and grabbed her arm to steady her. "Or did you trip over that Nalgene full of pinot grigio?"

Chaewon cringed at the lame couple joke, which was actually kind of mean. She knew the couple. They were on Brett's list. Both were lawyers at the government. Late thirties. No duct tape on their down jackets. They used to be more involved in YCC, but now they had more money than time.

"No problem. It's getting dark," said Chaewon with a smile. "By the way, thanks a lot for that donation to the repair fund."

"Least we could do," said the man magnanimously.

That's true, thought Chaewon. They had only given fifty bucks. But always play the long game, as Brett said. Christmas donation season wasn't too far away.

"We needed it! Windows are expensive. And winter is coming." She tapped her toque for emphasis. It felt like lame small talk.

"The Instagram pictures were hilarious," said the woman. "And who did the TikTok?"

Chaewon pointed at Taiya and her friends. "Our teenage brain trust," she said. "They're awesome."

"Who do you think was behind the attack?" asked the man.

"The email said Yukon Freedom Front and Y-F-F was spray painted all over the walls."

"Probably just one guy with spray paint and delusions of grandeur," said the man confidently.

"Get serious," said the woman. "Remember when we thought the anti-vaxxers were just a couple of weirdos? You know the guy down the street with the snowblower? Nice guy, comes over and does our driveway after big dumps? You should hear him talk about how the government is making him spend twenty-five grand to replace his oil furnace."

"When did you talk to him?"

"When you weren't raking the leaves."

Ahh, yes, thought Chaewon. This is why Brett called them "the Bickersons."

Now the woman was going through all the people she knew who had "gone off the deep end." The snowblower guy. The firewood delivery guy. A partner at one of the private law firms. Her hot yoga instructor's husband.

"Yeah, but they're still a fringe. How many votes did they actually get?"

"You're forgetting the iceberg factor. We only see one quarter of the story."

"I thought it was one eighth."

Chaewon took a sip of her beer and waited patiently for a chance to change the conversation to what YCC had planned to fight back. And to subtly work in how they would need money. But, as she listened to the Bickersons, she realized it might be a while.

24

Yukon Asian Food Mart, Wood Street

2:00pm, September 18th, Saturday afternoon. +10°C
2178 days sober

Winter was leaning on the wall beside the front window of the Asian Food Mart. He had chosen a spot in the sun, just out of the shadow of a giant Unimog camper covered with prepper stickers. If civilization collapsed, was the plan really to just park that thing somewhere in the Yukon forest and grow barley?

Tarfu was sitting at his feet, leash looped over Winter's wrist, scanning the neighbourhood for urban foxes or dogs to check out. Winter got back to thinking of a witty reply to Anna's last text. His ticket to Seattle was booked. He hadn't been looking forward to something so much for - well, he couldn't remember when.

He had met Taiya and Tarfu at YCC headquarters, just around the block, and walked over here. Taiya was inside the shop. Apparently they had a new kind of high-protein ramen from Korea. Winter hadn't known that some kinds of ramen were like white bread, and some had more protein and nutrients.

But he respected her obsession. For a long-distance expedition, every gram counted. If you found the perfect nutritious breakfast, then a special trip to a weird store to load up was worth it.

Actually, he didn't just respect it. He was kind of proud of her.

"But *you* have to stay out here, buddy," he said to Tarfu.

"Man, that sucks, buddy," said a voice. Winter looked up. He started. It was a homeless guy pushing a battered old mountain bike with the chain dragging on the ground. Short, First Nations, black hair in a slighty-off-kilter ponytail, wearing a torn red jacket with "Banff Leadership Forum 2019" embroidered on the shoulder. He was probably walking from the waterfront to the Centre of Hope shelter.

The guy leaned his bike against a parking meter and squatted to hold his hand out to Tarfu. Tarfu, as the world's friendliest dog, wagged his tail and allowed his head to be scratched.

Winter felt an uncomfortable urge to pull Tarfu away and walk around the corner. When he was a kid, his mother had always dragged them across the street whenever she saw a drunk Indian coming. Winter's grandfather used to do business out in the communities and seemed to know all the older indigenous guys in the line up at the bank. But his mother didn't.

"I used to have a dog like this. More husky, less lab." The guy looked up with a grin. He looked pretty rough. Not obviously plastered, but maybe just a bit of a buzz. It was hard not to stare at the scratches down the side of his face.

"Yeah, part lab for sure," said Winter. He recognized the guy. Or, rather, he recognized a much older version of a face from a lifetime ago. What was it, five years? The guy used to have prescriptions for Oxy from half the doctors in town.

Then he made the connection. "You're buddies with Henry."

The guy looked at Winter sharply. "You know Hank?"

"Since elementary school."

"That right?" he replied, as if this was some improbable fact. "Indian world is small. Real small. Hank's my cousin. Brother really."

He switched the conversation back to his old dog. It was back home, wherever that was. "Got hit by a car on the highway," he said with a melancholy sigh. "They didn't even stop."

Winter shook his head in sympathy. "That's brutal. Here today, gone tomorrow."

"Yep, just like us I guess."

A Subaru pulled into the angle parking a few spots down the street. It was newish and had a kayak on the roof. A blonde woman in her thirties got out. Winter knew her vaguely. A lawyer friend of Brett's. She threw her purse over her shoulder, and stepped onto the sidewalk. She pulled her key fob out of her purse, clicked it, and the car's locks beeped.

She jammed the keys back into her purse and walked away.

Without even looking at us, thought Winter with a smile. She sees *two* homeless guys!

"Hey," shouted Winter's temporary friend. He grabbed his bike and moved after her.

The woman didn't look back, but her pace clearly accelerated. Like an Olympic speed walker.

The guy started jogging, and shouted again. Oh god, thought Winter, I hope this isn't going to turn into a Good Samaritan incident. He suddenly had visions of cop cars, cops taking down the guy, him screaming as they kneeled on his back and then jammed him into the back seat, then getting interviewed with the guy in the background kicking the windows uselessly from inside.

The woman broke into a run and disappeared around the corner onto Fourth Avenue.

The guy's run petered out. He stopped in front of the Subaru on the sidewalk and leaned his bike against the car's hood. He leaned over and picked something up off the sidewalk, then put it on the Subaru's windscreen under the windshield wiper.

He turned and looked at Winter. Winter shrugged. The guy shook his head, picked up his bike, and trudged towards Fourth Avenue. He was not moving quickly, but there was a determined, maybe angry, energy to his step.

Winter watched as the guy, without turning his head to look for traffic, stepped with his bike out onto the crosswalk. Tires screeched as a big, black pickup with a heavy red fuel tank in the back skidded towards the white stripes.

The pickup stopped inches from the guy. He stopped and looked at the driver, who pounded on the horn and just let it keep sounding. The guy stood up straight, put his hand on the hood of the pickup and looked angrily at the driver.

Then he hoisted his arm in the air theatrically, gave the driver the finger, and finished -- slowly -- crossing the crosswalk.

Winter waited for him to disappear around the corner, then walked over to the Subaru and looked at the item under the windshield wiper.

It was the woman's credit card.

Winter tied Tarfu's leash to a parking meter and went into the store to borrow a pen and a piece of paper. He scrawled a message in all caps to jam under the other windshield wiper: "THE FIRST NATIONS GUY YOU RAN AWAY FROM WAS JUST TRYING TO SAY YOU DROPPED YOUR CREDIT CARD."

Did he need to add "FUCK YOU" at the end?

No. That was obvious.

25

YCC Equinox Vigil Camp, near Northern Lights LNG plant

7:32am, Fall Equinox - September 22nd, -4°C

Chaewon rolled over and reached out of her sleeping bag for her phone. It was cold to the touch and refused to turn on when she tapped it.

She pulled the phone back into the sleeping bag and jammed it between her thighs to warm up the battery.

She rolled onto her back and looked up at the tent ceiling. It was light enough to see, but not like summer. She heard the hiss of a stove from outside the tent. Taiya's sleeping bag beside her was empty.

"What time is it?" she asked.

"Seven thirty-two," replied Taiya from outside the tent. "Minus Four. You *almost* got up before dawn."

Yep, you couldn't say that in the summer. It had been dark during the night. Summer was over.

Her toque was twisted sideways from tossing and turning all night. She straightened it, then unzipped the sleeping bag and rolled out. She pulled on her pants and a down jacket, stuffed her phone into an inside pocket, then slipped her socked feet into her crocs and unzipped the tent.

With no trees to block the view, Chaewon could see the sunline on the mountains across the valley. In a few minutes the sun would be on them, melting away the frost crystals on the ground.

Taiya was crouching by her stove making coffee. The PowerBlimp hung limply in the background, its rotor not turning. She had taken a photo of it in the morning light for its Instagram feed.

"You're up early," said Chaewon.

"The cold woke me up," replied Taiya. "Brought my summer bag. Rookie move."

Chaewon joined Taiya in watching the Jetboil stove boil a litre of water. Taiya had her hair pulled back in a ponytail. Her scar stood out, curving from her collar up the side of her face and disappearing into her hairline. It was extra red this morning, maybe because of the cold.

Chaewon sat beside the stove. She felt the frost from the rocks seep through her pants into her thigh muscles. The coffee would taste good. "Not much of a vigil," she said.

"We're here!" Taiya always saw things in a positive light.

Brett had marketed the event as the Yukon Climate Collective Equinox Vigil. Relentless vigilance on behalf of our shared ecosystem. Brett even made them leave their vehicles at the office. He thought tents only would make a better image. Only Taiya's truck was parked in the snow dump across the road, since she had ferried them all to the vigil.

There were only a half dozen tents, but the photo from last night did look good on the website. Chaewon had to shoot it from just the right angle to get the fire, a couple of people and a tent in the background without too much empty space showing.

Chaewon looked for Brett. There was no movement in his tent, which he had set up a bit farther away. Past the tent of Prism, their Fall intern, and closer to the road. Chaewon had a sneaking suspicion he had snuck back to the comfy bed in his van. She pictured him and Echo snuggled under Brett's down duvet.

They both stared at Taiya's hissing stove.

"Who do you think trashed our building?" asked Taiya.

"Gotta be the Freedos. Amber probably sent Zach and his buddies."

"But swastikas?"

"They *are* bad people. Probably thought it was hilarious."

"Amber has never sent one of those official messages claiming responsibility before."

Chaewon thought about this in silence. Taiya was right. Not only did Amber not claim responsibility, it had taken a while for the media to find her. Echo said she seemed as surprised as everyone else about the attack.

Another tent unzipped and Nestor crawled out. He stood and stretched his big frame. "Nazis are everywhere. No one listened to Ukraine. Then we had to fight them."

He took a few steps and pissed loudly on a blackened stump.

At 8:01, Taiya's phone buzzed and she read the Signal from her dad: "R u ok? Just got email. Another attack at ycc hq"

She tapped a reply, then turned off the stove and ran to get her truck. Nestor was already at Brett's tent and woke him up. He crawled out looking groggy carrying his pants and boots. He glanced over at Prism's tent. "Wake up Prism too."

A moment later Taiya pulled up. They jumped into the back and a second later they were headed for the YCC building. As they approached, they could see fire truck lights in the distance.

But it wasn't YCC headquarters that was on fire. It was the car in front of it. Chaewon's car.

They joined a dad and two boys who were watching the firefighters clean up. The car was a smoking wreck, and anything that wasn't smoking was dripping with foam.

"Everything I owned was in there," said Chaewon to no one in particular. "I was moving out of the trailer."

Winter was the first journalist to arrive. He jumped his bike up onto the curb across the street and pulled out his camera. He framed the shot with the smoking car in the foreground, with YCC headquarters and Brett's powder blue van in the driveway.

"It's not a show," shouted one of the firefighters.

"Media," shouted Winter back.

"On a bike?"

"Budget cuts," said Winter, putting away his camera. "What's the story?"

"Four a.m. phone call," said the lead firefighter laconically. "Vehicle on fire. We got over here. Yup, there was a vehicle and, yup, it was on fire. So we put it out. Subaru electric vehicle. Total write off."

"Aren't battery fires supposed to be harder to put out?" Winter had read that somewhere. One of those internet things that might even be true.

"This one sure seemed like an old-fashioned gas fire."

"Why?"

"Because there was gas, and it was on fire." The firefighter might not have had media training, but he definitely had asshole training, thought Winter. The firefighter pointed at the bottom half of a red plastic jerry can sticking out of the foam behind the car. "See?"

"So they had a jerry can in the car that caught fire somehow?"

The firefighter paused for a second to let this media idiocy hang in the air. "No, notice where the jerry can is. *Outside* the car. Someone poured gas all over the car and set it on fire, and just left the jerry can to burn." He showed Winter where the gas had pooled under the car and along the curb and burned.

"Gasoline pour off and burn out too fast. But good enough for parked car," said Nestor in his Ukrainian accent.

The firefighter looked up sharply. "What are you? Some kind of Molotov cocktail expert?"

Nestor shrugged.

"It's her car," said one of the boys standing nearby, out of the blue as children do, to the firefighter. He pointed at Chaewon even though she was only standing five feet away.

"Someone must really not like you," said the firefighter. Chaewon stared blankly at him. "I mean, if I were an arsonist, I'd go after the building. Or that fancy blue campervan right there. Why a crappy old Subaru?"

The guy was right, thought Winter. I'd definitely torch the fancy van. Especially if I knew it was Brett's. "Why aren't the police here?" he asked.

"You said you're a reporter. When was the last time you wrote about the police solving a case of arson?"

Winter slowly rode his bike back up Third Avenue to the office. He felt sorry for Chaewon, even though she was Brett's yes woman. Taiya had been spending more time with her. Maybe she wasn't as much of a write-off as her association with Brett suggested. Taiya said Chaewon wanted to install a security camera after the last incident, but Brett hadn't got around to signing the purchase order yet. The neighbours probably didn't have cameras either. Some asshole was going to get off scot free.

He felt the anger building. It was so unfair.

But it wasn't his job to make the world perfect. He coasted for a second, taking three deep breaths like the podcast said.

He carried his bike upstairs to the newsroom. Who would do this? The first vandalism with the swastikas was one thing. But the second risked getting caught on a newly installed security camera. The attackers couldn't assume Brett wouldn't get around to installing security cameras after the swastikas.

Could it be Zach or one of his buddies? Possibly. But Amber wasn't stupid. Having her husband get caught for torching a car just wasn't worth it, even if she wanted to make a point.

But Zach's buddies? They weren't the coldest beers in the fridge. But were they capable of acting alone without Amber holding their hands?

Winter started his computer and re-read the 8:00am email that had started the excitement. The last Yukon Freedom Front email had come in at exactly 9:00am. Were we dealing with anally well organized vandals, or was it just a coincidence?

Winter's editor Artemis moved slowly out of the coffee room. She had a crutch under one arm, and in the other hand held her Yeti mug. A tea-bag string stuck out from under the lid, and tea slopped up out of the hole in the lid. Winter leaned back and pointed at his screen: "THE BATTLE AGAINST BIG MONEY AND FAKE CLIMATE NEWS CONTINUES."

Artemis crutched to Winter's desk. She squeezed the tea bag with her spoon, tossed it in the garbage, and read the email. "Arson is an artificial crime. A lot of buildings deserve to be burnt."

"Did you make that up?"

"H.G. Wells, I think."

Winter showed her the photos of Chaewon's Subaru. "Free publicity for assholes."

"Which assholes. Brett or the arsonists?"

"Both, I guess."

"Brett will hold a press conference. Could you cover it?"

"I was afraid you were going to say that."

"Try to hold back the tears," she replied. "Just focus on the facts."

26

F.H. Collins Secondary School parking lot
3:00 p.m., September 23rd, +1°C

Chaewon pedaled hard over the Riverdale bridge. Bonus of getting your car torched: daily workout.

The after-school traffic was already building. She zipped past slowly rolling cars, then curved right into the high school's parking lot. Taiya and her friends were standing in a clump beside Taiya's electric pickup. A lot of kids, and buzzing with energy like a field trip.

Brett wasn't in sight. He had inspired the kids after the attack on her car. Riled them up was maybe a better way to put it. If you didn't save the world, Brett said, no one else would.

This, however, had the ugly feel of retaliation.

And, now, where was he? He wasn't answering text messages. He wasn't planning to let the kids go do this themselves, was he? The Freedos, and everyone else, were going to be pissed. It crossed her mind that she'd never received a text from him about this one. Just verbal instructions to go get Krazy Glue and metal zip ties for the kids.

Chaewon braked and hopped off her bike in front of Taiya's truck, still breathing heavily. She swung her pack off her back and pulled it open. Taiya reached in, grabbed a tube of Krazy Glue and a pack of 25 zip ties and handed them to a tall, lanky boy in an Arctic Winter Games jacket. "Quartz and Second."

"Right!" The boy grabbed the gear, then squeezed into a minivan that looked like it belonged in one of those TikTok Most-People-in-a-Car videos. The muffler scraped as mom's borrowed minivan rolled over a curb.

Taiya quickly handed out glue and zip ties to the teams for the Two Mile Hill intersection and the Riverdale bridge, then moved towards her own vehicle: "Northern Lights team! Let's go!"

A student helped Chaewon lift her bike into Taiya's pickup, then they all piled in: three people in the cab and seven in the back. The boy sitting squeezed between Chaewon and her bike smiled. "LNG trucks, cement trucks, fat stupid commuters - it's gonna be sick."

A Toyota SUV and an old Chev van, also sitting low on their shocks, followed them out of the parking lot. Taiya steered into traffic. The bridge team was sprinting along the sidewalk beside them. As they rolled across the bridge, the first students were already blocking the southbound lane as others zip-tied themselves to railings and each other.

Taiya had selected the intersection in front of the Northern Lights facility for her group. Taiya had learned a lot at YCC, thought Chaewon. The protest would block commuters to the south end of town -- really get inside the heads of lots of people -- as well as access to the power plant and carbon-capture construction site. There would be some great images for the socials.

Chaewon handed out more zip ties and glue. Everyone already knew the hashtag and Taiya had told them the drill: wrists and ankles in a long knot of people; get all the way across the road; don't resist the cops but don't help them either - just lay there; if they cut you loose but don't arrest you, just run around with your spare zip ties and tie yourself into the knot again; and take lots of video to catch the cops being dicks.

The instructions weren't really needed. The kids had seen Extinction Rebellion on Youtube a million times.

A young girl -- Grade 10? -- in a puff jacket stuffed some spare zip ties down her pants. Chaewon recognized her from the last protest. "And get ready for the hate," she said with a smile that showed her braces.

Chaewon smiled back and gave her a fist bump.

Someone started the first chant: "Say it loud and say it clear, fossil fuel's not welcome here!"

Taiya and the van pulled into the parking lot by the intersection. But the Toyota SUV kept going. It pulled into the middle of the intersection and stopped right in front of a Nissan Leaf in the oncoming lane. The SUV's hazard flashers came on. Chaewon watched as the teenage driver stepped out and wound up for an outfield throw. The key arced through the air over the bushes beside the road.

Then he squirted some Krazy Glue on his hand and pressed it onto the hood of the SUV.

The honking started immediately.

Consequences were for old people, thought Chaewon. Although the kid's dad would probably have something different to say later.

Taiya grabbed the flare and little orange pylons from her highway emergency kit -- a gift from LDV -- and ran towards the SUV with the others.

Chaewon took some video of the kids zip tying themselves to the SUV and posted to the socials. Then she zip-tied herself to the girl in the puff jacket.

In the Nissan right in front of them, the toddler in the back seat unbuckled himself and crawled into the front seat for a better view. The mom in the driver's seat turned to push him back into the rear seat.

Behind the Nissan, a burly man with a big blonde beard got out of an orange 4x4 pickup with a big winch on the front bumper. He stood beside the Nissan with his hands on his hips and stared in angry disbelief at the demo. He waved his arm at the stressed looking mother wrestling her toddler.

"What the fuck!"

The teenagers started chanting: "O, I, L, Y … you ain't got no alibi … you oily (hey! hey!) you oily!"

The pickup driver spat onto the ground angrily and crossed his arms in frustration.

The first cop car arrived, driving up the vacant oncoming traffic lane. At the intersection, the traffic tailed back out of sight in all directions. Winter arrived on a bike moments later, followed by Nigel the photographer.

The two cops stood beside their car and took in the scene: two cops, several dozen people clustered around an SUV blocking the intersection. A crowd of drivers was growing around the Nissan. The lead cop spoke into her radio.

More police arrived and joined their colleagues. The lead officer came over and surveyed the bodies lying on the road, looking for the ringleader. Her eye passed over Chaewon even though she was the only adult there. The advantages of being a skinny Asian chick, thought Chaewon.

The cop turned to the tall boy and asked him if he was the organizer.

"Je ne parle pas anglais," the boy replied in a French Immersion accent.

The cop began the usual spiel. Breaking the peace. Blocking a public highway. "Blah blah blah!" shouted the girl in the puff jacket. Someone joined, then someone else, and it was soon a chant.

Chaewon checked her phone. Time was passing. The police couldn't do anything about this protest. Too many people and not enough cops. They were really making their point.

Echo and the CBC camera crew arrived. Echo looked around for Brett. So did Chaewon.

Echo spotted Chaewon on the ground by the SUV. "Can we interview you?"

"Sure."

"Can you stand up for a better shot?"

"I'm zip-tied to the bumper."

The cameraman stepped over the girl in the puff jacket and pointed his camera down at Chaewon. She waited for the light, then looked at the camera and tried to channel Brett: "This is a spontaneous protest by Yukon youth. They're protesting the vicious and cowardly attack on the Yukon Climate Collective. We call on all Yukoners to join the struggle to save our planet!"

A cheer went up. The girl in the puff jacket tried to fist bump Chaewon, but realized she couldn't because their wrists were zip tied together.

Eventually more cops arrived. Two tried to move the crowd of angry drivers back, while the others approached the clump of bodies. They ran through their usual protocol and -- when no one budged -- moved in on the student most on the edge of the clump. The lead cop reached behind her back and pulled some side cutters out of her belt.

The student rolled over on top of his wrist.

The cops carefully rolled him back.

"Police brutality!" shouted one of the kids.

"Film it!" shouted another.

The lead cop applied the pliers to the zip tie and squeezed.

Nothing.

She tried a new angle.

Still nothing.

"We've got stainless steel zip ties," said the student.

"So you speak English now."

"Those won't work. You'll need strap cutters."

The cop stood up and looked at her officers.

"The cops have got the wrong fucking tools!" exclaimed the man from the orange pickup. A cheer came out of the knot of students, matched by moans of frustration and cursing from the drivers.

The police milled around the lead officer's car, speaking into their radios.

Chaewon saw Winter step out of the crowd. Their eyes locked, and he stepped over bodies to get closer.

"Where's Brett?" he asked, an unusually urgent and angry edge to his voice.

"I don't know."

Winter pulled out his phone and dialed: "Brett, answer your fucking phone. You have your niece at ground zero of a protest and you have no fucking idea what Amber is about to do."

"Winter!" said a voice. It was Winter's high-school principal. "There's an article I should send you about this kind of--"

"Not now," interrupted Winter, looking around for Taiya.

A second later, someone shouted, "Hey, it's Amber!"

Cop eyes, driver eyes and protester eyes swiveled. Amber was stepping out of her black pickup, carrying an armful of wire cutters still with their tags dangling.

Echo elbowed her camera guy and they scurried to intercept her. "Amber! A quick question."

Amber ignored the CBC and walked right up to the lead cop. A crowd of people pressed closer to hear, while a man wearing a Make Speech Free Again baseball hat lifted his phone to film the scene.

Amber held out a pair of tin snips to the police then turned and spoke loudly to the phone. "There's a woman in labour stuck in traffic ten cars back. These climate extremists have gone too far. We've got to take back our country."

She handed the tin snips to the cop, and a cheer erupted out of the crowd of commuters. Amber waded into the crowd handing out tin snips.

The lead cop raised her hands to signal calm, but everyone ignored her. The crowd surged at the two cops doing crowd control, whose eyes bulged in alarm. One jumped into his car, while the other pulled a taser off his belt. Winter's ex-principal grabbed the officers arm, saying, "Hey, you can't--"

But before he could finish his sentence, the cop pulled back, raised the taser and pulled the trigger. A bang and a fizz later, the old man slumped to the ground.

The blonde guy from the orange pickup wrapped his powerful fingers around the arm of the boy with his left hand glued to the SUV. "Get away!" shouted the boy, turning to hold onto the grill with his right hand. The man shifted his grip onto the boy's collar and -- with a massive heave -- yanked the kid off the vehicle. The boy screamed as his hand pulled away from the layer of skin glued to the SUV.

"Fuck," said the Grade 10 girl in the puff jacket to Chaewon. "Like getting your tongue ripped off a frozen lamp post."

Their turn was next. A guy in a jean jacket leaned down and grabbed Chaewon's arm. Another pushed up his sleeves and moved in with the snips.

The Grade 10 girl sat up and sank her teeth into his arm.

The guy with the snips screamed and -- instinctively -- raised his knee into her face. Chaewon heard the sickening crunch of nose cartilage. It was the girl's turn to scream. Blood streamed down her face.

"Fucking bitch," shouted the man, looking at the teeth marks on his arm. He put his boot on the girl's chest to hold her down then snipped the zip tie. Chaewon gripped the girl's arm, but the guy in the jean jacket grabbed Chaewon's hair from behind and dragged her away.

Chaewon tried to stand up, but the man dragged her backwards so quickly she couldn't get her feet under her. Chaewon screamed. And writhed. And tried to reach backwards over her head for the man's arms.

"What I do with her now?" shouted the guy in the jean jacket. "She'll just run back."

He kept dragging Chaewon backwards. A spasm of real fear -- primeval fear -- ran through Chaewon's body.

"She's got more zip ties! In her ass pocket!"

They threw her face first into a chain link fence. The hand gripping her hair now pressed her face into the wires. She could feel the man's body press hers against the fence, and his warm breath on the back of her neck.

Then, the other guy pulled the zip ties out of her back pocket and used one to zip her wrist to the fence.

The guy in the jean jacket pushed her face harder into the wire; so hard, she felt individual links biting into her lip and cheek.

"Protest that, baby!" he said with a laugh. Then he released her and walked back to get another protester.

27

Cascadia Steakhouse, Vancouver

8:00pm, October 23rd. +15°C

Jim pulled out his reading glasses for the menu. If he had to spend two hours with these government people, he was going to have a great steak. One of the many wonderful things about being CEO was that he approved his own expenses.

He looked over his glasses at the waiter. "Got any beef that isn't sustainably raised?"

The waiter was a pro. "The prime bone-in rib eye is pasture raised and grain fed, but not certified sustainable officially," he replied evenly.

Jim looked at Karen. "Sustainable beef is like giving your wife a wedding ring made with conflict-free diamonds. Isn't the whole point that you want someone to have died for your diamond?"

It didn't hurt if the government people thought you could go rogue at any moment.

"Tell me more about the rib eye."

"Twenty ounce, four ounces of bone and sixteen of steak. Top grade Black Angus from our own farm in Alberta. Dry aged for 45 days. We use an 800-degree infrared grill for a more consistent high heat than open flame. The sides are family style, so you can order mashed potatoes or vegetables as you like."

"Deal."

"Rare, sir?"

"Is there any other way?"

Karen ordered the wild salmon.

Alex looked up at Jim. The CEO of Ńjür Nàdäk'ạ Devcorp was slouched comfortably in his chair, the only person in the restaurant wearing Carhartts. "How about the classic Tomahawk? It's forty ounces so we'll have to split it."

Jim looked back at Alex. Jesus, thought Karen, this is like the boys in high school bragging how big their dicks are. And couldn't the restaurant call it something other than "Tomahawk" these days?

Jim nodded. "Even better. Love that idea."

Jim ordered a few sides for the table and a bottle of his favourite Oregon pinot, then smiled at his guests. Time for some more small talk. Try to be nice, his wife said. It might get you farther. Find something everyone can agree on.

"Did I tell you I ran into Brett Schleicher in business class on the way to London?"

This piqued his tablemates' interest. "Protesting Air Canada's carbon emissions?" asked Alex with a wink.

"Yeah, by drinking champagne with me!" Even Karen laughed at that one. "He's doing a Masters at Cambridge in sustainability leader bullshit."

"Huh!" said Alex. "That will not be a cheap program."

Jim nodded in agreement. This Brett topic seemed like a crowd pleaser. He continued: "And how are things with Brett and the PowerBlimp?"

"Oh, fuck!" Alex laughed. "I'm just glad we gave a hard no on that-" -- air quotes -- "investment opportunity."

"Environment funded it," said Karen with a surprisingly girlish giggle into her pinot glass. "It generates more publicity than electricity."

Alex lowered his air quotes. "But as a publicity stunt for Yukon Climate Collective, it's great. Let's them act like they're solving the problem, not just whining about it."

Jim laughed: "Maybe I should get one for over our head office!"

"Only if you want your office filled with pissed off bush pilots, utility engineers and landscape photographers!"

They all laughed.

Good, thought Jim. Everyone's happy. Time for business.

"So, my board's been watching what's going on up North on the National."

Karen's game face slid quickly over her smile. "The Yukon Government Security Team believes the YCC attacker was an isolated individual."

"You won't mind if I point out that the Yukon Government Security Team isn't the CIA. It may be one guy, but he managed to provoke high school students into shutting down the whole town. Including our construction site. We had a concrete truck stuck in traffic for four hours!"

He projected his best CEO stare at Karen. She had the good sense not to say anything. He continued: "We just got lucky the TV crews didn't get the logo on our facility in the background. The last thing my board wants is our project getting national attention. Once the Greenies make you into a campaign, you can't get the toothpaste back into the tube."

"We've condemned the attack and spoken to the RCMP about managing protests. They're treating it as a priority."

Jim was unimpressed. "That's what they said when my bike got stolen in Grade Five. What happens when the Greens blockade us next time, and with their A-team not a bunch of kids with zip-ties? What are you going to do then?"

"Let's not speculate about what might happen. Like I said, we think it's an isolated individual."

"I don't call it speculation. I call it planning."

Alex leaned forward. "Look, Jim. We always knew this would be a controversial project. Our chief and council are pissed at the Greens. But we're in this one hundred percent. We need to know you are too."

"I am for sure." He turned to Karen. "We just need someone to hold up the premier when his backbone starts to turn to jello."

The steaks arrived a few minutes later. The two-inch thick Tomahawk sat majestically on its platter, with the bone curving artistically out of the meat.

"Wow," said Jim. "How long do you think an African village could hold out on this?"

28

In front of YCC headquarters

4:35pm, October 30th. -8°C
2221 days sober

Winter strolled down Third Avenue. His stories were filed, and it was time to do some thinking. He wore his headphones to ward off small-town conversation. CHON-FM's Wayne Bobalicious was streaming: today's Zeppelin shot was *Dazed and Confused*.

Why did things always bounce Brett's way? He made a bad decision to campaign against a project backed by First Nations -- what kind of clueless privileged white trust-fund kid did something like that these days? He was getting attacked by people who hated him, but it just made him more popular and got him national news coverage. People from Toronto who thought Yukon was a kind of potato were typing their credit card numbers into his crowdfunding site.

The clip of Brett and the burning car from the National was all over the socials. Like in his interview after the spray painting, Brett was supremely confident. His usual lines about always carrying on the fight and standing up for the planet. Like he was almost taunting the attackers to try again.

Winter mulled over the anonymous email he had received that morning. That Brett was doing a Masters in Sustainability Leadership at Cambridge University was something he knew already. What he hadn't known was that it cost £31,000 plus travel and hotel for four in-person study sessions. The calculator on Winter's iphone said that was more than $50,000 in Canadian dollars, quite a bit more expensive than Winter had assumed. Or that Brett had been spotted in business class on his way to England, which was titillating news. The email claimed YCC was paying for everything. That was the kind of accusation that, in Winter's small-town journalistic experience, might actually be true but which you could never get anyone to go on the record and confirm.

Winter had duly checked out the YCC's financials posted on the Corporate Affairs website. But YCC had a big budget, and the spending categories were so vague, you could easily bury a vanity Masters program if you wanted to.

Winter found himself standing beside Chaewon's burnt-out car. He pushed the scorched bumper with his foot. Deep in thought, he didn't even see Henry walk up to him.

"Hey man."

"Oh, hey." Winter removed his headphones. From the direction of Henry's walk, he was probably headed for the homeless shelter.

"What are ya listening to?"

"Streaming Wayne Bobalicious."

Henry made air quotes: "CHON-FM. The Beat of a Different Drummer."

Winter pointed at the car. "I know the woman who owns this car."

"Bummer. I saw the guy who did it. Couldn't believe it. He just rolled up on his bike, pulled a jerry can out of his backpack, poured the gas, sparked a lighter and took off."

"What? Did you tell the cops?"

"Tell the cops!" Henry laughed, inadvertently showing off his missing front tooth. "You've known me all these years and you still don't know I'm an Indian?"

Henry seemed to find the whole idea hilarious. "Excuse me, sir," he spluttered, laughing. "I'm a First Nations guy wandering the streets in the middle of the night and have something to report." Henry bent over wheezing with laughter, putting his hand on his knee for support. When he could speak again, he stood up and continued. "Oh, and sir, could you please also accidentally on purpose bang my head into the door while putting me into the back seat of your car?"

Henry convulsed with another bout of hilariousness. Winter waited for him to recover.

"What did you see?"

"Well, some dickweed pulled the fire alarm at the shelter. So I was walking around. And, yeah, saw this guy pouring gas on the car. After he lit it, he just jumped on his bike and took off back towards Main Street."

"What did he look like?"

"It was kinda dark. Big guy, tall."

A thought flashed into Winter's mind. Zach, riding a bike instead of a phallic black 4x4? That would totally throw off the cops.

29

Z-Dog Placer Mining, Whitehorse yard

7:00 a.m., October 31st. -12°C
2221 days sober

Winter steered his fat bike through the frozen mud puddles. The beam of his headlamp bounced crazily along the trail like the light of a dancing lighthouse. Millimetre-thick fresh ice cracked loudly under his tires in the morning still.

He could hear Tarfu's feet trotting on the frozen mud behind him.

It was pitch black. There was no moon to bounce light off the skiffs of early snow the wind had blown into nooks and crannies along the trail.

He put his bike down where the trail passed behind Zach's fence. The leafy barrier between the trail and the fence was gone. He could see the fence through a screen of leafless, frozen branches.

He turned off his headlamp for a moment to see if any other lights were bouncing around the compound. He told Tarfu to sit, then climbed the fence.

In a moment he had replaced the SIM card and batteries in the camera.

There was a new shipping container closer to the yard gate. If you had a heavy bladder of diesel in a container, that might be an easy place to put it. Also an easier place for your customers to turn around.

Winter moved the camera closer to the new container. It took him a moment to strap it to the pipe of a rusty sluice box that wouldn't be used till next year. Then he moved a barrel slightly and propped a few loose pipes beside the camera to make it less obvious to the human eye.

As he rode home -- McCrae trails, Miles Canyon suspension bridge, Yellow Trail -- the sky over the eastern horizon began to lighten. He thought about the fuel smuggling story.

Actually, carbon smuggling. That's what he would call it. Or maybe carbon profiteers, like war profiteers. Everyone hated them.

The cops barely bothered hiding their boredom when he asked if they were investigating rumours of diesel smuggling. The Customs spokesperson in Ottawa acted offended when he suggested the possibility that giant tanker loads of illicit fuel were somehow crossing the border. LDV had given a bullshit line that "the Yukon Government is proactively working with its partners to ensure the rule of law is upheld." Then her minion suggested he contact Customs and the cops for more information.

It pissed Winter off. Some people made sacrifices to fight climate change. Some struggled with higher fuel costs. Others with the monthly bills for expensive electric vehicles they were forced to buy. Meanwhile, for Zach and Amber, behind a high fence in a secluded industrial lot on the edge of town, climate change had turned into a lucrative new smuggling business.

The story wouldn't name Zach to keep the lawyers happy. He planned a story on unnamed villains making tens of thousands of dollars while everyone else complained about gas prices, backed up with references to "video obtained by the *Yukon Sun*."

That would go off around town like someone dropped their bear spray in the fire at a bush party.

It might even shame the cops into doing something.

Back home, Tarfu took up his usual position on the couch. Winter spooned a hefty dose of coffee into the French press, added boiling water and sat down at his Mac to check the photos.

The camera settings seemed much better this time. A magpie kept landing on a barrel and hopping around, using up a bit of the batteries each time. The camera captured various pickups rolling by, plus people walking. Zach, various Z-Dog employees and contractors, even Amber once or twice; wearing coveralls not Lululemon.

As Winter scrolled through the stills, the season gradually changed. The leaves disappeared, there were more night shots, and the sun got lower and the colours of the barrels appeared more muted.

The stream of changing images flashing across the screen was kind of artistic, actually. But so far no one caught refilling out of a giant tank.

Winter froze. What logo was on that pickup? He hit the back arrow and zoomed in: "Northern Lights."

He played the video for that one. It showed a Northern Lights pickup roll to a stop. Jim what's-his-name the CEO stepped out and leaned on the hood. Zach walked into the frame. They were talking intently.

Winter punched up the volume, but all he heard was muffled wind noises.

What could Zach be doing talking to Northern Lights? It couldn't be about business. Zach couldn't do anything for Northern Lights, unless Jim wanted the gravel in his parking lot sluiced for gold.

The rest of the pictures were useless. That magpie kept coming back, and fewer pickups showed up as the placer miners settled in for a quiet winter in Hawaii.

Fucking old camera. I need to borrow proper gear from the CIA, thought Winter.

30

Artemis' house on Black Street
8:00pm, October 31st. -12°C
2221 days sober

Winter tucked his fat bike behind the bushes in Artemis' backyard and walked around to the front door. He carefully extracted the box of chocolates from his pack and rang the doorbell.

"Fashionably late, I see!" said Artemis, opening the door. She was wearing an Indian outfit; a mustard-coloured silky sari over a crop top of the same fabric with a flare pant leg and embroidered slipper.

"You look stunning," said Winter, handing over the chocolates and leaning in for a kiss on the cheek. "Happy Diwali."

"Ah, sweets! You've been reading about my culture on Wikipedia. How thoughtful!"

"It didn't say anything about a case of Old Style being traditional, so I stayed safe."

"Well, I always celebrate Diwali on Hallowe'en so the white people don't get confused. A case of Old Style would have been perfect."

The entire *Yukon Sun* staff was already in the house, plus more of Artemis' friends. Winter slipped onto a bar stool in the kitchen and Artemis poured him a cranberry and soda.

"Are you wearing that to the bar for the after party?" he asked.

"It would attract male attention, but perhaps not the kind of male attention I'm looking for. Like the mine tour when I was the only girl at the Summit man camp. They even hit on a cripple dressed in oversize hi-vis."

"You know what they say about finding a man up North: the odds are good, but the goods are odd."

"And some of the goods are just liquored up amateur rapists," replied Artemis with a venomous smile.

"Dating not going well?"

"A real Yukon woman can only take so much policy analyst."

"Still want me to set you up with Nestor?"

"Go on a date with that sexy monster? Yes, please!" She fake-fanned herself as if overheating. "He could be the Minotaur and I could wear my Greek maiden costume."

"Before he agrees, he'll want to see a photo. Of your bike."

"Do you think I could get him to tie me up like in the Labyrinth? I need 25 percent less rope than most girls."

Winter's phone buzzed on the table. It was a text from Taiya's new wildlife camera letting him know it had snapped a photo. He had installed it on his way to the party -- without telling Taiya or anyone else -- hidden in some branches pointing at the YCC headquarters building a few blocks away. The photo was in grainy infrared night mode, but it was obviously Taiya.

Wasn't she supposed to be at a Hallowe'en party? Then he remembered. She'd been putting digital costumes on wildlife photos for some Hallowe'en fun on the YCC socials. It couldn't always be about fundraising. She must be posting them before going to her party.

"Hey Winter!" called Eamon, appearing in the kitchen door. "Another drink?"

"Yeah, thanks, I'll stick to the cranberry soda."

"Whoa, it's Hallowe'en. Don't go crazy!"

Out of his peripheral vision, he could see Artemis shaking her head at Eamon. Who now realized he had forgotten -- again -- that Winter didn't drink. Once an alcoholic, always an alcoholic.

"Don't worry about it, Eamon. Grab a chair."

He liked the newsroom people. They were funny and good to work with. But they made him feel old. Hallowe'en was a shitty time to be alone. The trip to Seattle couldn't come soon enough.

Eamon was sitting beside him now. "Is it true your family's been here since the gold rush?" He also was trying to be nice.

"We're BNR royalty. I can look in the family photo album and say, yep, there's the folks who actually stole this land from the First Nations in the first place."

Eamon and the sports guy laughed nervously.

Artemis jumped in. "Tell them about Great-grampa Slade and the cows."

He launched into the cow story. It was always a crowd pleaser. He was just at the bit where the scow broke up and the cows drowned when his phone buzzed. Then again three seconds later. And then three more pauses and buzzes.

"Just a sec." He picked up his phone and flipped the photos. The first shot showed a murky black figure, barely close enough to trigger the camera. Three seconds later, figure slightly closer with hand in pocket. Three more seconds, the whole picture was black except a super bright pinprick of light where the figure used to be. Then another photo that was all black except for an artistic swirl of light across the whole field of vision.

Winter stared at this for a second as everyone watched him. "Oh fuck."

The infrared exploded in a blaze of light in the next one. The whole right side of the photo -- where the YCC building was supposed to be.

He held his screen out of Artemis to see. "Firebomb at YCC. Taiya's in there."

"When? Now?"

But Winter was already grabbing his jacket and running for the door. He biked down Black Street, weaved between the trucks on Fourth Avenue then sprinted for YCC.

The glow of the flames grew as he pedaled closer. Winter stopped for a second on the sidewalk in front of YCC to look for Taiya. The building looked like a Youtube video from Ukraine. The building was black, but the windows were rectangles of bright flame light. The flames spilled out of the smashed window where the Molotov cocktail had gone in.

Where was Taiya? He ran around the building shouting. No sign of her. He opened his phone and tapped on Find My Friends. He stamped his foot in impatience as he waited for the dot and map to materialize.

There it was. Right inside the building. Oh god.

He ran to the front door. Fire.

He ran around to the back frantically. Locked. He took a step back to kick it down, when he felt an arm around his neck. The arm pulled him backwards over an extended leg and Winter went down -- hard -- onto the gravel. Winter tried to stand up but the figure had already flipped him onto his stomach.

Winter writhed and screamed, but his assailant had already got his arm in a lock and was kneeling on his back.

"Calm down, buddy," said an angry male voice. "RCMP. You're not going anywhere. Except the back of my car."

"My daughter--"

The cop pressed Winter's face into the gravel. "Shut it."

Winter put all his strength into rolling over and tried to shout. But all he got was a mouthful of dirt.

"We got a live one. Help me with the cuffs," shouted the officer. Then he leaned in behind Winter's ear. "You moron, you're supposed to break in *before* you burn the place down. How about another gravel sandwich?" The cop put his hand on the back of Winter's head and pressed it into the ground with a powerful twist.

Winter lay still.

"That's better." Winter heard a car pull to a rapid stop. A door slammed. "Stay on the curb ma'am," said the cop. "Live police operation."

"Absolutely officer," said Artemis. "But I'm from the media. First I want to get some video of some fuckwit cop using excessive force to arrest the dad of the girl trapped in the burning building."

31

Northern Destiny Chinese Restaurant
9:30pm, October 31st. -13°C
2221 days sober

Taiya, Artemis and Winter sat in a booth at the Northern Destiny Chinese Restaurant.

Did "Northern Destiny" refer to how a young couple from Lâm Đồng province in Vietnam found themselves cooking buckets of General Tso's Chicken in the Yukon Territory?

"You should have known your daughter was too savvy to get trapped in a burning building," said Artemis.

Winter chewed carefully. His jaw ached if he opened it too wide. He'd just come back from the bathroom where he had tried to pick the gravel out of the cuts on his face. He had cleaned up his face, but couldn't see the streaks of dirt and blood with a few bits of wet toilet paper on the side of his neck. For some reason Henry popped into his mind. "Two minutes of my life being treated like a First Nations guy. I shouldn't complain."

Taiya had been in the kitchen getting a glass of water when the Molotov cocktail came through the front window. As she'd been told a dozen times on Air North, she did not pause to collect her personal belongings before exiting the burning aircraft. She had bolted out the back door, leaving her jacket, laptop and phone to burn.

Winter was proud of her presence of mind. She had run down the street to Northern Destiny and phoned 9-1-1 right away. Which explained why the cops had arrived just seconds after Winter. She had also left a voicemail from the restaurant phone for Winter, but by the time it came through he was face down in a police chokehold.

The door banged open, and Nestor and a cold draught swept into the restaurant. Without taking off his coat or toque, he slid into the booth beside Artemis, who scrambled to move her crutches. Nestor did a brief double take at Artemis and her sari, but quickly turned back to Winter.

"Chaewon ask me to check on computers. I found your bike," he said. He looked back at Artemis. "Break your leg?"

She twisted her hips to swing her stump out from under the table. "Car accident."

"You need better crutches. These are crap."

"What?" Artemis, for once, appeared to be speechless.

"In Ukraine, many legs gone." He held out his sleeve to Artemis, who -- after a second looking back at him in puzzlement -- grabbed it and held as he squirmed out of his jacket. "My friend makes very high-tech crutches. Tell me your mobile. I send link."

While Artemis scrambled to tap her number into Nestor's phone, Taiya asked Nestor, "What about the computers?"

"All destroyed."

"The data?"

"Data good. Remember, Brett ask last month to put all your data in cloud."

"How was the rest of the building?" asked Winter.

"Not bad. Very ineffective attack. Just gasoline bomb. Big mess, but no problem for fire people."

Artemis finished entering her number in Nestor's phone. She winked at Winter. "Worse than ineffective. Counterproductive."

Nestor turned and looked at Artemis quizzically. "Why counter?"

"Yep. Not just another hot amputee." That joke seemed to fly over Nestor's head. "Think about it. Because they didn't do any real damage. And now everyone will be sympathetic to YCC."

"More money and volunteers," said Winter.

"Ah, like when Russians bomb children's school. Bad for children, good for Ukraine."

After dinner, and despite an invitation from Artemis to join the party, Nestor slipped away claiming he had an early-morning fat-bike ride. Taiya left for Brett's Hallowe'en party. Winter walked Artemis home.

"You should come back in to the party," she said. "It's perfect for Hallowe'en. You already look like a zombie."

Winter smiled, then winced and closed his jaw. Once he got home, he sat in front of the TV with Tarfu and turned on the sports highlights. The Canucks were in last place again. Maybe the world wasn't out of kilter after all.

He was snoozing when his phone buzzed. He had to look around for a second to remember where he was.

The call was from Chaewon. Spinning something this late on Hallowe'en? He answered the call.

"Hey Winter. I'm calling about Taiya." Winter sat up abruptly. So did Tarfu as he sensed Winter's alarm. "She's safe, but she kind of needs your help."

"What? Can I talk to her?"

"Umm," Chaewon muttered uncertainly. "I'm afraid she can't talk right now."

"Come on, Chaewon," said Winter harshly. "I'm her dad for fuck sakes!"

"No, I mean she really can't talk right now. I'm holding her ponytail and she's puking into a bush."

A pause. "Sorry Chaewon. I'll be right there."

"We're at Brett's cabin."

"Of course you are."

Winter hung up and looked at Tarfu. "Get a towel and a bucket. We're picking up your special friend."

Where to get a car at this hour. He ran through his list of close friends. It was quite short, actually. But that was something to think about later. Tarfu was already standing at the door. He phoned Artemis.

"Are you able to drive?"

"Of course I can fucking drive," replied Artemis in an annoyed voice. "You may not be able to notice this without Facetime on, but I've only had one leg amputated."

"No, I mean have you been been drinking?"

"What? No. What's going on?"

"Taiya's puking into a bush at Brett's party."

Brett's driveway was full of cars. Music pulsed out of Brett's cabin, and Winter could see people dancing in the living room. A few hardy souls in toques and down jackets stood around the bonfire holding beers.

Taiya was sitting on the deck. Vomit stains oozed down the front of her jacket. Chaewon appeared to be holding up her head and wiping her face with a towel. Sierra and another of Taiya's friends shuffled guiltily to one side.

Tarfu ran up to Taiya, whose arms moved vaguely to welcome the dog. Tarfu jumped up on the deck and started licking Taiya's face.

"Gross!" said Sierra. She stank like weed and was holding a can of cheap cider. Winter ignored her.

Winter and Chaewon stood Taiya up. She couldn't walk, so they each lifted an arm over their shoulders and walked her to the car as she mumbled and slurred. Taiya's limp body was surprisingly heavy, and she smelled like vomit. And also, Winter noticed with growing anger, like weed. Her boots dragged behind on the gravel.

"I'm fine," slurred Taiya.

"Thank you for taking care of my daughter, Chaewon," said Winter. "I really appreciate it."

"It's what friends are for."

Winter felt his anger rising, and almost replied with something cutting about friends who let teenage friends get drunk and stoned. But Chaewon wasn't Taiya's uncle. That was a conversation for Brett. First thing tomorrow when Taiya was safe. He suppressed his rage and nodded an acknowledgement to Chaewon.

Sierra ran over to the car. "I texted her moms too."

Winter looked up at her. Was that a bad joke? Apparently not. "Thanks, Sierra. That's really super."

Winter, bucket and towel rode in the back with Taiya while Tarfu sat in the front.

They pulled into Winter's driveway, then began to extract Taiya and drag her into the house. Just then a Tesla pulled in behind them, illuminating the trio in its lights.

"Lord Vader has tracked us back to our base," said Artemis. Karen and Misty stepped out of the car.

"My baby!" wailed Misty as she ran to Taiya.

"Watch out, Misty," said Winter, "we need to get her inside, warm and cleaned up."

"You're not taking her into your house. You got her into this!"

Misty stood in Winter's way and let loose. Why didn't Winter text us? Did he know she was going to a party? The risky rafting job. "And you encouraged her to work with your brother at YCC ... the RCMP called. She could have been killed tonight!"

"Not now, Misty."

"Yes, now," said LDV. "What was she drinking out there?"

"Cider."

"Any hard liquor."

"Who knows."

"You should have asked. How are we supposed to know if we should take her to the hospital?"

"Fuck off Karen."

"We're not the irresponsible alcoholics here. Misty has custody. Either you put Taiya in our car or we're calling the cops."

Misty turned and shouted in Winter's face. He flinched as the spit flew. "She's got midterms! She's supposed to go to university! And you let her do this?"

Stay calm, thought Winter. "I did not *let* her do anything."

"You got her into this climate stuff. She got arrested at that protest! You want her to have a criminal record too?"

"Calm down. You don't get a criminal record for getting arrested at a protest."

LDV grabbed Winter's left arm and yanked him to look at her. He felt a powerful urge to deck her. "We've talked about this before. We're calling the lawyer on Monday to revoke your access. If you contact Taiya again, we'll sue your ass off."

Winter pulled his right arm out from behind Taiya's back and made sure Artemis had her weight.

Then he turned, planted his feet, and twisted all his torso muscles to pound his right fist into LDV's nose. Just like his old minor hockey coach used to say: punch *through* the face you're hitting. LDV went down like a protester tasered by the cops.

He pointed the finger on his unbroken hand at Misty. "Recovery position on her side. Don't leave her. If you let her fucking choke on her own vomit, I'll kill you." Then he turned and stomped off into the darkness.

32

Yukon Sun newsroom, Third and Main

10:15am, November 4th, -25°C
0 days sober

Artemis propped her crutch against the desk and slumped into her chair. Zero days sober. Or that was her guess. For a guy whose most intimate relationship was with the IAmSober app, this was bad news.

No one had seen Winter since he punched LDV four days previously. Artemis was getting worried. Or, rather, even more worried.

She opened her computer and played the Northern Lights security video on her laptop again. No one had claimed responsibility for the latest attack, unless the email was sitting in Winter's inbox. The tit for tat retaliations were escalating. The YCC kids blocked traffic. Freedos firebomb YCC. Someone, presumably a Green extremist, breaks into Northern Lights.

Amber had commented publicly this time, calling on the government to keep families safe from Green extremists rather than raising the cost of living with carbon taxes that just made the Chinese laugh.

The video started. It was night. The camera was on a pole pointing down on the equipment in the Northern Lights construction yard. A lone figure in a white hazmat suit walked into the field of vision. The person was wearing a ski buff up to their nose with goggles on top. She watched as the figure calmly climbed into a front-end loader, shone a headlamp around until they found where the secret start code was scrawled in Sharpie on the dashboard, started it, and proceeded to flip over a pickup and demolish the Atco trailer that housed the construction office.

Then the figure dismounted, lit a Molotov cocktail, and threw it into the engine compartment of the loader, and walked away. Briskly but not hurried. Five minutes, hundreds of thousands of dollars of damage. Just another day at the office.

She opened Winter's wildlife cam videos from the YCC headquarters fire. The person with the molotov cocktail in that one was wearing black, not a hazmat suit.

When she moved to the Yukon, she was hoping for quirky northern adventures. But this was getting out of control.

Eamon poked his head into her office. "Winter still taking a few days off?"

Artemis nodded. That was the way she had put it to the newsroom and Eamon, at least, still seemed to be buying it.

The cops had visited of course. She had been a good citizen and was happy to answer questions. She had shared the photos of the constable kneeling on Winter's back -- which did not make them happy -- and, as for LDV getting hurt, all she had seen was LDV aggressively grab Winter's arm while he was trying to help his daughter. No idea why she fell over. Death threats? Sounded like hysterics to her.

Eamon was still standing there. "Funny," he said, "I thought I saw him going into the 98 with the Breakfast Club on Sunday morning."

Great. So Winter went straight to the only dive bar that opens at 9am, thought Artemis with a frown. Time to reset Winter's app to zero days sober.

She assigned the latest attack to Eamon. Even he could write a story describing a video. Then she grabbed her crutches and headed over to the 98 Hotel.

She flinched as the cold wind blew down Second Avenue. The winter had hardly started and it was already -25°C. An early cold snap. So much for global warming this week. It was time to get out her real winter coat.

The bartender was in her forties, wearing a "My other ride's a D9 dozer" tank top from the Chamber of Mines, and was busily wiping the bar. Morning shift at the Breakfast Club. She had probably seen a few things over the years. Artemis showed her a photo of Winter.

"He's barred. As of Sunday morning. Fucking asshole."

Artemis looked around the bar. She never came in here. Seemed fine at ten in the morning.

What the hell. She leaned her crutches against the bar and hopped onto a stool. The bar was beautifully inlaid with coins surrounding jumping salmon.

"I'll have a Caesar."

She sipped her drink, pulled out her notebook, and jotted down the events. First, someone spray painted swastikas on YCC. Then Chaewon's car was torched in front of YCC; unfortunately, Brett's obnoxious van was undamaged. Which prompted the YCC students to block traffic. After that, someone in a black jacket firebombed YCC headquarters, which seemed to have prompted the guy in the white hazmat suit to go on a rampage at Northern Lights.

What was the pattern here? More attacks on YCC than on miners or Freedo-friendly targets. Which got Brett lots of sympathy. Then, each time someone from the Green side retaliated, ditto for Amber.

Also, each attack was bigger than the one before. What did that mean for the next one, assuming someone would retaliate for something?

She sipped her Caesar. The perfect brunch cocktail, as they said. She took a bite out of her celery. Cui bono? That was the question to ask, she thought. And who did benefit from all this mayhem? Amber and the Freedos got publicity and got their base fired up. The government didn't benefit; this wasn't Russia where they were looking for an excuse to arrest a bunch of people. The media benefited since they had real news instead of reporting on infrastructure photo ops. Brett and the Greens benefited too, in a way. Their stuff got trashed, but Brett was now almost a regular on the national news.

Her musing were interrupted as the only other guy in the bar walked over and took the barstool beside her.

"New in town?"

Artemis looked at the bartender. "Could I please have a fork to jab in this gentleman's eye in case he becomes a pest?"

The bartender silently removed a fork from the drawer and slid it across the bar.

The guy stood up. "Whoa. Frosty inside today too." He picked up his beer and retreated to his table.

33

Grainger Sports Pub parking lot

11:00pm, November 4th, -32°C

"Fuckin' Habs fans!" laughed Zach, looking back over his shoulder at the neon beer signs in the sports pub's frosted windows. The frigid packed snow squeaked like Styrofoam as he climbed into the passenger seat of the old black F-350. "Did you see their faces when Brendan Lambert scored the winner?"

Casca sat up off her blanket on the seat. She wagged her tail and jumped up to lick his face. The dog's frozen breath floated in the cab. Zach put his arm around her and gave her a good rub with his big snowmobile mitts.

The old BNR smiled and rummaged for the key in his pocket. It was nice to see a local boy like Lambert in the big leagues. The pub walls were covered with his old jerseys.

"The Habs could've traded for him. They went for that Swedish pretty boy instead," he said.

"With the purple hair," said Zach. "It's a fucking crime, Dad."

The old BNR inserted the key. The radio came on in the background as he waited for the diesel spark light to blink out. It was an early cold snap this year, but they'd only been there for a few beers. The truck should start fine.

The radio was playing the news. He reached out to turn it off but something made him hesitate and he let the radio play: "Allegations that Saskatoon police took an intoxicated indigenous man on a so-called Starlight Tour are unfounded, an investigation by the city police force's Public Complaints Commission has found. Last winter, Gerald Tomlins, a citizen of the Whitecap Dakota First Nation, was found frozen to death on the outskirts of Saskatoon. Lawyers for the-"

The spark lamp went out. He clicked off the news and turned the key. The old diesel roared to life. The old BNR turned the heaters up to max.

"The guy probably had a rap sheet as long as his arm," said Zach.

"No one'll miss him." The old man put the truck into gear and let out the clutch. "Feel like some KFC? The pub food is way too expensive."

At the drive thru, they each ordered two-piece boxes. Zach tore off a piece of his drumstick and gave it to Casca as the old BNR turned onto the Alaska Highway and accelerated. He peered intently into the dark through the frosted windshield as snowflakes swirled in the headlights.

Suddenly, a shape popped out of the swirling snow into the light cone of the headlights.

The old BNR slammed on the brakes and steered – not too much, it was icy – away from the shape. Zach braced himself on the dashboard, and Casca and her blanket slid off the seat onto the pickup floor into a tangle around the gearshift.

"Caribou?" asked Zach.

"No, some guy. Looked native," said the old BNR.

They pulled over, put on the hazard lights, and got out of the vehicle. Zach turned on the flashlight in his phone, and they walked back along the dark, quiet highway.

A figure trudged unsteadily towards them.

"You could get killed!" shouted Zach. "It's fucking dark."

The figure continued to trudge towards the light.

"Are you okay, man?" asked Zach.

Henry stepped into the light, and swayed slightly on his feet. "It's fuckin' cold, man. Old school," he slurred. He had his hood up, but his jacket wasn't that thick. He was wearing running shoes instead of boots. "Just walkin' home."

His spiky black hair stuck out from under the hood. His wispy black beard was covered with frost, and the gap from his missing tooth stood out as the phone light bounced off his teeth.

Zach and the old BNR exchanged glances. The old man nodded.

"Let me and my dad give you a ride home," said Zach. A thought occurred to him. "We were just at KFC. Want some dinner?"

"That's okay, just a mile or two to go," muttered Henry.

"No, no. It's Thirty-Five Below. We'll give you a ride."

Henry made a few more objections, but Zach steered him towards the truck. Finally, Henry agreed to get in.

Casca stood on her blanket again. But this time her ears went back and she growled.

"I forgot the old girl doesn't like Indians," whispered Zach with a laugh to his dad.

"I used to have a dog," said Henry, speaking to no one in particular.

"She's just shy about strangers," said Zach, pulling Casca down onto the truck floor and steering Henry into the cab. Zach was 6' 5" and muscular, and Henry seemed like half his weight. Zach boosted Henry into the middle seat.

Henry held his hands out and rubbed them in the warm air coming out of the dashboard vent. Casca sat at Zach's feet watching Henry. The old BNR turned the truck around in the Airport Chalet parking lot and headed north up the highway.

They approached the Hamilton Boulevard junction. "You headed to Macintyre?" asked Zach.

"Yep, my auntie's place."

Zach eyed the approaching intersection, wondering if their passenger would notice if they turned or not. "Want some chicken?"

Henry took a piece out of Zach's box. He held it with both hands and bit eagerly into the crunchy skin. He hadn't eaten since breakfast.

The F-350 roared past Hamilton Boulevard and continued north past Kopper King. Henry was warming up as the dashboard fan blew hot air all over him. He took some fries and chewed them hungrily.

He was starting to feel very sleepy. His head nodded forward. Zach held him up as the truck turned onto Fish Lake Road. By the time they got to the end of the road, Henry was leaning on Zach's shoulder and snoring lightly.

The old BNR turned the truck around and drove back a few hundred yards towards Whitehorse. He stopped without pulling over beside an embankment. It was snowing lightly, and the wind was starting to come up. The snow swirled in the headlights. The tracks they had made just a few minutes before were already starting to drift in.

He looked into the distance. No headlights were visible on the road.

Zach opened the door and, holding Henry upright with his left arm, stepped out into the snow.

"We're at your auntie's place," said Zach.

Henry lifted his head and blinked. "What?" He peered confusedly out the car door. There were no lights. "This isn't my auntie's place."

"Close enough," said Zach. He planted both hands on Henry's coat, and hauled him out of the pickup cab. The KFC box and cold fries scattered over the snow.

Henry tried to wrestle free and stand up, but Zach held his slender frame in a tight grip and kept Henry off balance. "Let fucking go-" said Henry, becoming agitated.

Zach dragged him over to the embankment.

"What the fuck, man, let me go," shouted Henry, alive and squirming. His hands tried to reach up and grab Zach's arms or face, but Zach was holding him in a straightjacket grip by the upper arms.

Zach brought Henry up almost to standing position, then kneed him violently in the balls and tossed him down the embankment. It was too dark to see, but Zach could hear Henry slide to the bottom of the ditch and moan. Then he got back in the truck with his dad, who gunned the pickup back towards town.

34

Eamon's Chevy Bolt

11:05am, November 12th, -24°C
1 day sober

Eamon turned the car onto the Alaska Highway. He glanced sideways at Winter. The "taking a few days off" story from Artemis was obviously a smoke screen, and a pretty unbelievable one at that. Winter looked rough. Like he'd been aged a few years then dragged through buckbrush by a quad. His face was drawn and he looked thinner. He hadn't smiled yet and sat staring silently at his phone, tapping it occasionally with the fingers sticking out of bandages around his hand.

His face was covered with scratches and he had a black eye that was maturing into the greenish-yellow stage.

It was no time to ask him to finish that story about his great-great-grandfather and the ghost cows of Miles Canyon.

Artemis had been all full of fake cheeriness when she suggested Winter and Eamon go out together to check out the body discovered on Fish Lake Road. Just a routine story. Might turn into a murder trial or missing persons case later, but today was just a little piece about a body.

Hardly worth even driving out for, in Eamon's opinion. He wondered what Artemis was thinking.

Winter was deep in thought. Not about Eamon. But about Taiya. He stared at the "1 day sober" banner on the app. Oh god. A powerful wave of shame swept over him. He wanted to puke. Memories of Misty and LDV floated across his brain. And the police interview. And the lawsuit.

Artemis pointed out that Taiya was in Grade 12 and the custody rules wouldn't apply to her soon anyway. Too bad no one had figured that out in his driveway before LDV started threatening lawsuits and asking to be punched out.

At least Artemis said LDV was walking around with splints up her nose. Those were supposed to be painful.

Winter tried not to dwell on the bitterness. Let it flow over, just like they said in the fucking annoying podcast.

As long as he hadn't done anything else while blacked out. His phone had a giant crack, he didn't know where the black eye came from and he'd woken up with the worst hangover of all time in a strange basement with a Yukon government briefcase and somebody else's jacket.

He turned his mind to Brett. It really was all his fault. Who allowed their teenage niece to get legless at their own house? And Brett seemed completely blasé about leaving high-school kids in risky positions. Working late, alone, at YCC headquarters, the most vandalized building in Whitehorse? He had to admit he almost agreed with LDV about Taiya getting arrested at the YCC zip tie protest.

But Brett would just float through all this smelling like roses, as he always did.

Unless someone held him accountable.

"Held him accountable." That was bureaucratic talk. "Payback" was what Brett really needed. Payback. Payback with extreme prejudice, and a plane ticket out of the Yukon.

Winter caught himself. These were negative thoughts. The podcast guy said not to wallow in negativity.

OK, something positive. Getting to the bottom of the YCC attacks. That would be a good project. Some front page stories. Some creeps outed for their bad choices. Working closely with Artemis and the news room.

Step One was finding Henry. Maybe he could remember something specific about the biker he saw. Or maybe he'd also seen the firebombing. In the meantime, hanging around with Eamon doing some boring stories to get back into the flow, like Artemis wanted. Which was nice of her. Just too bad Eamon was so dull.

They turned onto Fish Lake Road and Eamon accelerated.

"Drive in the middle of the road," said Winter dully. "BNR wisdom. The shoulders are soft."

Eamon drove along until they saw a cop car, then pulled over behind it. Winter sighed, opened the door, and walked towards the cops. They looked surprised someone had shown up. Eamon grabbed his camera and hurried behind.

He didn't know any of the cops. But they all did a double take when they saw Winter.

Eamon walked over to the police. They were standing a decent distance from a body-sized lump covered with an emergency blanket. "What's the story?" he asked.

"First Nations man, late 30s, identity unknown, frozen to death."

"What was he doing out here?"

The cop shrugged. Other than freezing to death? Hard to say.

"How frozen?" asked Winter. He jammed his hands into his jacket pockets and leaned against the warm cop car engine compartment. "Today or rock solid?"

"A day or two at least."

"And people just kept driving by?"

The cop shrugged. "We got a call this morning."

Winter looked over at the body. An elbow poked stiffly out from under the blanket. It was an olive jacket. Suddenly Winter strode forward and, before the cops could react, ripped off the blanket.

The body lay huddled on its side on the edge of the road with its arms crossed. An olive drab jacket with a dusting of snow. The face was frozen in a contorted grimace. The eye balls were frozen open and hoar frost covered the lashes. The corpse had spiky black hair and was missing a front tooth.

Winter staggered back over the cop car, leaned on it, and threw up by the front tire.

35

Winter's bedroom

5:58 a.m., November 27th, -13°C
16 days sober

Winter opened his eyes. The room was bathed in morning light. It might be fake light from his sunrise clock, but it sure beat waking up in pitch dark to the buzzer on his old clock radio. The electronic seagull and wave noises hadn't started yet, so the light must have woken him a few minutes early.

He reached out to turn off the clock. It would be nice to just roll over and sleep in.

Tarfu lifted his head up off his bed on the floor. Their eyes met. Did Tarfu sense a moment of weakness? Probably.

Winter pulled his hand back from the clock. He stood up and looked through the window at the thermometer on the window frame: -13°C. Much warmer than the night Henry froze.

Would Henry have survived if it was warmer that night? Maybe.

Who would do that kind of thing? There were no witnesses and a light dusting of fresh snow that morning over the whole scene. One more incident for the cold case task force to pretend to work on.

Whoever they were, they stood an excellent chance of getting off scot free. A lot people were getting away with too much shit these days. Which was an excellent reason to get out to Zach's compound and catch some diesel smugglers in action. The trails would be perfect this morning, packed from yesterday's riders and frozen firm overnight.

He dressed quickly. He put a piece of bread into the toaster, grabbed the peanut butter and waited for the toast to pop. An image of LDV with splints up her nose crossed his mind. That had been a stupid thing to do. Colossally stupid. He would have to live with the consequences. And even if she was awful, she didn't deserve that. He had to admit she took being Taiya's stepmother seriously.

Winter looked around for something else to think about. He checked Tarfu's foot. The dog had been limping for a day or two, but seemed fine now.

He finished his toast, had a glass of water, and grabbed his fat bike from the garage. It was a half moon and he didn't need his headlamp as he pedaled from his house to Chadburn Lake road. Tarfu trotted silently behind him. The streets were empty and the only noise was the studs on the five-inch tires grabbing the frozen road. Winter downshifted and pedaled up the first hill.

He felt the cobwebs disappearing as his legs pumped. It felt good. His frozen breath shot away into the dark air. At the top of the hill, he stopped pedaling and coasted to a stop. He looked up at Grey Mountain, gleaming under the moonlight in the perfectly clear air. What a great day to be alive.

After he broke the story about Zach, Amber and the diesel smuggling, the next job would be Brett. That asshole had to be hiding some financial shenanigans, or worse. Maybe enough so that he would actually keep his distance from Taiya, or maybe even fuck off back to Ontario.

Winter pedaled across the Miles Canyon suspension bridge. The Yukon River rushed noisily through the ice-encrusted canyon walls. He pumped uphill towards Zach's compound.

He checked quickly for lights, told Tarfu to sit, then climbed the fence. He swapped out the camera card and batteries then returned over the fence.

He pedaled a minute down the trail then stopped. He inserted his new card reader into his phone and plugged in the camera card. He scrolled through the photos. There weren't many and the camera was pointed right at the correct shipping container. Finally, he had the settings correct.

A few photos of Zach walking by, then Amber, then their dog. Then, a pickup with a big tank on the back.

Jackpot! Winter recognized the truck. It belonged to an RCMP officer on Zach's Oldtimers team.

The camera took a still shot then ten seconds of video. He watched the truck pull up and the cop step out wearing civilian clothes. In the next video, Zach stepped into the frame and unlocked the container.

Next would be dragging a hose over to the truck.

But the next video cut off after 2 seconds.

The batteries had gone dead in the cold.

Winter felt a powerful urge to hurl the SIM card into the trees.

He looked down at Tarfu and sighed, remembering the old gold rush line Gramma used to say: "Bury me here, where I failed."

The podcast guy would tell him to de-catastrophe-ize his situation. Whatever shit Winter was in, it was nowhere near as bad as the guy that wrote that suicide note.

Winter blew out a long sigh into the cold air. Why was he doing this? To publish a big exposé on fuel smuggling? To show up the government and the police for doing nothing despite everyone knowing what was going on? To get a journalism award, the first since the accident?

He knew what his younger self would have said: "This isn't Watergate."

And that the BC-Yukon Community Newspaper Association Award was not the Pulitzer Prize.

But what was the alternative? Just sit around the newsroom and be the lazy old alcoholic journalist republishing government press releases as news?

He jammed the SIM card into his pocket and put his mitts back on. Maybe the fresh batteries would hold out long enough to catch Zach in action next time.

Winter looked over at Tarfu, who was standing expectantly down the trail. Ready to run behind Winter's bike, chase a rabbit or nap on the couch.

Tarfu was exceptionally good at his job of being a dog. There was a message in there somewhere.

He just needed better equipment. And why stop with Zach and his diesel scam. Brett had to be sitting on top of an even bigger scam. One that involved big-city donors. One that might even get national headlines. And, just maybe, one that would keep Brett away from Taiya.

Tarfu turned and trotted down the trail. "Yeah, yeah, I'm coming," said Winter.

36

Pike's Place Market, Seattle

2:15pm, December 4th. +55°F
23 days sober

Winter checked his phone again. Anna was definitely ghosting him. It had been a terrible idea to come to Seattle for the weekend, even if the tickets were non-refundable. Too much time alone to think.

He stood with the tourists at the fish stall in Pike Place Market, watching the guys toss a salmon from the ice to the cutting table. The coho curved gracefully through the air. One last graceful jump, except the destination was getting made into sashimi rather than spawning in the stream it was born in.

That fish had one job -- spawn -- and it had failed. All those years swimming, eating, dodging Orcas; wasted.

All Winter could think about was Anna ghosting him. His stomach tightened. He must have sent her some messages while on his bender. But their Signal conversation deleted messages after 24 hours, so he couldn't even look in his sent messages to see how bad it was.

He wandered through the market. He found the pack of blue raspberry flavoured condoms in his jacket pocket and tossed them in the trash. He wandered past the artisanal honey and Pacific Northwest crafts and out onto the street.

Thirty-two hours until his flight left.

He wandered along Seattle's streets. He tried to remember what the mindfulness podcast said. The thoughts about Anna were going to come into his mind. Just let them pass through. Focus on walking. Breathing.

He paused at a crosswalk. Another thought came into his mind: the meeting next week with the lawyers about his assault investigation and LDV's lawsuit. The good news, his lawyer had joked, was that Winter had hardly any assets for LDV to go after. The bad news was they needed their retainer paid up front.

Let that thought pass by too.

It was replaced by Brett. The careless and self-centred guy who somehow got Taiya and everyone else in shit, but emerged spotless himself. He was even getting more publicity and donations. He'd been on national TV news shows more than he had ever been before.

He looked up. A sign said "Seattle Spy Shop." He decided to go in.

37

A gravel pit about one kilometre from Brett's cabin

9:00pm, Winter Solstice - December 21st. -22°C
40 days sober

The packed snow crunched under the tires of Taiya's electric pickup as it crept quietly into the gravel pit. Winter powered off the motor and sat in the dark listening to the winter silence. Half a kilometre to Brett's cabin. Six minutes at hiking speed. Say ten minutes on skis in deep snow.

Tarfu stood up on the seat, ready to go. Winter rubbed the dog's head with his mitt. "You stay here, buddy." Winter folded the dog's blanket and spread it on the seat.

He grabbed his pack, slipped out of the vehicle and clicked on his skis. He looked into the forest. The trees cast black, angular moonshadows on the white snow. The ski tracks from his last visit were blown in with fresh snow. In the daylight, they would be invisible. But now the shadows found the corners of the slight impressions, darklighting his path to the Brett's cabin. To whatever he was about to find on the cameras he had planted on his last visit.

Assuming Brett hadn't tried to read the copy of *An Inconvenient Truth* on his bookshelf and discovered the pages had been cut out to make room for a spy camera.

Winter slipped his mitts through the pole straps and stepped into the snow between the trees.

He was breathing heavily by the time he got to the band of willows along Brett's driveway. The snow was unusually deep for this time of year. Like last year. For once, the oldtimers and the climate activists agreed: the Yukon was getting warmer and wetter.

No lights in the cabin and no vehicle in the driveway. He took off his skis and jumped over the plow bank, trying not to leave obvious footprints, and walked to the cabin.

The key was where he found it last time. Under a frozen pot of dead pansies on the deck. Exactly where you would expect Brett to put it. He pulled on his thin liner gloves and opened the door.

Winter checked over his shoulder for headlights coming up the driveway and slipped into the cabin. He bent to take off his boots, then remembered how silly it would be if Brett came home and he had to find his boots before slipping out the back door.

He kicked the snow off his boots and headed for Brett's office.

He checked the bookcase. Al Gore's book was still on the shelf, up high with a good view of Brett's desk. The hole in the spine for the camera looked obvious, but only if you knew it was there.

While the key was conveniently under a frozen pot, Winter had not found Brett's wifi password written on the fridge. If he had, he could have done all this from home. He pulled a router out of his pack and crawled under the desk to plug the internet cable into the back of Brett's router.

He slipped the laptop out of its insulated sheath. As he waited for it to power up, he checked out Brett's office. Laptop in its usual place. Covered with stickers from climate conferences and Save-the-Caribou protests.

Printed selfies were pinned to the bulletin board. Greta Thunberg at a conference. David Suzuki in a shopping mall. Justin Trudeau. Even one with what appeared to be a wax mannequin of Nelson Mandela.

Fortunately Brett paid more attention to his selfies than his bookcase.

When the wifi connected, the light-bulb camera in the kitchen popped onto the screen but not the book camera in the office. As the light bulb transmitted its files to the laptop, Winter pulled down Al Gore to swap out the batteries and SD card. Hopefully it had caught some good footage before its power died.

Files successfully transferred, he put his gear back in his pack and slipped out of the cabin.

Back at the truck, he powered up the laptop and the truck's heat.

He fast-forwarded through the book-camera videos. The quality was excellent. The book had a perfect view of Brett's desk. The problem was that the laptop was screened by Brett's back when he sat at the desk.

How stupid! Why hadn't he thought of that? One time, Brett leaned back and sideways far enough for Winter to see the screen. But it was just a news story about Leonardo DiCaprio visiting a retreating glacier in Greenland.

He checked battery icons. Being stuck out here with a dead truck and a frozen laptop would be a disaster.

He opened the folder with the kitchen light-bulb camera files. The fish-eye lens had a good view of the whole kitchen.

Winter viewed the files in increasing frustration. Brett making coffee. Brett drinking coffee. Brett loading the dishwasher. Brett making breakfast. Brett cleaning an egg off the floor. Brett sitting at the table reading a magazine. Brett clipping his toenails.

About 20 files in, Brett picked his nose. Winter watched as Brett, at two-times normal speed, flicked the booger into the firewood box.

Fuck! This was useless.

Then the next file was different. It started in the dark as the door opened with a bang that made the mic indicator spike to max. The camera's infrared night lens captured two greenish, slightly blurred figures wearing toques and parkas clatter into the kitchen wearing cross-country ski boots.

One was definitely Brett. The other was a woman, Echo maybe.

Winter waited for them to flick on the kitchen light but they never did. Instead, they clamped into an embrace. The kitchen table scraped on the floor as they almost fell onto it.

The woman pushed Brett back against the fridge and dropped to her knees. Fridge magnets clattered noisily to the floor. Framed by the dark green rectangle of the fridge, she squirmed out of her down jacket and pulled Brett's ski tights down to his knees in one swift yank.

The woman's toque had a ponytail hole in the back. Where had he seen that before?

Oh god, it was Brett's new intern from Queen's.

He scrambled to hit the pause button. Cabin porn in green night-vision monochrome. There was probably a whole section of the Alaskan internet dedicated to this.

Boss-sex with a younger woman. He made a note of the filename, but there was no need to watch it. Some things you can't unsee.

The next file was date-stamped the next morning. It showed Brett shuffling into the kitchen in his slippers and bathrobe carrying his laptop. The light was on this time, and Winter could see the intern's parka and shirt on the floor by the fridge.

Brett moved towards the table. Winter willed him to put the laptop on the nearest side, where the camera could see its screen. Which he did. Winter fast-forwarded through the coffee making and cereal pouring.

Then Brett sat down. At the far end of the table. He reached across and pulled his laptop away from the camera.

Winter cursed. All this for nothing.

He put it on double speed and kept watching, just in case.

Brett slurped excess milk from his cereal bowl and drank some coffee staring out the window into the dark.

Winter began to feel sympathy for cops surveilling drug dealers.

Then Brett popped open his laptop. The camera couldn't see the screen. But it could see the keyboard.

Winter jolted forward and watched as Brett held his coffee in one hand and henpecked his password into the keyboard with his other.

Winter grabbed a pen from the glove box. It was frozen. He found a pencil and watched the sequence at half speed: 1 - G - r - e - e - n - pause to drink coffee - r - o - c - k - *

Of course that was his password.

Winter jumped out of the truck and skied as fast as he could back to Brett's cabin.

In Brett's office, he tossed his toque over *An Inconvenient Truth* and tapped the password into the laptop. With an ear listening for a vehicle in the driveway, Winter searched Brett's Yukon Climate Collective emails. Long exchanges with Anna and her finance person about Clima not renewing this year's funding. Suck up emails to other funders. Short, witty emails -- no doubt taking lots of editing to get just right -- to journalists to get them to cover YCC in just the right way.

He opened Messages and watched as the latest texts from Brett's phone appeared. Half the conversations were with other climate bunnies in town, including some flirty, puke-worthy messages with his intern. He considered creating a groupchat and sending a screenshot to all of them.

A word search in Finder for "Cambridge" brought up an expense claim for his Masters program. YCC was paying for that? Did the donors know? He copied the whole folder to a thumb drive.

He did the same for YCC's financial statements and Brett's personal taxes. He found the statement from Brett's trust fund and took a moment to soak in the numbers. Jesus. And mom had spent a decade complaining about a few hundred bucks a month.

He was about to close the computer when he noticed more icons at the bottom of the screen. A Virtual Private Network program and the Opera browser. That was the one Nestor said to use to avoid getting tracked. He opened it and watched as it reopened the tabs that were open last time it was used.

Headlights appeared through the trees. Winter froze. Then the headlights disappeared. It was a car on the road, not Brett's driveway.

Focus.

There was a tab for Brett's bank. Another was for a Bitcoin wallet. The last was for Protonmail. That was the ultra-confidential email platform the Yukon Freedom Front emails came from. Did Brett also have a separate, top-secret email account?

The inbox loaded onto the screen. The top email was from him, Winter Slade at the *Yukon Sun*. He blinked and looked again. It was the reply he had sent to YukonFreedomFront@protonmail.com after they claimed responsibility for the latest attack.

How did Brett hack their email?

Wait, thought Winter, the dark realization seeping into his mind like Forty Below cutting into your body through a thin jacket: Brett doesn't know how to hack email; he *is* the Yukon Freedom Front.

The bastard. Winter was on his feet in a second, his fingers gripping the edges of the laptop. He so badly wanted to hurl it through the window.

Three deep breaths. Think it through.

Brett was attacking his own organization to get sympathy and donations. It made sense. He never seemed personally afraid of being attacked. It was Chaewon's crappy Subaru, not Brett's fancy new van, that got torched. He wasn't in the building when the firebomb came through the window, but he was ready with an eloquent statement.

Winter burned with a cold rage. Brett had attacked his own organization. And everyone had fallen for it. From the National to Echo. And Taiya had been in the building when he threw the firebomb. In the building!

Winter pulled out his phone and snapped some photos of the screen. Then the sent items. Then he pulled back and got one with the laptop and selfie board to prove it was Brett's cabin.

Taiya would be heartbroken. She only had one uncle and it turned out he was the kind of guy who would firebomb his own headquarters while she was volunteering inside it.

Fucking asshole. There was an empty cardboard box on the floor beside the desk. He booted it savagely into the wall.

But what should he do now?

He picked up the crumpled box, straightened it out, and put it back beside the desk. He turned away, then his head whipped back. What did the box label say?

"Holy fuck..." he muttered.

He whipped out his phone and dialed Brett. No answer. Of course. He dialed Taiya. "Taiya's phone," said a voice. It was Chaewon. "Where's Taiya?"

Chaewon didn't answer for a second. "Hello to you too. She forgot her phone in my office. She's already at the protest."

"Brett?"

"Don't know. He's got something special planned tonight."

"What kind of something?"

"He wouldn't tell me. Something big. Make sure you're there early-"

Winter hung up.

Something big. Was that why there was an empty box from Alaska marked "Caution - Explosive Material" in Brett's office?

He leaned over the Macbook and clicked on Find My iPhone. He watched as the map loaded. A blue dot appeared. On the side of Chadburn Lake Road by Schwatka Lake.

Winter quickly but carefully closed the browsers, powered down the laptop and -- standing to one side -- pulled his toque off the book camera.

Then he sprinted for the truck.

1982 - JULY

1982-3

Wayne's wall tent, Big Kalzas Lake

5:00pm, Tuesday, July 20th, 1982. +20°C

Shawn slowly banked the floatplane into its final approach to the lake, gazing up at the twin peaks towering over the landscape. It was just a 50 mile hop from Little Salmon Lake to Wayne's wall tent. Wayne and Kendrick would be happy to see the beer and steaks. Unlike most flights, he wasn't carrying a heavy load. Just some gas, a little nylon pup tent and a sleeping bag. And lots of beer. And other necessities: a Sara Lee frozen chocolate cake, a bottle of Canadian Club, and some mix. They would catch a few lake trout, cook up some surf and turf, and celebrate!

Shawn saw Wayne's wall tent. The smoke drifting up from the campfire showed a North wind. Good. Wayne's aluminum boat was out on the lake. It had two guys, and it looked like they were trolling. He rocked his wings as both men waved up. The lake had some light chop. Also good. Better than glassy smooth when it could be tricky to gauge your altitude as you landed.

He curved across the lake and over the outfitter camp on the other side. Nobody there. Too early in the year.

He double checked the water rudder was up, pulled back the throttle, extended his flaps and put the plane on the water.

By the time he had taxied over to the beach, Kendrick and Wayne were waiting. He wondered again why the party wasn't in town. Why not steak at the Cellar and then party it up at the Kopper King? The KK would be hopping with T&A tonight.

But Wayne loved it here. He would just hang out for days. He always had a bunch of bullshit Native tradition stories about his grampa and uncles hunting here every year when he was a kid.

Kendrick also seemed to love it here. It beat hanging out at home with the wife and kids, I guess. If that was married life, staying single sounded pretty good.

Kendrick was also super uptight about word leaking out. There were no barmaids to overhear all the geology chatter here.

The beach was perfect. Light gravel, no sharp rocks for the floats, and big trees twenty feet back to tie the plane to. He powered down the engine and let momentum carry the floats onto the beach.

"I hope you didn't forget the beer!" shouted Kendrick, stepping forward once the prop stopped spinning.

Shawn hopped down onto the floats. "No chance of that!" He tossed a stubby to Kendrick and one to Wayne. "Let me get this thing tied down, then it's party time!"

They quickly put the beers in the lake, wrapped the potatoes in tinfoil and put them in the fire. Wayne gutted a lake trout and Kendrick unwrapped a couple of steaks. Shawn popped the top off a fresh beer for each guy, then produced a shrimp tray complete with a little bowl of cocktail sauce. "Got it from a guy from Skagway. Pretty fancy for appetizers, huh?"

Shawn bit into a shrimp. That cold, crisp crunch. Still just a bit frozen in the middle. He dipped the remaining chunk of shrimp in the sauce. Perfect.

"Sure beats stale crackers and warm Imperial cheddar," agreed Kendrick with a laugh.

When they had finished dinner, Shawn set his empty plate on a stump and got up out of his chair. "Gotta take a leak," he announced. His first step was a bit wobbly. A dozen empty stubbies of Old Style already lay beside the fire, plus a few High Tests. One case dead already and another on the way.

He took a step and unzipped.

"Not there!" shouted Kendrick with a laugh. "Give us at least twenty feet!"

Shawn hiked up his pants and walked over to a big old pine. He unzipped, leaned on the tree, and let go. Ants scurried everywhere. Shawn steered his stream over the ants, watching as they scrambled to avoid the foamy liquid, or were carried over the bank onto the beach. He gave their nest a good soak, then kicked the sand violently as he zipped up. The ants swarmed over their exposed larvae.

Shawn returned to the fire. "What's for dessert? Sara Lee or some CC?"

"How 'bout both?" suggested Wayne with a laugh.

Kendrick cut up the cake, while Wayne slopped CC generously into three battered enamel camp coffee cups. It was getting a bit chillier. Shawn pulled on his jean jacket and accepted the mug from Wayne.

"This is more rye than Coke!" exclaimed Shawn.

"Is that a problem?"

"Fuckin' A, man, fuckin' A. That's all I'm saying." He relaxed into his lawn chair and raised his mug to Kendrick, and then to Wayne.

Shawn couldn't tell but Kendrick cringed inwardly. He was not a fan of Shawn getting emotional after a case of beer, which usually meant overly long sweaty hugs and beery declarations of eternal friendship.

When Shawn was sober, hugs were off limits. He didn't actually know any homos, as he called them. Except maybe that guy in high school who was now -- get this! -- a hairdresser in Vancouver. It went without saying that homos were totally unnatural. If any were stupid enough to show up at, say, the KK, any normal guy would be totally justified in taking them out into the parking lot for a good butt kicking.

In fact, it was practically a duty. And anyone who didn't think so was probably a homo too.

But, late at night and when liquored up with his friends, hugs were different.

Shawn came back from another trip to the pine tree. He picked up the CC bottle, saw that it was empty, turned and hurled it into the lake. It soared through the air, seemed for a second like it was going to hit the plane, and plopped loudly into the water behind the tailfin.

"Close call!" laughed Kendrick. He was much less wobbly than his companions, having poured out his second mug of rye behind a tree and replaced it with 100% Coke. "You would have killed *me* if I'd hit the plane!"

"Aww, man, I love you guys." Shawn approached Kendrick and gave him a huge bear hug. Not a shoulders only triangle hug, but a full body contact hug with a sweaty steak-sauce covered hand on the back of the neck. Shawn held the hug for longer than Kendrick liked. "It is just fucking great to have a friend like you," Shawn slurred, "out here in the bush, finding fucking treasure."

"Love you too, man," said Kendrick, with a bit less enthusiasm.

Shawn let go of Kendrick, and staggered over to Wayne. Wayne stiffened but Shawn was oblivious. He wrapped his arms around Wayne too. "I love you, too, man," he said. "I know we've had our ups and downs, but I love you. It doesn't matter that you're an Indian. We're all, you know, humans. Right? Same human fucking race."

Wayne softened and hugged Shawn back. "I'm glad you said that, man." Kendrick saw Wayne's face over Shawn's shoulder. Oh god, he thought, they're both going to start crying.

Wayne stepped around the fire and hugged Kendrick. "I love you, brother. We found it, man, we found it!"

"We sure did," said Kendrick, returning the hug.

"Fifty-fifty man," said Wayne. "I'm Skookum Jim."

"You bet."

Wayne heard something in Kendrick's tone. He kept his hands on Kendrick's shoulders. "Fifty-fifty, you and me, say it."

"Fifty-fifty, you and me," said Kendrick.

"No! *Really* say it. Like you mean it."

"I mean it!"

A switch seemed to flick inside Wayne. "I am not going to be the dumb Indian on this one," he shouted. "Skookum Jim found the gold. But his white buddy tried to rip him off. That other guy said they didn't want Indians to stake claims. Skookum Jim had to stand up for himself. I led you guys to the place. *I ... led ... you ...* to the place." He was shouting now. "I'm not going to end up with a few bucks for gas like the guys who showed Al Kulan the Faro deposit."

"C'mon man," said Kendrick, trying to calm Wayne down.

"Don't c'mon me. I'm not stupid."

"I said fifty-fifty." Then Kendrick said something he immediately regretted. He wasn't as cut as the other guys, but he still had five or six beers and a stiff rye-and-coke under his belt. "Our lawyer in Vancouver says it's complicated. We need more partners."

"We have a lawyer in Vancouver?" Wayne was amazed. "You mean, *you* have a lawyer in Vancouver. I knew it."

Kendrick opened his mouth to say something, but his mind went blank.

Wayne beat him to it. "You fucking asshole." Wayne grabbed Kendrick's jacket and tried to throw him to the ground. Kendrick resisted. He grabbed Wayne's jacket and tried to push him away. But Wayne's grip wouldn't loosen.

Kendrick was taller, but Wayne was heavy set and stronger. His fingers tightened on Kendrick's jacket. He instinctively put his right leg forward, and twisted Kendrick's upper body over it. Kendrick felt himself going over and tightened his own grip on Wayne's jacket.

Kendrick fell, landing half on the empty beer bottles and half on the fire. Wayne landed on top of him.

Wayne was in a rage. He flailed at Kendrick as Kendrick grabbed his sleeves to stop Wayne's punches or at least prevent a full swing.

Shawn stepped in, grabbed Wayne by the back of the collar, hauled him off Kendrick, pushed him over a lawnchair and sent him sprawling away from the fire. He felt a burning sensation on his foot, and looked down to see an ember melting through his Adidas shoe. He kicked it off into the sand.

Kendrick rolled off the fire and lay on the ground, panting and ripping off his smoking jacket.

"You assholes," said Shawn bitterly, panting and standing between the two. "You fucking ruined it."

Wayne stood up and stomped down the beach, cursing. Kendrick stood up, and went the other way.

The next morning, a bright ray of sun poking past the big pine tree woke Shawn in his tent. He had a splitting headache. Kendrick was huddled in the fetal position beside him with no sleeping bag, just his scorched jacket. Shawn's pillow and sleeping bag were covered in puke. The sun was already warming the tent and the vomit into a horrible hot box.

It was going to be a terrible flight back to Whitehorse, thought Shawn. He flipped his pillow so it was puke-side down and retreated into the darkness of his sleeping bag.

1982-4

44 Tagish Road, Riverdale
1982: 5:00pm, July 29th, 21°C

"Car!" The boys playing street hockey on Tagish Road heard Shawn's Trans Am before they saw it. The goalie dragged the net off the asphalt and stood on the gravel to watch the muscle car cruise by.

Shawn had the window rolled down with his arm on the sill, and the tunes were pumping. "Thanks dudes!" he said with a thumbs up as he cruised past the boys and turned into the driveway of number 44.

The car was well known to the neighbourhood kids. A black 1976 Trans Am with gold highlights, with a Pontiac 455 V8 under the hood and the classic gold screaming eagle design on top.

The game restarted but not before the twelve-year-olds tackled one of humanity's great debates: Trans Am or Mustang?

Kendrick looked up at his house from the passenger seat. No sign of the wife or kids. The neighbour waved. You couldn't make an inconspicuous arrival in Shawn's Trans Am.

He carefully opened the passenger door. It was so long it risked banging into the fence, and he didn't feel like a conversation with Shawn about scratched paint. Shawn popped the tiny trunk and Kendrick extracted his gear.

Shawn slammed the trunk and turned to high-five him. "Nice flying, Kendrick. You'll be ready for a solo soon!"

"Thanks, can't wait!"

Kendrick watched as Shawn backed out of the driveway before taking off with some gratuitous gravel spraying for the kids.

He turned and walked into the house. The kids were watching TV in the basement. His wife's easel and water colours were still set up in the living room. He had made a point of remembering where the brushes were sitting before he flew into Kalzas, and they appeared not to have moved.

In the kitchen, no sign of dinner. But two empty cans of soda sat on top of the garbage. He glanced at his watch. 6pm. Blast warning, he thought to himself.

He moved warily towards the back door. Maybe he'd take the whole family out to dinner. The Cellar for steak? Too expensive, and too dark on a summer night. Chinese food at McRae would be fun.

"What the hell is Wayne all upset about?" It was the wife. She had been down the hall, not in the backyard. Her tone was, as usual these days, sharp and accusatory.

"Wayne's upset?" he replied, as slowly and calmly as he could. He turned to get a beer out of the fridge. Upset about what? Kendrick thought they had smoothed things out pretty well after the blow up at the wall tent.

He opened the fridge and leaned in to get a beer.

"Well, you don't usually look for a lawyer unless you're upset." There was that tone again. "He's pissed off about his shares in one of your mining projects."

Oh shit. He was glad his face was hidden in the fridge.

When had she spoken to Wayne? She thought he was a doofus. She did like Wayne more than Shawn, however. She always called Shawn's Trans Am the "black penis extension."

Then it clicked. Wayne had gone into her cousin's law firm, and either the cousin or his wife who worked there as a secretary had blabbed it.

So Wayne was still pissed off. Pissed off enough to talk to a lawyer.

He pulled the beer out of the fridge and opened it.

"I might have to go to Alaska for a while."

"Business?"

"Yeah."

"Or another fishing trip?" She was uncanny. "You better sort out your shit with your business partners before you go drink beer and chase halibut in Haines."

"I'll talk to Wayne about it." He smiled at his wife. Underneath that angry frown somewhere was the beautiful woman he had married. It seemed like a very long time ago. He raised his beer in a toast. "Salud!"

She pulled two boxes of Kraft Dinner out of the cupboard. "What's with the Spanish all of a sudden?"

WINTER

40

Northern Lights LNG plant

Midnight, Winter Solstice - December 21st. -24°C
40 days sober

The blast wave from the LNG plant explosion flashed almost instantly over the protesters and carried on across the valley. The cell phone video shown in the inquiry afterwards, taken by people who happened to be filming the protest at the time, was reminiscent of old black-and-white film footage from atom bomb tests. There was a blast. Then a circular shock wave emanated from the epicentre, where the explosive device pierced the high-pressure LNG tank, and travelled nearly instantly over everything in its radius.

The cellphone videos, when investigators played them back slowly, recorded two explosions. First the smaller one from the explosive device. Then, the bigger one. With the tank ruptured and no longer at high pressure, the liquefied natural gas boiled into vapour, rushed through the rupture, and exploded into flame.

It was a classic BLEVE -- Boiling Liquid Expanding Vapour Explosion -- and the videos would feature in Canadian pipefitter training videos for years.

What was different from the atom bomb test films was that, instead of the mock Japanese houses, the blast wave swept over YCC protesters waving signs, cops drinking lukewarm coffee from Tim Horton's, and the Freedos and their elaborate protest-theatre rigs.

An off-duty firefighter sat in a Freedo hot tub on one of those rigs, some distance from the epicentre. The blast wave blew off his toque and sent the beer cans on the edge of the tub clattering onto the flatbed. The plastic bowl of Cheesies launched like a leaf when a helicopter takes off.

He stared, amazed, at the soaring flame, then scrambled out of the hot tub. He tiptoed across the frigid flatbed deck, found his phone, and texted his crew chief: "bleve @ northern lights. no shit"

Another flare of flaming natural gas shot into the sky as Winter skied down the embankment. Tarfu cringed. Winter was reminded of some asshole tossing gas onto the campfire, times a million.

It was pandemonium at the protest. Screaming. Headlamps darting left and right. Ominous bangs and hisses from the burning LNG tank.

Tarfu darted into the crowd to look for Taiya. Winter looked for Taiya's red camo Team Yukon jacket. He saw one red camo jacket limp past. It was Taiya's biathlon coach.

"It was a drone!" shouted the woman. "I saw it."

Winter ignored her. Flaky eye witness interviews were for later. Someone else would say they saw a sasquatch do it. And, anyway, he already knew exactly who did it. He kept looking for Taiya.

Then he saw Tarfu dart to the left. Taiya was kneeling beside a yellow North Face mountaineering parka in the blowing snow, silent in the middle of all the screaming, speaking quietly to the parka owner as she pressed her mitts onto their head. The bright light from the flaring gas showed a growing bloodstain seeping over Taiya's knees onto the snow.

"Drag them farther away!" he shouted to her.

"Can't move her. Might be a spine injury."

Winter waved at the flames shooting into the sky. "Rule number one: don't become a casualty yourself. It might blow up again any second."

They dragged the victim farther away behind a parked vehicle.

"Will you call 9-1-1?" shouted Taiya.

"A million people already have. I'm going to look for Brett."

"I hope he's okay."

Winter looked at her. Another time. He skied back up the embankment. He looked back. Tarfu was staying with Taiya. That was good.

Winter found Brett just where he had last seen him. Brett was on his knees frantically stuffing black shapes into the duffle bag of his sled. Chaewon was trudging up the embankment towards him.

Brett looked up at the two of them. "Oh good, can you help me get this stuff back to the van?"

Chaewon opened her mouth to ask a question.

Winter just launched himself, skis and all, right onto Brett.

Normally, wrestling in skis and poles would put you at a disadvantage. But Brett was so surprised he quickly found himself on his back as Winter kneeled on his chest. Brett raised his arms in front of his face to fend off Winter's fists so Winter drove them into Brett's chest. He threw off his mitts and poles and kept pounding.

"Stop it!" shouted Chaewon. Like many female patrons of the Kopper King over the years, she grabbed one friend's raised right arm and dragged him off another.

"What's wrong with you? This isn't kindergarten!" Also words that have been heard before in the KK parking lot.

Both men scrambled to their feet, although it took Winter a second longer since he still had his skis on. In the flickering light from the LNG fire, you could see blood from Brett's nose in black stains across his cheek and down his jacket. He clamped his mitt to his nose.

Chaewon positioned herself between them, her arms outstretched in both directions like a traffic cop signaling "stop" to the madness.

"What the fuck, Winter? What's your problem?" said Brett angrily from behind Chaewon's protection. Winter eyed him, still but ready to pounce, as soon as he saw a chance to get past Chaewon to add a black eye to that bleeding nose.

Taking a quick glance at Brett to make sure he wasn't about to do something stupid, Chaewon — arms still outstretched — swiveled to face Winter. He was still looking intently at Brett. Chaewon could tell he *was* thinking of doing something stupid with whatever part of the primitive human brain he was using at that second. Chaewon moved her head to intercept Winter's angry stare "Winter, look at me! Back off!"

"You just blew up an LNG plant! With people standing around!" shouted Winter at Brett.

Brett waved at the black shapes lying scattered in the snow. "No! These are just fireworks." Brett explained the plan to set off fireworks at midnight to remind everyone how dangerous an LNG explosion would be. And to make the protest more fun and newsworthy.

"Something else set off the explosion. I didn't even have time to launch any fireworks," he added. Case closed, he seemed to be saying.

Fuck, thought Winter. The guy is more slippery than Soapy Smith.

Winter switched his stare to Chaewon. "Ask him why he firebombed his own headquarters. With Taiya inside."

"That's crazy talk!" exclaimed Brett.

"Winter!" said Chaewon. "That makes no sense."

"Yeah," added Brett. "Why would I burn down my own office? Get yourself under control."

Winter could feel the situation slipping away. Brett was already acting like the victim and Chaewon would take his side.

Winter tapped his pocket. "Then how do I have screenshots proving your computer sent the emails taking responsibility?"

"Bullshit!"

"And the email claiming responsibility for the swastika attack. Typed before the attack but set to send after."

Chaewon's head snapped to look at Brett, then back to Winter.

Brett answered, with slightly less convincing bravado this time, "You're just making this stuff up!"

Winter now looked at Chaewon. "Ask him if he fucked your intern. First in his kitchen. Then on the fake sheepskin seduction rug by the woodstove."

Again, Chaewon's head snapped back towards Brett; this time at whiplash speed: "You had sex with Prism?"

Brett shook his head. "This is all just bullshit."

"I have video," said Winter, tapping his pocket.

Chaewon was now swivelled completely toward Brett. "Did - you - have - sex - with - our - intern? Yes or no."

"Come on, Chaewon. Am I the kind of guy who needs interns for sex?" asked Brett.

This line of argument did not land as well with Chaewon as Brett thought it would. A question from last August suddenly came back to her: "And last summer, did you sleep with either of those sorority girl interns?"

Brett was silent.

Chaewon took a step towards him. She was no longer traffic-copping Winter, but was facing squarely at Brett.

Chaewon replied, "Did you have sex with the sorority girls?"

Brett, betrayed by an idea that had percolated in his mind throughout the previous summer, fatally misunderstood the question. "At the same time, like an intern orgy? Of course not!"

In a split second, Chaewon closed the distance to Brett, clamped her hands in his arms for leverage, and lifted her right knee — with enthusiasm — into Brett's balls.

Brett went down hard. Maybe if he hadn't been wearing ski tights. Maybe if she was a bit shorter. Maybe if Chaewon's leg muscles hadn't been tuned by years of mountain biking and backcountry skiing.

But all of the above was true. Brett's universe collapsed instantly into a single, infinitely intense wave of pain. Nothing else existed, not even an LNG fireball.

As Brett lay in the snow, Winter showed Chaewon the screenshots. "But why did you hide cameras in his cabin?"

"I needed evidence."

"Of what?"

"Of whatever he was doing. Your donors are also paying for his trips to Cambridge."

The wail of police and ambulance sirens sounded faintly in the distance. At the Northern Lights plant, the initial pandemonium had worn off and the headlamps now clustered around the injured. It was like kicking an anthill while hiking. The ants scurried around in a panic at first, but soon shifted to carrying their larva to safety.

Chaewon flicked on her headlamp and shone it on Brett's bag. It was just the kind of fireworks you'd find at an Alaskan Fourth of July party.

Brett's universe slowly expanded as the pain retreated from infinite to measurable, albeit massive, levels. From just clutching his balls in frozen agony, he was able to writhe. And then moan. And then complain. And, finally, ask for things.

"Don't tell the police," moaned Brett.

"We're not negotiating," replied Winter. "Here's the deal: you get a blue ticket, like in the gold rush. Tomorrow morning, you resign from your job at YCC, get in your van and leave the Yukon. Forever."

"No way!"

"And your trust fund pays for Taiya's university."

"I said, no way!"

"Or an exclusive story goes on the *Yukon Sun* front page, I file a sexual harassment complaint on behalf of interns with bad taste at the Human Rights Commission, and an anonymous creep uploads the video to Alaskacabinporn.com."

"You'd never do that. Taiya would be devastated."

"I'm telling Taiya anyway. I owe it to her to tell her what a fucked up family she's been born into. It's just whether the cops and everyone else find out."

Chaewon and Winter left Brett and headed back towards the protest. Chaewon suddenly stopped and turned to Winter, grabbing his arm. "If Brett didn't blow up the LNG plant, then who did?"

41

Yukon Sun newsroom, Third and Main

10:00 a.m., December 22nd, -34°C
41 days sober

Chaewon's glasses fogged up as soon as she stepped out of the cold and into the building with the *Yukon Sun* offices. The temperature had dropped like a rock to Minus Thirty-Four overnight and the forecast said an old-school cold snap was coming. Time to get more contact lenses. Mind you, her eyes were so puffy from crying half the night she probably would have worn glasses anyway. It was also good her hair was under a toque.

She walked slowly up the stairs and pushed the door open, and saw Artemis immediately.

"Merry Christmas," said Artemis.

Chaewon smiled uncertainly. Her tone didn't seem very merry.

"Don't worry," continued Artemis. "I'm the kind of Hindu who celebrates Christmas."

"I was just looking for Winter."

"He's out at their cabin at Marsh Lake. Taiya drove him."

"Strange time for a cabin weekend?"

"Strange temperature too. It's the BNR version of mindfulness. Chop wood. Melt water. Think deep thoughts over instant coffee and evaporated milk."

Chaewon considered this. That would explain not answering text messages.

"Any news on who blew up Northern Lights?"

"No, but it must have been Green extremists. The Freedos actually like Northern Lights -- jobs, power and all that. They would bathe their children in liquefied natural gas if they could. The only thing they don't like is subsidizing First Nations business, but that's not enough for them to blow it up."

Artemis explained how she had called the bomb expert at the Anchorage paper. It was Alaska; of course they had a bomb expert. From the videos, the guy figured it was a relatively small bomb packed in some kind of napalm. When the bomb went off, it ruptured the tank and at the same time set the napalm on fire. Then when the LNG turned to gas and came shooting out the hole, the napalm set it on fire.

"Sounds complicated," said Chaewon.

"Not really. Could be Chinese intelligence, could be a Do-It-Yourselfer. You can buy everything you need off the internet or from some survivalist in Alaska. The guy told me the crazies have been playing with propane bombs for years. Including one on the Skytrain in Vancouver way back in the 2010s. This was just a giant version."

Artemis waved Chaewon over to her monitor. "She won't let us interview her, but check out Amber propagandizing on Global breakfast news in Vancouver."

Chaewon watched as Amber appeared on the screen over a caption that just said "Whitehorse, Yukon." Artemis tapped her pen on the desk in annoyance. "Just a regular concerned citizen. The caption should say 'deranged Freedo activist.'"

Chaewon watched Amber listen carefully to the reporter's question, her eyebrows flexed and her lips pursed as if she was thoughtfully considering her answer. Then she answered a completely different question. "The government has given a lot of money to Njür Nàdäk'a and the First Nations--" She paused to let the dog whistle echo for a second. "But the jobs and cheap power are important. Regular Yukoners can't afford to put gas in the car to drive the kids to school right now, even if they have the carbon ration points. After giving all that money to the First Nations, the government needs to protect the facility properly."

"And is the government doing enough?" The hint of a smile flashed across Amber's face. This was the kind of question she would answer.

"No. The government is totally in bed with the Greens. Families can't make ends meet, and the government is spending big money on experimental climate technology instead of on tracking down these Green terrorists. We all know violence is never the answer. But if the government doesn't do its job, I think we can all understand why concerned citizens are going to have to protect themselves."

Artemis blew a raspberry at the screen and stabbed the pause button. "She doesn't exactly threaten an armed insurrection, but all the Freedos watching know exactly what she means." Artemis sipped her coffee and stared at Amber. "She's like Sinn Fein. Clueless Canadian TV hosts with good hair just don't get it."

"Shin who?"

"Oh, in Northern Ireland during the IRA bombings. The IRA would blow something up, then their politician friends would go on TV and say, oh, we didn't do it personally but here's some propaganda for your viewers."

Chaewon stood silently watching the frozen screen. She could see how that would work. Her mind leapt to some radical Greens she used to hang out with in Vancouver. But how did Artemis know about stuff like Shin Fane? Once again, Chaewon resolved to spend some more time on Wikipedia.

Artemis looked up at Chaewon. "By the way, where is Brett? For once we can't find him for a comment."

Chaewon wondered: had Winter told Artemis? She decided now was not the time to announce Brett's departure. "He's on vacation."

"The morning after a massive explosion at one of his rallies?" Chaewon shrugged. "OK, well, in that case, since you're here, do you have any comment for YCC on the explosion?

Chaewon paused. The options flashed through her mind. Option A: no comment and leave the building until she could talk to the YCC board. She should ask the board who was in charge now that Brett was gone. Option B: pull an Amber and say YCC had nothing to do with it but they could understand how people were angry about how carbon capture let the LNG industry dodge the need to transition to Net Zero.

Instead, she chose Option C: "We are totally opposed to violence."

"Unequivocally?"

Chaewon wondered precisely what that meant.

"Totally," she said.

"And I can quote you on that on behalf of YCC?"

"Yes."

"And how are you going to respond to the bombing? Plans for your next rally?"

Chaewon smiled. She had a plan – a very good one, she thought; Brett would never have thought of it – and really wanted to tell Artemis. She would be impressed. But Chaewon just smiled.

"Can't say or won't say?" asked Artemis, also smiling.

A thought crossed Chaewon's mind. She had a good idea, and didn't actually need Artemis' approval. She just smiled, zipped up her coat, and said, "Wait and see!"

42. Winter's family cabin at Marsh Lake

10:30 a.m., December 22nd, -35°C
41 days sober

Winter opened the woodstove and put more spruce on the fire. At this temperature, the stove needed to be roaring continuously to keep the drafty old cabin just at sweater temperature. He didn't come out to the cabin in the winter very often anymore. A fifty-kilometre ride was okay in the summer; not on a fat bike in the winter.

But it was nice when Taiya drove. The cabin brought back good memories. Even mom and dad got along at the cabin at Christmas. He remembered his mother hiding the presents in the woodshed, then trying to explain on Christmas morning how the mandarin oranges in the stockings must have frozen solid on Santa's sled.

Even better, it was nice that Taiya didn't seem to mind ignoring Misty's ban on visiting him.

Taiya sat on the moose rug by the woodstove. The plywood floor was frigid, but the hide was thick. She was flipping through the *Yukon Sun* archives on her laptop again.

Winter was sitting in the kitchen reading the *Sun*. The business columnist had calculated how much a family that hadn't been smart enough to convert their oil furnace to a heat pump was now paying every winter. That wasn't exactly news. The science columnist, on the other hand, had been doing some actual research. She reported that Alaska weather nerds were looking at something called the Aleutian Low. The column said this unusual zone of very low pressure out in the Aleutians often foreshadowed unseasonably warm weather and precipitation in the Alaskan interior.

He scrolled down to the comments. There was only one: "More scientists out to lunch. Forty Below doesn't seem like global warming!!!"

Every lugnut thinks they're smarter than a scientist.

He opened his weather app: Minus Thirty-Four now, dropping to Minus Forty for a couple of days, then warming sharply on Christmas.

Maybe even a couple of degrees above freezing. Consistent with the Aleutian Low idea.

The kids with their new Christmas snowboards would be sad if the runs on Mount Sima turned to slush.

Winter spooned some Nescafe Gold crystals into a cup, added a half inch of evap, and poured in the boiling water. He sat down on the couch beside Tarfu.

He hadn't told Taiya about Brett yet. What would Artemis' book on journalism ethics have to say about covering up a prominent public figure boffing the interns in order to blackmail that figure into getting out of your teenage daughter's life?

Discuss that in a 700-word column with a strong point of view.

Unless it was your daughter, of course.

He sipped his coffee and mused on Chaewon's question: if Brett didn't blow up Northern Lights, then who did? Brett also claimed he was not the guy in the white hazmat suit who trashed the Northern Lights worksite with the front-end loader. The obvious suspects were Green extremists. People who were, like Brett, against LNG and Northern Lights no matter how much carbon they claimed to be capturing. But, unlike Brett, competent and technically sophisticated. People who could drive heavy equipment and operate explosives more sophisticated than Fourth-of-July fireworks.

In this line of thinking, Brett started everything with a series of attacks on YCC. The Green extremists, whoever they were, thought the Freedos were attacking YCC. So then they retaliated against Northern Lights. Now the Freedos were probably plotting a counter-retaliation.

Once again, Brett had made a mess and would be out of town when the shit hit the fan.

On the other hand, this line of thinking required there to be technically skilled Green extremists actually living in the Yukon. Extinction Rebellion in Europe had more important oil tankers to glue themselves to. And this storyline left Amber and Zach as, if not the good guys, then at least responsible citizens doing some peaceful protesting. Which made this line of thinking obviously suspect. They had to be up to something.

Winter stood up and warmed himself by the fire. Amber was twice as smart as Brett. If Brett came up with the idea of attacking his organization, then what if Amber came up with the idea of attacking the LNG facility that most Freedos thought was a good thing.

She would have seen all the sympathy, donations and press coverage Brett got.

They had lots of America First friends in Alaska. With all their trucks and snowmobiles, getting explosives and everything else they needed across the border would be easy. They probably had Alaskans building it for them.

God, it would be nice to break that story. It would be national news for sure. Especially if you could beat the cops to it. Which would not be hard. Zach knew half the cops in town from Oldtimers Hockey. And if they weren't on his team, they sledded at the Pass together. Their stock line was that they couldn't comment because the case was under active investigation, while behind closed doors the case moved at glacier speed.

Taiya looked up from her laptop: "Hey Dad, no one ever told me about this murder investigation. When Grampa's friend got shot."

"Before I was born. But your Aunt Brenda remembers it."

"They never found out who did it?"

"Unsolved. The twist was that he wasn't shot with the usual kind of hunting rifle. It was a Swedish Mauser. 6.5 millimetre or something weird like that, not a thirty-aught-six or three-oh-eight."

Taiya sat up and turned around. "An unsolved murder, here?"

"There are a dozen unsolved murders in the Yukon. That stuff about the RCMP always getting their man is gold rush bullshit." Winter explained that the police thought that, because of the Swedish gun, it might be a Norwegian outfitter who had a camp on a nearby lake. But the guy had an alibi. "Grampa was at a fly-in fishing camp in Alaska when it happened. He always said he regretted being away, since if he'd been out at the guy's camp maybe it never would have happened."

"Or he would have been shot too."

"Which would mean Grampa wouldn't have a fancy house in Rosedale. And your friends wouldn't have summer jobs cleaning up an abandoned mine." And my mother wouldn't have been able to complain for years about child support, he thought to himself.

"And we wouldn't have this cabin."

43

YCC's new temporary headquarters
2:00 p.m., December 23rd, -41˚C

Chaewon returned to her little office in the ancient Quonset hut serving as temporary YCC headquarters. She shut the door behind herself. God, I hate public speaking, she thought. She slumped into her chair and exhaled loudly. It felt like stress and adrenaline was pouring out of her body with each big breath.

She needed to get over this. Public speaking was now a big part of her job. Interim Executive Director, Yukon Climate Collective. The board and staff just seemed to assume it was her. Which made her feel proud. Maybe, she suspected, if she were a man the board would even have skipped the "interim" stage.

Public speaking today was even more brutal than usual. She had to spin and tell half truths to the staff: "Brett had some urgent family issues that meant he had to go back to Toronto."

Which was true. But a more honest way to put it would have been to say his "family issues" were that members of his family were threatening to turn him in to the cops for attacking you, his closest friends at the Yukon Climate Collective. Including throwing a Molotov cocktail through the window and nearly dousing his niece in flaming gasoline.

He hadn't known his niece was in there. But it didn't matter.

The good news was that everyone at the staff and volunteer meeting seemed to buy the story. At least for now.

Nestor had been helpful, actually. He had asked two questions. And not in a hysterical sky-is-falling kind of way. Which Prism the winter intern was obviously about to do — she looked far more verklempt than an intern should do if their boss resigned to spend more time with his family.

The first was a question of fact about when Brett was leaving; earlier this morning, which was easy to answer.

And then what the plan was for the next rally. She made a mental note to thank Nestor. If he hadn't done that, Prism would have asked why Brett was leaving. And Chaewon would have been sorely tempted to say: "Because the media has video of you blowing your boss."

She looked at the frost on the inside of the Quonset's single pane windows and zipped up her down sweater. The Saran Wrap taped over the window to stop drafts was completely ineffective. Little circles of frost covered the nailheads running around the window frame. The new building didn't have 240-volt chargers. Her new car -- a well-used electric Mazda -- was plugged into a lawn mower extension cord. At Minus Forty-One, that was barely enough power to keep the battery warm; it didn't recharge at all.

The worrying thing was that Brett claimed he was not the guy in the hazmat suit who had trashed the Northern Lights construction site with a front-end loader. Which was believable, Winter had pointed out, because Brett couldn't drive a front-end loader.

But he had inspired some other nutcase out there. Could it be someone she knew? Inside YCC even?

And this nutcase had pissed off the Freedo nutcases who threw a Molotov cocktail at the refugee hostel last night. Things were getting out of control.

It was also good news that the staff loved her idea for their next rally. It would be a "Climate Peace" rally. After Nestor's question, she had told the staff about the idea. No one complained or said they needed to do something in revenge for the attacks on YCC by, they thought, the Freedos.

That was good. The movement needed some anger to succeed, but Brett let the last few rallies get too angry. Maybe, thought Chaewon, I should call Amber and see if we can de-escalate.

Her thoughts were interrupted by a throaty rumble, which she felt even before she heard it. Prism's scream cut through the paper thin walls of her office.

"The Freedos are here!"

Chaewon jumped out of her chair and whipped open her office door. Taiya was locking the front door while everyone else ran to look out the windows. Chaewon peeled the Saran Wrap off one of the front windows and scraped a rectangle of frost off the glass with her thumbnail.

The low-angle sun peeked through the clouds and ice fog onto two flatbed trucks which had just parked on the street in front of the building. Men in winter construction overalls and giant mitts were lifting blue construction fence off the front truck and carrying it into place along the sidewalks on the front and side of the Quonset hut. Nickelback was blasting out of the speakers on the other truck, and people in toques were already in the hot tub. A woman in a pink camo snowmobile suit walked along the fence, a big mitt clenched in her teeth as she zip-tied the sections together at top and bottom.

It was Forty Below, but the mood seemed festive. Amber stood behind the fence, directing the work. She wore blue, hi-vis insulated construction overalls, bunny boots and a big toque with Freedom embroidered on the front. She grinned cheerfully, shouting jokes over the music to the guys putting up the fence. The men high-fived with their huge mitts after each section of fence went in. This was the benefit, Chaewon thought, of having members whose day jobs involved actual outside work. Prism was too scared of having her phone freeze to do more than scurry from car to building at this temperature.

Two more women zip-tied a banner to the fence; facing out so Chaewon couldn't read it. Chaewon checked Amber's X feed. The banner said FreezeIn@FortyBelow. Amber's messaging was smart, as usual; it would appeal to the media and her base. A protest at Forty Below would be clickbait for the media. And the base would love the image that they were blockading the freedom haters at YCC to stop them from sabotaging the economy, twisting the minds of young children and executing various nefarious foreign-funded Green schemes.

She glanced sideways at the staff and volunteers. They were scared. As if violent climate change deniers were about to break in the front door to trash the place and the people in it. Which, Chaewon had to admit, had been her first thought too.

Zach and an RCMP officer stood beside the hot tub truck. They were chatting like it was the Canada Day parade and Zach had a particularly creative float.

Winter, Nigel the photographer and the rest of the media stood across the street taking photos and tapping things into their phones.

Then the Nickelback stopped. Two guys dragged some concert speakers up to the fence and pointed them at the Quonset hut. She heard the CHON-FM jingle - "the beat of a different drummer" - then Wayne Bobalicious, then music. Loud music.

"What is that?" asked Prism as if she'd bought tickets to the wrong music festival.

"AC/DC," replied Chaewon. Should she tell Prism to phone Wayne and ask for more female singer-songwriters? No, that would be mean. And it was recorded anyway.

One song ended and another began. They are trolling us with indigenous radio, she thought. With the cops right there doing nothing. She zipped up her fleece, unlocked the front door, and stepped out.

She was across the front yard in a second. If she had seen a video of herself, she would have said it reminded her of the lunch ladies at her elementary school in Seoul scurrying across the playground to stop some children from having too much fun.

Zach was just on the other side of the fence. His bulk blocked the RCMP officer from seeing Chaewon approach.

The cop was laughing: "Well I wish I was in the Hot Tub of Freedom with you too! But we got a job to do."

The guys in the hot tub laughed too. "Fuckin' A man!" said one one them, raising his Kokanee in a toast. "To the R-C-M-fuckin'-P!"

Chaewon stepped out from behind Zach. "So officer, public drinking is legal now?"

The smile drained off the officer's face, quickly replaced by the usual impassive police stare.

A wave of laughter and shouts came from the hot tub.

"Fuck off!"

"Go back to China you hippie bitch."

"This isn't beer. I pour Bud Zero into Kokanee cans so I don't get peer pressured into drinking alcohol when I don't choose to."

Much hilarity in the tub over that one.

Chaewon put her hands on her hips and looked at the cop. "Well, aren't you going to make them remove this fence?"

"We're keeping the peace and won't interfere with a peaceful protest. As Yukon Climate Collective will know."

Fucking fascists. Chaewon was about to reply when another man appeared at the fence. He was huge, a foot taller than Chaewon, and three times as wide. He wore ripped insulated overalls. The fingers of one glove came through the fencing and gripped it, while the other held a sawed-off hockey stick. Intense, angry brown eyes stared out from the gap between his toque and an out-of-control black beard.

"You heard him," said the man, his fingers tightening on the fence. "Back to China, you hippy bitch."

"I'm Teslin-"

The man cut her off with a roar, a frightening, primeval kind of roar. He banged his hockey stick on the fence, which shook ominously.

The comedian in the hot tub joked, "Uh oh, looks like she's making Randall angry." A smirk flickered across the police officer's face.

Chaewon steeled herself and looked back into the eyes. "I'm Teslin Tlingit, and I have a right to be here."

Instead of another primal scream, the big man leaned closer into the fence. He stared intently at Chaewon. "This fence won't be here forever," he said, tapping the hockey stick on his boot.

Chaewon pulled her right hand out of her pocket, extended it to the Freedo, and lifted her middle finger. Then she turned on her heels and stomped back to the front door. Behind her she heard another roar as the man violently shook the fence.

She didn't look back. "Show us your granola!" shouted the comedian in the hot tub as she slammed the door behind herself.

Everyone crowded around her to congratulate her on her braveness. She didn't feel brave. She felt terrified. She looked around for Nestor, but he had slipped away. Not because he was scared, she thought, but because he was on some Nestor mission. Nor had Prism slapped her on the back. She was typing furiously on her phone.

Chaewon felt her own phone buzz in her pocket.

A text from Winter: "you've gone viral"

"?"

Links arrived. Video of her exchange with the cop and the hot tub clowns was already on Discord, X and even Parler.

She watched the number of shares spiral upwards. And the insane misogynist comments come in.

Winter texted again: "your intern is live tweeting the hostage taking"

It was a video from inside the building taken through the icy window. It showed Chaewon with her hands on her hips exchanging words with the cop as Dirty Deeds provided the soundtrack. Caption: "So brave!"

"Prism!" shouted Chaewon. "Back to work!"

44

Winter's kitchen in Whitehorse

6:00 p.m., Christmas Eve - December 24th, -18°C
43 days sober

Winter clicked on his headlamp, opened the oven door and peered in. Was it possible for a grown man to fuck up the smallest turkey you could buy?

He looked at the two place settings on the kitchen table. Poisoning Taiya with a salmonella turkey would be a classic wrap up to a shitty year. She cried when Uncle Brett suddenly left the Yukon, and kept asking about Brett's lame excuse: "urgent family matters." He would tell her, but not at Christmas dinner.

Assuming she got here; Misty and LDV had to buy her story about visiting a sick friend on Christmas Eve. He checked the thermometer through the window. Minus Eighteen. The temperature was rising fast. After a stretch of Forty Below, Minus Eighteen felt warm. Maybe the Aleutian Low was really a thing.

Tarfu barked in the living room, then there was a knock on the door. Mormons? Christmas carolers hitting the streets now that it was only Minus Eighteen?

Winter stepped past the little spruce Christmas tree and looked through the frost in the window in the door. All he saw was orange down jacket. Whoever it was, they were huge. He opened the door.

Nestor quickly stepped in, carrying a home-made box of blue styrofoam insulation held together with duct tape.

"Merry Christmas! I make varenyky! Perogi in English," he exclaimed cheerily. His Ukrainian accent seemed thicker than usual. He gave Winter the box. "Should still be warm."

Nestor kicked off his Sorels and stuffed his toque and mitts into his left parka pocket. From his right pocket, he produced a bottle of Khortytsa vodka. "Ukrainian. For the others."

Winter blinked. Others?

Nestor laughed. "Taiya, such a girl!" He hung his coat and stepped past Winter into the living room.

Artemis crutched up the driveway a few minutes later, followed by Chaewon on a fat bike. The Freedos had taken their fence away that morning as suddenly as it arrived. It was almost like a Christmas truce after a week of mayhem on social-media and the paper's comments section.

Then Taiya's truck pulled into the driveway and she ran up the steps. Her scar was livid in the cold, but she was grinning excitedly. "Your people, Dad!"

"You're like Sarah Palin," said Artemis, pulling a tupperware of brussels sprouts wrapped in a towel out of her pack. "Not many people like you, but those who do are strangely fond."

Winter felt himself tearing up. "Don't you have better places to be?"

Chaewon turned toward the door to hang her parka. "Will went to Mexico for the holidays." She turned back to the group with a smile that wobbled just a bit.

"At least you've got a boyfriend for the winter," laughed Artemis. "Let's not talk about why Winter's people all happen to have open calendars on Christmas Eve."

The group crowded into the tiny kitchen. Nestor grabbed three chipped coffee mugs and slopped Ukrainian doses of vodka into them; Taiya was driving.

Nestor carved the cooked pieces off the turkey, after laughing at how dull Winter's knives were. Little of Winter's dishware matched, and every inch of table and counter was soon covered with dishes of different shapes and colours holding varenyky, potatoes, brussels sprouts and Yukon cranberry sauce.

Steam filled the room. Winter opened the window an inch, but the sharp thin draft of Minus-Eighteen air quickly disappeared into the heat. Chaewon stripped down to her tank top. Artemis held the sleeve of Nestor's sweater as he squirmed out of it, giving Taiya a wink as she did so.

After dinner -- where Artemis enforced a rule on no talk about Freedos, explosions or politics -- Winter pulled out his laptop with the wildlife cam video that almost showed Zach filling a cop's tank with smuggled diesel. Chaewon and Artemis squeezed in beside Winter to see the screen. He could feel the warmth of their bodies. In the corner of his eye, on Chaewon's smooth brown skin he saw a small collarbone tattoo -- three delicate flying ravens interspersed with Korean characters -- peeking out from under the strap of Chaewon's tank top.

Nestor and Taiya leaned over Winter's shoulder from behind.

"Better luck next time," said Artemis. "A court of law would say that's not smoking, and it's probably not even a gun." She put down her vodka and reached for her phone. She showed them a video of the firebombing of YCC headquarters which she had just obtained from the police. It was from a security camera across the street and showed a grainy figure walking across the street.

Winter and Chaewon had the same thought: Once you know who it is, it's obviously Brett's body shape and gait.

Then a pinprick of light as the Molotov cocktail was lit, then a flare of light filled the screen as the camera's night vision adapted to the burst of flames.

"Who is it? Looks like tall, skinny Sasquatch," said Nestor.

"Impossible to say," replied Artemis. "Also impossible to say why it took the police a month to figure out they should check the neighbourhood for security cameras."

Chaewon frowned: "When they talked to me, they seemed more interested in us violating the court order about protesting on Northern Lights property."

Nestor downed his vodka and clapped Chaewon on the shoulder. "Police are part of system! Drinking buddies with Zach and Freedos. Same Oldtimers' team. Same snowmobile weekends at White Pass." Nestor stepped around the table so he was looking directly at the group. He raised his hand in front of them and snapped his thumb and fingers into a circle. "There is zero chance the police arrest the Freedos."

"The police didn't do a thing at the blockade," said Chaewon, her face glowing red from the vodka. "We need to get the Minister to intervene."

"No!" said Nestor, slapping the table. "Must mobilize people to take direct action. Forget the minister. Forget the Liberals, Conservatives, NDP. All same shit. Even Green Party. Traitors, bribed by system, just like Lenin say about Social Democrats. Only solution is mobilize the people to direct action."

A silence hung in the air, until Artemis spoke: "That's the Lenin translation of what they say in Alaska politics: the only things in the middle of the road are yellow lines and squirrels with F150 tire tracks on their backs." She paused and looked at Nestor. "Are you named after Nestor Makhno?"

Nestor smiled and nodded. "My parents are professors in Kyiv. They love him."

Artemis turned to the group. "Famous Ukrainian anarchist." She raised her fingers in air quotes: "Man is only free if he is prepared to kill every hangman and every power magnate."

"You know him!" exclaimed Nestor.

Artemis leaned back in her chair and smiled. "So you're also a political theorist. Where have you been all my life?" She pointed at the vodka bottle beside Nestor and waved her finger in the air to signal another round.

1982 - AUGUST

1982-5
Big Kalzas Lake
4:00am, August 12th, 1982, +12°C

Wayne rolled over and squirmed deeper into his sleeping bag. He jammed his sweater over his ears to block out the sound.

But it didn't work. Some magpies and a squirrel were having the Pay TV fight of the century in the tree directly above the tent. He looked at his watch.

Four in the morning.

Jesus.

He unzipped the sleeping bag, sat up and reached for the .22 rifle. A .30-06 would be overkill for a squirrel, he chuckled to himself.

He made sure there were five rounds in the clip, then unfastened the wall tent's flap and stepped outside.

It was a beautiful, sunny morning. The lake was glassy and the day was already warming up.

He looked up into the big spruce over the tent. The shredded carcass of some bird was hanging off a branch. He could see black feathers, a claw dangling and some bloody shreds of flesh tangled in the spruce needles. The squirrel was darting back and forth trying to protect its prize, loudly scolding the magpies flitting between branches. The magpies in turn were screeching, trying to distract the squirrel so they could swoop in.

Wayne chambered a round, leaned the rifle against another tree and aimed at the squirrel.

The squirrel darted away, disappearing behind the tree trunk.

"They always do that," muttered Wayne to himself. "It's like they know."

He switched his aim to a magpie on a branch. Breathe in, breathe out, hold it, slowly squeeze trigger.

The .22 cracked and the magpie fell out of the tree and landed with a light thud. In one swift motion, hardly moving the rifle, Wayne popped the bolt, pulled it back, and chambered a second round.

The squirrel reappeared higher up the tree. It was partly obscured by a branch. Wayne aimed and squeezed the trigger. Just as he was squeezing, the squirrel saw another magpie and turned to dart away.

The bullet almost missed. A quarter inch lower and it just would have just grazed the squirrel's stomach. But it wasn't a quarter inch lower. The bullet ripped a wound channel through the squirrel's abdomen.

The squirrel fell through the air. It landed on a lower branch, and reached to hold on, but couldn't. It bounced off the branch and landed squirming at Wayne's feet.

"Gut shot," said Wayne to no one in particular. The squirrel might live for hours or even a day or two.

He moved to step on it and put it out of its misery, but then realized he was in bare feet. He reached over for the axe beside the fire, and brought the blunt side down in a swift movement onto the squirrel's head.

Then he picked the squirrel up by its tail and threw it in a high arc over the willows and out of sight.

The surviving magpie was going to eat well today.

He sometimes felt a bit guilty shooting a moose or a bear. But not a squirrel. They were just annoying.

He realized there was no point in trying to get back to sleep. Might as well go fishing. Maybe he'd have grayling for breakfast. The lake looked perfect.

He reminded himself to go fishing again the morning he got picked up. His aunties back in town would love to have a couple of grayling.

He dressed, grabbed some pepperoni sticks and a beer for breakfast, and pushed off. Just as he was about to pull-start the outboard, he heard the buzz of a plane.

At this hour?

At the far end of the lake, he saw a plane come in to land. It buzzed over the surface of the lake for a long time, as if the pilot was nervous to land. Then the engine slowed abruptly and the plane came down fast. It began taxiing towards the outfitter's camp.

Wayne started the engine and began motoring along the shore towards the outfitter's camp. Might as well say hi. He hadn't spoken to anyone in a few days.

The plane nosed into the beach at the outfitter's camp. The pilot got out, carried a rifle case and a jerry can onto shore, then started turning the plane around. Wayne waved, but the pilot didn't wave back. He must not have seen the boat yet.

Wayne motored closer. The plane had American call letters. What was someone from Alaska doing here at five in the morning?

The pilot walked a rope off one of the floats onto shore and lashed it around a tree. He walked back to the plane – there was something familiar about how he walked – then he suddenly stopped when he saw Wayne's boat. Wayne waved.

The guy didn't wave back. Weird.

Wayne motored closer. The pilot was on his knees fiddling with something on the ground.

Then the pilot turned towards Wayne, lifted one knee off the ground and put his left elbow on it.

With his right hand he swung a rifle up to his shoulder. The pilot watched Wayne through the scope.

Wayne froze. What the hell? This was a sick joke. He gave a friendly wave with his right hand, while throttling down the outboard with his left.

The pilot slid the bolt forward. A 6.5 millimetre cartridge slid into the Swedish Mauser's chamber with a click. The first bullet hit Wayne's left arm. It ripped through his bicep and smashed through the bone before exiting into the outboard and flattening itself on the engine block.

Wayne's adrenaline surged. His brain told his left arm to goose the throttle and turn the boat into a 180.

But his arm just hung uselessly at his side.

With his right arm, he grabbed the tiller and yanked it into a left turn while dialing up the power.

The boat lurched as maximum power pushed the stern to the right.

Back on the beach, a nervous hand worked the rifle bolt, ejected a spent casing into the willows and chambered another round.

The boom of a second shot echoed across the lake. Wayne heard the bullet whoosh past. He crouched beside the motor and raced away from the plane at maximum power.

He heard the boom of a third shot and a metallic clang as the bullet punched through the aluminum hull.

The pilot fell from his knees into the prone shooting position. This shot needed to count.

He lined up the cross hairs on Wayne's back, raised the aim just a touch for the distance, breathed out and paused. Then he squeezed the trigger.

The fourth bullet hit Wayne in the back, just below the left shoulder blade. It ripped through his lung and exited through his shirt pocket. The entry hole was a clean round hole. But inside Wayne's chest, the bullet hit a rib where the lead tip mushroomed into a jagged star burst. The hole out the front of Wayne's chest was the size of a quarter.

Wayne knew in an instant it was all over. If you shot a moose in the stomach, it could run away. Shoot it in the lungs, and it will bleed out in no time.

He lay in the bottom of the boat looking up at the sky. He ripped off his hat and jammed it over the wound to stop the bleeding. He knew it was useless.

Strangely, he didn't feel any pain. Just the warmth of the blood.

He watched as a seagull soared across the blue sky over the boat. That reminded him of lying on the beach with his cousins when he was a kid at his auntie's fish camp.

Good times.

The engine idled as the waves gently rocked the boat.

Wayne was starting to feel the pain now. The seagull was gone. He was getting sleepy. Very sleepy.

WINTER CONTINUED

46

Z-Dog Placer Mining, Whitehorse yard

7:10 a.m., Christmas - December 25th, +4°C
44 days sober

"Sit Tarfu! Sit!" Winter hopped off his bike and let it fall into the wet snow beside the trail. He wiped the rain off his face. Tarfu stared back at him, looking wet, sad and bedraggled. The trail from Miles Canyon was packed by snowmobiles and should have been easy, if not for this warm spell. The temperature had rocketed above freezing. Then, that morning, the rain came.

He reached out and rubbed the dog's neck. "I know, buddy. Fucking Aleutian Low. I don't like it either."

The paved roads had been like skating rinks, literally. The asphalt was chilled to Forty Below by the cold snap so the rain touched it and froze instantly. If not for the studs on the fat bike tires, riding would have been impossible. Then the trails had turned from hard-packed snow into slush pits. His feet were soaked from pushing his bike and postholing through packed snow into ice water pooling just above the frozen soil.

The drizzle and warm temperatures had melted the edges of the footprints from his last visit into Sasquatch-sized footprints that gaped like blackholes in the washed out light of the cloudy half moon.

The camera better have worked this time. These nocturnal visits to Zach's compound were getting old. And risky.

He clicked the leash onto Tarfu, extended the cord, and looped it around a tree. Now would be a bad time for Tarfu to run around the fence trying to get into Zach's compound.

Then Winter scaled the fence, clicked his headlamp on low and walked over to the camera. No snowdrifts or random placer mining equipment had materialized to block its view of the fourth container. Hopefully the new batteries lasted long enough in the cold to get some good pictures.

He popped the old SIM card into the pocket on his jacket sleeve and clicked the new one into place. He popped the battery tray out and shook the old batteries into his palm.

Vehicle noises! He looked up to see two pairs of headlights barreling along the road towards the gate to Zach's compound.

The gate was wide open.

Shit! Why didn't I check more carefully, thought Winter. He had assumed no one would be up and around at seven in the morning on Christmas Day. It seemed Zach had the same idea.

When the vehicles came in, their headlights would point right at the fourth container. Right where Winter was crouched.

He clicked off his headlamp and scurried through the slush behind the container.

Seconds later two big 4x4 pickups with snowmobiles in the back rolled up to the fourth container. Winter heard a door open and boots hit the snow. The faint sound of Guns N Roses filtered through the cold, damp air.

"You back up over there. I'll get the hose." It was Zach's voice.

Winter felt his heart pounding. I'll just wait here till they leave, he thought.

Winter heard the clang as Zach used a crowbar to pry the frozen container door open. There was some muttering, clanking and then the whir of an electric pump.

"One hundred gallons, coming up!"

"Thanks man. The fuel guy will think I reinsulated my house next time he delivers!"

Oh fuck, thought Winter. It's the cop from Zach's Oldtimer's team.

"You should get a bigger Tidy Tank. I could give you more."

"It's plenty. Save me more than a thousand bucks," said the cop. "What do I owe you?"

"Oh, don't worry about it. Amber brings over twenty thousand litres a time. So it's not like we're running short."

Winter listened to the two men shoot the shit for a minute as the pump did its work. In the distance, Tarfu barked. It was the bark he gave when he'd been left in the backyard too long.

The knot in Winter's stomach tightened.

"What the fuck?" said Zach suddenly, his chatty tone turned serious. "Footprints beside the container."

Boots sloshed closer in the wet snow.

"And that looks like a wildlife camera!"

"What the double fuck! And the footsteps go behind the container."

No point in waiting. Winter took off for the fence. The yard was filled with junk. But it would be stupid to turn on his headlamp. He had to hope this didn't end with him tripping over a pipe.

He vaulted over an aluminum ladder lying half covered in snow.

"There he is!" He glanced back to see two guys and their iPhone flashlights chasing him to the fence.

Don't look back. Just run.

Tarfu saw him coming and started barking.

He pulled his mitts off and jammed them into his pockets as he approached the fence He leaped onto the chain link, grabbing the cold metal with his hands and driving his toes into the fence. But his winter boots were too fat, and his right toe slipped out. He found himself hanging from the fence by his hands.

A glance over his shoulder showed the iPhone flashlights bouncing closer.

His hands screamed on the cold, biting wire as he pulled himself up. He put his left knee on the fence, then lifted his right boot.

The toe went into the gap between the wire this time.

He vaulted himself over the fence. A wire sticking out of the top of the fence jabbed deep into his down jacket.

He landed in the other side in a pile of wet snow as down feathers drifted down around him.

Winter rolled out of the snow onto his knees and scrambled for his bike. He unclicked Tarfu's leash and stuffed it into his pocket. Zach and the cop got to the fence.

Don't look back. He heard frustrated cursing as someone kicked the fence behind him. "Around the other way!" shouted Zach.

Winter jumped on his bike and took off down the slushy trail along the railway. The black stumps of burned trees poked out of the snow along the railbed. If they had a gun, it would be an easy shot.

But they didn't. The shouting and abuse slowly faded into the distance.

Winter pedaled until the trail went into a pocket of trees that had somehow survived the fire. He stopped and jammed his bleeding hands into his mitts. He gave Tarfu a head rub and laughed, feeling the nervous tension drain out of his body. "We made it buddy. But if they saw you, we may have to put you in the dog witness protection program."

Then he heard a sled engine start in the distance.

Fuck me. He pushed off and pedaled as fast as he could. He shifted up through the range, but even in top gear fat bikes aren't built for speed. Especially on a slushy trail.

Winter's lungs sucked in the burning cold air. Three kilometres from McCrae to the Miles Canyon bridge. How far had he gone already?

If I make it to the next junction, he won't know which to take.

In the distance, the motor of a high-performance mountain sled revved as someone backed it off their pickup in a hurry.

Winter hit the first trail intersection.

Even in the moonlight, Winter's tire ruts in the slushy snow showed exactly which way he had come from.

Oh fuck.

47

Schwatka Lake Float Plane Base

7:35 a.m., Christmas - December 25th, +4°C

The rider had the snow machine's throttle pinned as it roared along the dark shore of Schwatka Lake. Going anything less than max throttle would be stupid in this weather, especially towing a skimmer; you'd risk sinking into unseen overflow on the lake. Driving on the road along the lake would be better, but it was pure ice and the track wouldn't grip. The sled curved onto the shore and came to a stop behind a floatplane dock frozen into the ice. The rider tapped the kill switch and the engine sputtered to a stop. Silence rolled back over the dark lake.

The red warning lights on top of the dam blinked slowly in the darkness. Behind and above, the PowerBlimp's lights flashed. The moonlight filtered through gaps in the shoreline willows and made a kind of dappled camouflage on the snowmobile. And the skimmer it was towing. And the figure sitting perfectly still behind the handlebars.

The rider may have looked still, but under the old-fashioned -- but very warm; *way* too warm today -- beaver hat and goggles the brain was moving fast. Rehearsing thoughts it had already processed many times.

The distance was 1.2 kilometres. That would be 1.2 minutes -- 72 seconds -- at 60 kilometres per hour. Or 2.4 minutes at the drone's actual speed, 30 kilometres per hour. Then factor in lifting the heavy payload to three hundred metres. Plus hover time.

The big question a week ago was how the batteries would perform at Forty Below. At Plus Four, it was no problem. Especially since kamikaze drones don't need power for a return flight.

The Solstice bomb had been easier. One drone you could carry in a backpack. Just ski in close in the dark. No snowmobile for people to see or hear. But this target had fences and security cameras that meant distance. And that meant bigger batteries.

It would be worth it. A power outage on Christmas morning would get everyone's attention. The Greens would blame the Freedos. The

Freedos would blame the Greens. The rider smiled, then swung off the machine and stepped back to the skimmer. Mittened hands undid the bungee cords over a large, custom-made plywood box and unbuckled its lid.

Inside the box and its layer of insulation, two drones nestled in drone-shaped carve outs in a foam mattress. Underneath each sat a microwave heat pad; unnecessary this morning but warm batteries couldn't hurt.

The goggles now went up onto the beaver hat and the mitts came off. Polypro liner gloves -- usually for finger work in cold weather; today to cover fingerprints -- lifted one of the drones out of its nest.

Underneath was the payload, shaped like a mickey of Captain Morgan Original Spiced Gold rum; which was how the plastic bottle started its life. With its covering of magnets, it looked kind of like a flattened black pineapple. The figure turned the drone upside down and squeezed a warm tube of Gorilla Glue construction adhesive onto the bottom of the payload.

Two gloved fingers hovered over the timer buttons on the lid of the Captain Morgan bottle. This was where you found out if you fucked up the electronics. The fingers pressed down. The figure breathed out as a red LED began to pulse. Fifteen minutes.

Ten seconds later, the harsh buzz of drone engines sawed into the still Yukon morning air.

The snowmobile rider -- now a drone pilot -- watched the drone's blinking light head for the dam then switched to watching through the controller screen.

Between balaclava and beaver hat, the drone pilot's eyes glinted in the blueish screen light.

The eyes focused intently on the control screen. The wind was light, and it was easy to keep the blinking lights of the PowerBlimp in the middle of the navigation crosshairs.

The PowerBlimp quickly got bigger. It was like an elongated, football-shaped donut, hanging in the sky with a rotor spinning in the middle. With a few quick thumb maneuvers, the drone pilot slowed the drone and crept it slowly into the donut hole.

Slowly. Watch for wind gusts. Don't get hit by the rotor.

The drone pilot lowered the drone slowly. When it was a foot or two above the bottom of the donut hole, the pilot cut power. The camera image bounced as the drone hit the bouncy inflated donut, but then stabilized. The rotor moved across the screen in regular motions. It looked like the glue was working.

The drone pilot tossed the controller into the box and pulled out the backup drone: power, timer, construction glue, launch.

This drone also flew towards the PowerBlimp. But, instead of rising to the blimp, it turned left and searched the Yukon Energy parking lot for the transformer park.

The square shapes of a row of massive transformers appeared in the night-vision cameras. It reminded the drone pilot of the scene from *Star Wars* before the Stormtroopers blew up the rebel power supply on the ice planet Hoth.

The drone pilot lowered the drone towards a transformer.

Either the payload's magnets and glue would clamp onto the metal skin of a transformer, or the drone would touch the wrong wire and end up like an electronic version of a fried squirrel.

In either case, power outage on Christmas morning.

The drone pilot reduced power until the drone shuddered and the camera stopped moving.

No fried squirrel yet.

The drone pilot tossed the second controller on top of the first and bungee'd the lid down. Seconds later, a thumb jabbed the sled's start button and the snowmobile was roaring across Schwatka Lake.

48

Snowmobile trail on the old White Pass railway line, north of McCrae

7:50 a.m., Christmas - December 25th, +4°C
44 days sober

Winter pedaled furiously down the trail above the river with Tarfu racing after him. A sled engine roared in the distance. The PowerBlimp blinked in the distance like a beacon of safety. If he could just get across the Miles Canyon pedestrian bridge, he'd be safe. It was too narrow for a snowmobile and the water was too fast to freeze over.

He looked down and to the right. A turn and steep hill was coming.

His eye swept over the river. The river! An awful feeling of doom pulsed across his body from the pit of his stomach. The river was frozen for miles upstream of Miles Canyon. Even if he got across the bridge, Zach only had to drive 500 metres upstream to the solidly frozen part and zip across the ice.

Winter had never felt this kind of fear before. He pictured himself trying to fend off Zach's bulk in the deep snow. Zach would just drag his body to Miles Canyon and throw it in. They'd find it in the spring somewhere downstream.

Or Zach would just beat him to death and toss his body in the bush. One of those Whitehorse missing persons reports where someone's dog drags a skull out of the bush ten years later and they check the dental records.

He glanced back. The bright light of Zach's sled bounced along the trail in the distance. Getting closer.

Maybe there was a stretch of trail too steep or narrow for a snowmobile?

No. Too bad they weren't on Money Shot. But that was on the other side of the river and too far away.

Winter kept pedaling. He turned right down the steep hill. Weight back. Watch the brakes. Don't wipe out. Not now.

Zach would be able to ride this on his sled. Tricky but doable. He'd just have to stand on the uphill side to balance on the turn.

An idea hit him.

At the bottom of the hill, he let the bike roll ten more metres. He hopped off and pulled Tarfu's leash out of his pocket. He double looped one end around a tree about the height of the top of a snowmobile windscreen. Then he jumped across the trail, pulling the cord out of the handle as he went. It was long enough. Just. He tied the other end around another tree.

He lifted his bike and heaved it downhill out of sight. He watched as it bounced over a stump before sliding to rest under some willows.

He clicked off his headlamp and ran another ten metres down the trail before stepping behind a tree. "Come, Tarfu, come!" he hissed. The dog came and stood beside him. Winter put his hand on Tarfu's collar and crouched behind the tree.

Zach's sled engine revved in the distance. It would just be a minute before the headlight appeared.

Then, suddenly, Winter saw a bright flash in the sky to the south. Tarfu started as a boom echoed across the valley.

Focus, he told himself. "It's okay," he whispered to the dog. "Just wait." He looked back uphill to see the headlight bouncing off the spruce trees at the top of the hill.

The machine turned right and eased down the hill. Zach's black figure hopped onto the uphill side and balanced the machine around the corner. Easy. Standing with a knee on the seat, Zach pressed the throttle and accelerated down the trail.

Right into Tarfu's leash. With a sudden twang, the leash tightened across Zach's chest. Two hundred and twenty pounds of momentum versus a leash designed for a medium-sized dog.

The leash snapped, but not before arresting Zach's forward movement. His body stopped, and the snowmobile kept going.

Zach hit the ground like someone dropped a moose quarter off the back of a pickup.

The sled, no thumb on its throttle, decelerated quickly. It bounced along the snowmobile trail then slowly nosed into the deep snow and tilted onto its side.

Winter jumped out of the trees. He recognized the machine: a Tundra. He jumped on the sled. He stood on the high side running board with both feet and wrapped a mitt around the mountain bar on top of the handlebars. He threw his entire weight into leveling the machine. No movement.

Zach rolled onto his knees, still gasping for breath.

Winter threw his weight again. This time, the sled leveled. Just enough. Still with both feet on the high side, Winter slowly squeezed the throttle. Enough to move. Not enough to spin out and bury the rear end. And definitely not enough to drive it straight into the willows.

The machine started to move forward and level out.

Winter pulled himself in, put a knee on the seat and steered the machine back toward the trail. He glanced back for Tarfu, and saw the dog's eyes reflect the red glow of the tail light.

Somewhere behind Tarfu was Zach, either still on his knees gasping for breath or about to leap out of the darkness in a massive roid rage.

Winter punched the throttle and the Tundra took off down the trail with Tarfu racing after it.

49. Cascadia Steakhouse, Vancouver
7:30 p.m., December 27th, +2°C

Karen followed the hostess to the table. Her steps felt long and lumbering compared to the slim eighteen-year-old hostess, who was skittering over tiles wet with Vancouver rain in her heels and little black dress. Karen could hear her left foot squelching with each step.

It was a weird winter. Yesterday, it was actually warmer and rainier in Whitehorse than Vancouver. Today, the temperature was dropping again. Fast. The drive to the airport was a mess; three cars in the ditch just on the airport road itself. Then three hours sitting on the plane as they dealt with ice on the runway. The forecast predicted high winds. God only knew how long the flight delays would be on the way home.

The hostess waited for Karen to take her seat so she could smile and tell them the server would be there shortly. Her duty done, the hostess tugged her dress hem down her thigh -- ineffectually; little black dresses riding up teenage thighs was part of the Cascadia Steakhouse business model -- and scurried back to the front door.

Jim watched the teenage hips walk away for a second, then turned to Karen and smiled. "Your nose looks nice."

Karen decided to take this as a compliment. "Thanks. The specialist says it's all healed. A good excuse for a trip to Vancouver."

"Did you get to pick a new nose out of the catalog?"

This was more annoying. But it was probably some strategy that Jim, for some reason, didn't think was counterproductive. He prided himself on keeping people off balance. Which was another way of saying he was an asshole. She smiled back: "I got hit by Winter, not a Mac truck."

"Did your family come too?"

"Misty yes. But Taiya refuses to fly."

"I love flight shaming. The fewer the people at the airport, the better, in my opinion."

Karen decided to change the subject. "How did your board react to the bombing?" She listened as Jim explained the board's concerns about the Yukon's investment environment. It was a corporate version of good-cop-bad-cop. The board always wanted to pull out, while Jim was the Yukon's friend and just needed a little bit of help to keep the project alive. Just something small like tax credits or a tweaked regulation.

Then it was Jim's turn to change the subject: "Any news on who blew up the PowerBlimp? Other than someone with a sense of humour?" He said this with almost casual unconcern, as if a vandal had spray painted something funny on a building across the street.

This puzzled Karen. Back in Whitehorse, everyone in the Cabinet Office from the premier to the front desk was in the middle of a multi-day panic attack. The LNG plant bombing wasn't a one-off by some crank. Nor was the PowerBlimp attack. That made it clear they now had an actual right-wing Freedo terrorist group operating in the Yukon. One that had some fairly sophisticated technical capabilities, judging from the drone parts and half-burnt electronics the police found.

And one that had some artistic flair. The kamikaze drone video released from somewhere deep on the dark web had gone viral. Karen herself had watched it half a dozen times: Dark sky with the lights of Whitehorse in the background, blinking red PowerBlimp lights hanging in the sky, getting closer as the drone rises and moves closer, opera music getting louder as the drone creeps into the PowerBlimp's rotor opening. Then blackness, followed by the Yukon Freedom Front logo and white noise.

When it happened, social media exploded. People were pissed that the power outage took so long to fix. They were just lucky it happened during a warm spell and the worst thing that happened was that people had to talk to their families on Christmas Day instead of surfing the internet.

Karen waited for the server to fill the wine glasses and leave the table before replying: "Other than the Yukon Freedom Front claiming responsibility, the police investigation is just beginning. Forensic experts from Ottawa found drone parts, but they're from a pretty common commercial drone."

"Our security guy says every extreme ski video maker in Alaska would have one."

Karen decided to push Jim. She still owed him for the nose catalog joke. "The bombers seem to like you. They mentioned you and Northern Lights twice in the rant they included in their email claiming responsibility."

Jim seemed unfazed. "With friends like that, who needs enemies?" He pulled a list out of his pocket and spread it on the table beside his wine glass. "We had an emergency board meeting. We have a few members who have mining experience in terrorist shitholes like Yemen and Colombia. They came up with a list of things you could do to help Northern Lights stay in the Yukon."

Karen stared back silently.

Jim continued. "You know, to help you out. So you don't go into the next election with everyone thinking you lost control of the situation and blew up the economy too."

"Thanks Jim," said Karen, suppressing an eye roll as she pulled the list over to her side of the table. This was not an episode of her public service career she would be telling the kids in the Yukon Model Parliament about.

50

Lower Boogaloo

Chaewon leaned on her poles, breathing heavily, and squinted into the low mid-day sun to the south. The wind roared in her ears. Tiny ice pellets and dead leaves rattled off her sunglasses and Goretex jacket. If it wasn't so windy, she would probably be able to hear her heart pounding. With deep snow under a frozen crust, this was much harder than her usual workouts.

"Feeling cooped up? It would be fun to go for a ski!" Taiya had texted. Was this fun? Only for BNRs who were also biathlon champions.

Taiya was waiting at the top of the hill. Chaewon took another step, felt the crust collapse under her weight, then felt her thigh muscle scream as she tried to lift her ski up through the crust.

Chaewon stopped and leaned on her poles again. A two-minute break. That's all she needed.

Despite the terrible conditions, she thought, it did feel good to get away from the craziness in town. The science columnist who kept writing about the Aleutian Low was getting death threats. Winter's stories called it the Icepocalypse. First the rain. Then the cold came back, turning Whitehorse into a skating rink. You couldn't walk the streets unless you put traction cleats on your boots. The ditches were so full of cars that the towing companies weren't answering the phone anymore.

Even the moose couldn't handle it. The crust was so thick they had trouble walking, while the wolves just scampered on top. So people on the edge of town were waking up with moose in their driveways, eating their caragana bushes. The police were asking people not to call 9-1-1 just because a moose in the driveway wouldn't let them near their car.

Looking back, those seemed like just some quirky northern stories. Because then the wind came and the really scary stuff started happening.

Tall skinny Yukon trees with a few hundred kilos of ice on top started toppling over. Everywhere in town; only the neighbourhoods leveled by the Wildfires didn't have trees down across roads, vehicles, houses and -- this was the big deal -- power lines. Ice-covered trees knocked down hundreds of power lines all over the Yukon. Entire neighbourhoods went black.

And stayed black. There weren't enough power crews, and they couldn't borrow crews from Alaska or Western Canada since they were all in the same weather system.

So, when temperatures plunged again, if you had electric heat you were screwed. If you had an electric car you were screwed. And if you had oil heat, you were also screwed. Your furnace needed electricity for the oil pump and fans. Only the real preppers had cut-off switches and wiring to plug a portable generator right into their furnaces. Canadian Tire sold out of generators in minutes. Even if you already had a generator, or traded a kidney for one, you had to go into your basement with a headlamp and Youtube instructional video on your phone to wire it in.

Generator theft was rampant. When an old lady put a 12 gauge bear slug into the knee of a guy with a cordless grinder in her backyard, the cops didn't know where to put her. Even the jail's backup generator had run out of diesel.

Then, even if you did have heat, you needed a camp stove or a barbecue with a full tank of propane left over from the summer. Otherwise you couldn't cook. The cops found an entire family frozen dead in their house with carbon monoxide poisoning from using a barbecue inside. Some people just turned off the water, abandoned the house and moved in like refugees with a friend who had a woodstove.

Which was why Chaewon was sleeping in Winter's basement with his ski collection while Eamon couchsurfed in the living room.

Chaewon finally made it to the top of the hill. Taiya was sitting calmly on the trunk of a fallen tree.

"Oatmeal raisin muffin?" offered Taiya. "With egg whites for protein. I cooked them on the barbecue. It sort of worked."

Chaewon slumped onto the tree trunk beside Taiya and accepted the muffin. Did the BNRs realize how not normal they were?

She could feel the damp sweat in her armpits. Her legs felt like spaghetti. Skiing through crusty snow had revealed some leg muscles she didn't know she had, and they would not be happy tonight.

Taiya offered her some tea from her thermos.

"Thanks," said Chaewon, trying to smile. They sat quietly in the wind, each lost in their own thoughts.

Then Taiya broke the silence. "Does it seem weird to you that someone can blow up the PowerBlimp almost in the middle of town, then post a video on the Internet, but the police can't find them?"

"Winter said the video was posted on some anonymous equivalent of Youtube. Probably using TOR or some VPNs. Not easy to trace."

"My dad thinks it was Zach. He wants to publish an exposé in the paper."

"You saw Amber. She said it was fake news. Somebody else pinning it on them." Chaewon laughed. "She basically said her husband was too stupid to pull off such an elaborate attack. Had to be the government trying to make the Freedos look bad."

"Yeah, but that's what she *would* say, isn't it?" Taiya folded up the muffin bag and stuffed it back into her daypack. The temperature had dropped some more. She could already feel the cold seeping through her jacket.

"Your dad will need proof," said Chaewon. "Or he'll get sued."

"Or worse. He was lucky to get away from Zach on the snowmobile." Taiya stood up. "Well, that was a nice picnic!"

Chaewon laughed. "Picnics only last two minutes at Minus Twenty-Four."

Taiya stuffed the thermos and cups into her daypack and zipped it up. She hopped on her skis over beside Chaewon. "Selfie!" she exclaimed as she reached into an inner pocket for her phone.

She stared at the screen for a second. Then another second. She held it out for Chaewon. Apple Photos had produced a "memory" from a few years before. It showed Taiya and the YCC kids skiing at White Pass. Including a drone video. And a picture of the drone landing at the feet of its operator: Nestor.

Taiya looked up at Chaewon. "How could Zach have blown up the PowerBlimp if he was chasing my dad on a snowmobile at the time?"

51

Winter's house

4:00 p.m., December 29th, -33°C
48 days sober

Winter listened to the traction cleats on his boots bite into the ice on the sidewalk as he walked. There was a dead electric car sitting in the middle of the street, covered in a layer of frozen rain. The street was strangely empty; no traffic, no lights in the houses.

He stopped and looked back at his house at the end of the street. Through wind gusts he could hear the whirr of the generator, and see Artemis and Eamon sitting at the living room table. The whole news team was in his living room, clustered around the wood stove, with their laptops plugged into an extension cord running from a generator chained to a tree. The office was frozen solid.

Taiya's truck was parked out front beside Chaewon's Mazda. They would be back soon.

"Come on, buddy," he said to Tarfu. The dog tentatively put a foot on a stretch of icy sidewalk, decided it was too slippery, and looked up unhappily at Winter. "You said you wanted a walk."

Winter heard the sound of a diesel engine. An old, black F-350 4x4 turned onto the street. It had chains on its tires and crept slowly along. He watched it as it rolled to a stop beside him. The window rolled down.

"Winter!" exclaimed the old man with a smile. He was wearing an old-school parka with a well-worn beaver hat. Oil-stained insulated work gloves sat on the dashboard. His dog Casca napped on the seat beside him.

"Shawn! You're the only guy on the road!"

"My buddy's stuck. Gotta pull him out."

They shot the shit for a moment. Was Shawn still flying the plane? Was Winter still playing Oldtimers? How was Winter's dad? Your house frozen up?

"Well," said Shawn, "better go get the tow strap on my friend's truck."

Winter gave a thumb's up and tapped the hood of the truck. The diesel revved up as Shawn drove away.

Winter smiled to himself as childhood memories came back. Zach might be a dick, and a terrible human being to spend a hockey tournament in Watson Lake with, but Winter actually liked his dad. He remembered when Shawn coached their minor hockey team, with Winter's dad as assistant coach; when he could make it. Shawn even gave Winter a case of Old Style Pilsner when he turned nineteen, and that was something you didn't forget.

Winter's phone rang. It was Taiya's tone. He answered. Tarfu stopped and watched as Winter's body stiffened. Something was up.

Winter turned and started running back to the house. Tarfu took off after him, skittering awkwardly on the ice.

52

Chaewon's previously-owned Mazda, Annie Lake Road

7:30 p.m., December 29th, -40°C

Chaewon leaned forward and clenched the wheel, the cold seeping through her mitts, her shoulders tense as she peered through the frosted windshield. Her previously-owned Mazda's temperature gauge said -30°C, its lower limit. The engineers in Japan didn't design the car for Forty Below. Which it probably was out here. Annie Lake was always colder than in town.

The battery warning light blinked distractingly in the darkness at the bottom of her peripheral vision. Eamon had unplugged her car from the generator so they could use the cord for their laptops. All the heaters were off to get more range. If only Taiya had waited until they got home to tell Winter, they could have stopped him from running off after Nestor. Now they would probably end up freezing in a powerless car on the side of the road.

Taiya reached over with the windshield scraper and widened the slit in the frost through which Chaewon was watching the road. She pointed at the familiar sign for Annie Lake Road. Chaewon felt the regenerative brakes kick in; that was a few more metres of range. Taiya pulled the mitt off her right hand with her teeth and tapped her phone screen with her liner gloves. Still no blue dot for Winter's location. The last place she had seen it was where coverage ended on Annie Lake Road.

Taiya broke the silence: "We know ... we think ... he's going out to Nestor's place," she said, her breath pushing through her buff and hanging in the air. "Do we just drive up to the front door and say we were in the neighbourhood?"

Chaewon took a moment to reply. The fact that Winter had taken Taiya's truck suggested he was in a hurry. "Maybe he's decided to sneak in and plant one of his cameras. It's like he thinks he's James Bond."

Taiya considered this. Planting cameras had worked with Brett. But Nestor was different. Very different.

"But why take Tarfu?" Taiya asked. "You don't take a dog on a James Bond mission."

The Mazda rounded a corner under the shadow of Needle Mountain, and turned towards Annie Lake. They were still a few clicks from the turn off to Nestor's cabin.

"There's my truck!" exclaimed Taiya, signalling Chaewon to pull in behind it. They were on the causeway across the Annie Lake swamp. Taiya knew it well. She and her dad spent plenty of Saturday afternoons skiing around Annie Lake when she was younger. The truck batteries must have died here.

"Follow his tracks from here, or drive straight to Nestor's?" asked Chaewon.

Taiya opened the Canada Topo app on her phone and checked the distance. "Follow him. He'll be breaking trail through an icy crust. Maybe we can catch him before he even gets there."

Taiya opened the door and immediately heard barking from Taiya's truck.

"What the fuck, Dad?!" exclaimed Taiya, jumping out of the car to run over to the truck. Tarfu was wearing his winter sled-dog pullover and jumping up and down excitedly on a pile of jackets Winter had left on the seat. Taiya looked back at Chaewon. "He's half husky, but still. It's cold!"

"Maybe he's not planning to be gone long."

Taiya tapped the window. "Let's move you over to Chaewon's car, little guy. It's warmer." She opened the truck door and Tarfu jumped out. But instead of waiting at Taiya's feet, the dog immediately took off at full speed following Winter's tracks.

"Tarfu! Come!" shouted Taiya. The dog showed no signs of hearing and pelted away into the darkness. Taiya kept calling for a minute, then stood quietly looking along Winter's ski tracks. "Has my whole family lost their minds?" she finally said. She stomped over to the car, opened the hatchback and grabbed her skis.

Chaewon grabbed hers too. They were going to wish they had the gear in Taiya's garage. Fatter skis. Warmer boots. A dark thought crossed Chaewon's mind. Maybe even Taiya's biathlon rifle.

There was no 9-1-1 on Annie Lake Road and, even if there was, it would take them an hour to respond.

Taiya popped her headlamp over her toque, looked at her watch and strode away in Winter's ski tracks. The reflective tape on Taiya's white Arctic Winter Games snowpants flashed in Chaewon's headlamp beam as she got into stride. Chaewon scrambled to click on her skis and catch up.

They followed Winter's and Tarfu's tracks onto the lake at a brisk pace, with Chaewon struggling to keep up. The first part was easy going on an ice-solid snowmobile trail leading to a dog musher's cabin. Up ahead, they heard thirty dogs howl into the cold dark sky. That had to be the dogs in their pens spotting Tarfu running past.

The dogs barked at them in turn. Then Taiya and Chaewon followed Winter's and Tarfu's tracks into deeper snow. He had been breaking trail from this point. They would be able to ski a lot faster.

The moon poked out from behind the mountains to the southeast. Taiya and Chaewon clicked off their headlamps. In the stark moonlight, they could see the mountain that sat just behind Nestor's cabin. Each stride brought it a bit closer. Along the lakeshore, there was a black band of dense spruce trees. They could see Winter's tracks curve into it and disappear.

Chaewon banged her mitts together to get more blood into her hands. She looked at the trees. This was crazy, she said to herself. How did I get into this situation? The sense of foreboding that had started as a tummy rumble at the truck was now nearly overwhelming.

"Maybe we should head back," she said. "Get help from that dog musher cabin."

Taiya turned sharply. Frost covered her buff, eyelashes and the wisps of hair poking out of her toque. "We can't! My dad is up there. We *must* be about to catch up to him. We've got to stop him from doing something stupid." Chaewon stood silently in Taiya's ski tracks. "Chaewon, I need your help," Taiya pleaded.

Chaewon felt her pulse racing. She nodded.

They continued along Winter's ski tracks. They weaved through the trees in the direction of Nestor's cabin. The tracks curved around dense stands of spruce and angled gradually up the sides of the small hills and eskers left when the glaciers retreated from the valley after the last ice age.

It was darker in the forest. The mountain behind Nestor's cabin was getting close. Very close. They had to be almost there.

Winter's tracks curved up a small rise into a stand of leafless aspens. Taiya herringboned quickly up the hill, deftly keeping her skis where Winter had already broken the crust.

Behind her, Chaewon was breathing heavily as she floundered uphill. Her skis kept crunching through the crust. She cursed as she tried to pull her ski tips back to the surface.

"Shhhh!" hissed Taiya. "I can see the cabin."

Winter's tracks continued straight at the building, which was about 100 metres away. It was a small but tidy modern cabin, with a big kitchen window facing them and a porch facing the other direction. Smoke drifted straight up from the chimney beside a Starlink satellite data dish. The windows were bright squares spilling light onto the snow. Not the warm colour of an old propane lamp, but harsh white LED light from Nestor's solar panels and batteries. They could see the kitchen and table clearly, but there was no sign of Nestor or Winter.

Behind the cabin, Nestor's truck was parked beside the woodshed. Red LEDs glowed where the extension cord connected its block heater. Behind the vehicle was Nestor's garage, with snowmobile tracks leading to the garage door.

Winter's tracks curved towards the cabin. They skied closer.

Chaewon saw Taiya freeze. A distorted rectangle of light illuminated the snow in front of the cabin's door. Which was wide open. Little swirls of steam escaped into the frigid air along the top of the open door frame.

Who left their door open at Minus Forty? A knot of fear tightened in the base of Chaewon's stomach. Where was Winter? Where was Tarfu?

"What the-"

Without turning around, Taiya made a sharp gesture for silence. She listened, but there were no voices. Chaewon felt her heart pounding as Taiya clicked off her skis and stepped quietly onto the porch. A pair of snowshoes sat on top of fresh tracks coming from the forest and a white sack with a frozen marten sticking out of it lay on the porch, as if dropped there in a hurry. She stepped over a chainsaw and the marten and looked into the cabin.

Taiya's head reappeared and she signaled for Chaewon to follow her.

"Where are they?" whispered Chaewon. "Should we go back and call 9-1-1?" But Taiya was already gone.

Chaewon felt an almost overpowering sense of dread as she clicked off her skis and stepped onto the porch, like she was the woman in a horror movie walking on a creaking floor.

She poked her head into Nestor's cabin. The hallway looked normal. Painted plywood walls and floor. Ski and winter boots on the floor. Coats and coveralls hanging on a row of pegs along the wall with a squirrel gun laying horizontally across the pegs. A jumble of skis propped in the corner.

She continued into the kitchen, passing a workstation with three monitors and a jumble of computer gear.

Taiya was beside the woodstove, looking down into a rectangular hole in the floor. Beside the hole, a two-foot by four-foot piece of plywood flooring had been lifted out and pushed to the side. A handful of flooring screws and a cordless drill lay by the wall.

Chaewon looked into the hole. In a big plywood box framed between the floor joists, there were plastic bins holding drones, wires, bits of electronics and plastic jugs of various liquids.

"A hidden compartment?" stammered Chaewon, her eyes wide as she stared at the gear.

"A classic Yukon cabin feature. But most people are just hiding gold or old guns." Taiya kneeled on the floor and stuck her head into the hole. There were more bins pushed under the floor. She pulled her head out of the hole, then leaned back to sit on the kitchen floor. "Did Dad find this and then leave to tell the cops?"

Chaewon didn't answer. Instead, she pointed at Taiya's knees. Small blotches stained the white snow pants. Chaewon dropped to her knees, pulled off her mitt, and ran her hand along the floor. There were droplets.

Of blood.

Chaewon followed the trail of droplets. They led out the door and across the deck. Towards Nestor's garage.

53

Annie Lake

Chaewon followed the drops of blood onto the deck, where they continued onto the driveway. Just off the deck there was a large patch of disturbed snow she hadn't noticed on the way in, when the open door grabbed their attention. It looked like someone had fallen and made a messed up snow angel.

In the middle of the snow angel, there was a large blotch of blood. Bigger blobs of blood on the ice led away to the garage. Chaewon stared at the furrows, picturing Nestor dragging Winter to the garage. She hesitated to look up and make eye contact with Taiya.

The silence hung in the dark, frigid air. Finally, she turned to Taiya, who was standing frozen in the doorway staring at the garage and whispered, "What do we do now?"

Taiya didn't answer.

"We take Nestor's truck and call 9-1-1," continued Chaewon, taking a step towards Taiya. Taiya still didn't respond. "We need help!"

Taiya dragged her eyes off the garage and focused on Chaewon. "That's two hours." Her worried eyes bounced back to the garage.

"But what can we do by ourselves? It's just you and me versus Nestor."

"What's he going to do to my dad?"

The thoughts flashed through Chaewon's mind. Nestor was a nice guy. He liked Winter. They were mountain biking buddies. But it also turned out Nestor was the kind of guy who blew up LNG plants. She remembered the stories about Nestor and the war in Ukraine.

"We'll tell him if he lets Winter go, we won't say anything. We won't tell the cops, and he can just leave the Yukon."

"That wouldn't work."

"It worked for Brett."

"What?!" blurted Taiya. Chaewon froze. She wasn't supposed to tell anyone that. Taiya grabbed her sleeve and hissed, "Chaewon! What are you talking about?"

"Winter caught him--"

"Tell me later," interrupted Taiya, suddenly releasing Chaewon's sleeve. "We have to focus. How do we get my dad out of there?"

"We tell Nestor we'll forget everything if he lets Winter go."

Taiya's face hardened. "Nestor won't buy it," she said.

"Sure he will. It makes sense."

"Getting bossed around by two girls?"

Suddenly, the garage door motor cut through the silence. The door clanked upwards, revealing a strip of light along the ground. Chaewon dived behind the woodpile, and watched as Taiya stepped back into the hallway and pressed herself into the coats hanging on the wall.

The opening garage door revealed the front skis of a snowmobile and two Sorel boots. The door lifted higher. The Sorels were Nestor's and he was silhouetted in the harsh LED garage lights, standing beside the snowmobile with an axe in his hand. The sled had a skimmer attached behind it. Beside Nestor, Winter was slumped in a folding camp chair. Orange duct tape wrapped his legs and wrists to the chair. Where his face should have been was the North Face logo of a black sleeping bag stuff sack that Nestor had jammed over Winter's head.

It was like a scene from an Islamic State snuff video, if Islamic State operated in Antarctica.

Nestor leaned over the snow machine and pressed start. The engine caught the first time and coughed exhaust into the garage. He pulled his Carhartt bib overalls over his boots and zipped down the side zips. He hefted Winter, chair and all, and dumped him into the skimmer.

Nestor leaned over Winter, the axe hanging menacingly in his right hand. He was speaking to Winter in the skimmer, but his words disappeared into the rattle of the sled engine.

Chaewon looked back at Taiya, who was still pressed into the coats hanging along the hallway.

Suddenly Tarfu appeared from around the back of the garage. He saw Winter in the skimmer and ran into the garage. Tarfu nuzzled his human, who squirmed in response.

Nestor moved towards the dog from behind.

But Tarfu saw him coming, and turned to place himself between Nestor and Winter. The dog snarled and barked aggressively, his ears pinned back and his eyes not moving off Nestor.

Nestor inched closer. Then he lunged forward to grab Tarfu's collar with his left hand.

Nestor's fingers brushed Tarfu's collar, but the dog dodged sideways and squirmed away. Tarfu circled back in the entrance to the garage, continuing to bark. Nestor adjusted the grip on his axe and moved slowly toward the dog.

"What should we do?" hissed Chaewon to Taiya.

But Taiya ignored her. Chaewon watched as Taiya reached up to the row of coat hooks over her head and wrapped her fingers around Nestor's squirrel gun. Chaewon watched, stupefied, as Taiya lifted the .22 off the rack.

Taiya felt the cool, familiar heft of a gun in her hands. She quickly ejected the clip, checked it was full of ammo, and clicked it back into place. Like she'd done a thousand times in biathlon.

She pressed her back against the wall, hidden by the coats from Nestor's view. This breaks every rule I've ever been taught on the gun range, she thought. She realized her heart was pounding and her breathing rapid and shallow.

It's also my only option. She took a deep breath and let it out in a controlled exhale.

With a sudden, deft movement she pulled back the bolt and then rammed a round into the chamber. Her thumb clicked off the safety.

Then she took one step out of the coats into the middle of the hallway. She stood sideways, feet shoulder width apart, and raised the gun to her shoulder. She stuck out her hip, jammed her left elbow onto it for support and sighted the rifle where Nestor's hand gripped the axe.

Just like biathlon. Nestor's hand was about the size of a standing target. She hit those four times out of five and at twice this distance. She exhaled, paused, and squeezed the trigger.

The gun cracked, twice as loud in a hallway as on a biathlon range.

In biathlon, however, the targets don't move and you're not nervous because they have your dad duct-taped behind a getaway sled.

Taiya's shot was low and to the right. The bullet missed Nestor's hand by an inch, grazing his pant leg before slamming into the wall.

With a normal hunter, Nestor might have had a chance to jump out of the way of the second shot. But Taiya cycled the bolt in a split second, her body hardly moving. Her brain raced through the logic in an instant. Aim at his lungs. The kill zone, like a moose. But I don't want to kill him. She lowered the gun to Nestor's stomach, paused her breathing, and squeezed the trigger just as Nestor was jumping.

Again, her shot was a bit low. The bullet hit the edge of the metal fly zipper on Nestor's coveralls. The impact caused the soft lead bullet to mushroom on one side and cartwheel into Nestor's flesh. It entered the scrotum, took off the top corner of his right testis and ploughed through the epididymis before entering his inner right thigh and tearing a wound channel through the gracilis muscle. The bullet exited through Nestor's Carhartts and bounced, spent, off a jug of chainsaw oil under the workbench.

Nestor landed in a heap. "Blyat'!" he screamed, writhing on the garage floor clutching his crotch.

Tarfu barked furiously at Nestor as Taiya strode quickly to the garage, keeping the rifle on her shoulder as she chambered the third round. She kept the gun aimed at Nestor as she entered the garage. She stepped onto the snowmobile running board with her right foot and raised her left knee onto the seat.

Nestor stopped moaning and looked up, recognizing Taiya. A surprised look flashed across his face.

"That's right," said Taiya. "Shot by a white stocking."

Watching him, Taiya transferred the rifle to her left hand and reached for the handlebar with her right. Nestor opened his mouth to say something else, but Taiya pressed the throttle and left him in a cloud of sled exhaust.

She stopped in front of the woodpile where Chaewon was crouched. "Get on."

"But you shot him in the thigh," stuttered Chaewon, staring at Winter lying duct-taped in the skimmer behind the sled. "Upper thigh. What if he's bleeding out?"

"I know!" shouted Taiya, almost crying. "But what if I just grazed him? It's not safe here!" She looked back over her shoulder. No sign of Nestor. Yet.

Taiya discharged the gun into the front tire of Nestor's truck and slung it over her back. "Chaewon! I am *not* doing wilderness first aid on that guy. Get on. We'll call 9-1-1 when we get out."

Chaewon stumbled out from behind the woodpile and jumped on the sled. She grabbed Taiya's hips and held on as Taiya punched the throttle and roared down the driveway with Tarfu sprinting behind Winter and the skimmer.

54

Winter's family cabin at Marsh Lake

8:00 p.m., December 31st, -42°C
50 days sober

Tarfu heard car tires crunching on the snow outside the cabin and jumped up onto the couch for a better view. Winter looked up from his laptop. It was Chaewon's Mazda with Artemis in the passenger seat. He looked at his reflection in the window. Two black eyes, a swollen nose, a gash on his lower lip that refused to heal and a pair of tinted concussion sunglasses that seemed to make no difference at all.

He pulled off the sunglasses as Taiya opened the door.

"Figured we'd find you out here," said Artemis.

"It's kinda crazy in town," replied Taiya.

"Yeah, the national media can't figure out what to do. They want to camp out on your dad's front lawn with cameras until you come home, but it's Minus Forty-Two, all their batteries are dead, and the power's out at their hotel."

"We had to run out of the lawyer's office like we were celebrities."

Artemis had a bag slung around her shoulder with boxes of rapidly cooling Indian take-out and two bottles of non-alcoholic apple cider. She crutched up the stairs. "This is the most fucked up New Year's party ever. A teenage girl on the run from her mothers and the national media. A dad who looks like he's been dragged behind a snowmobile, which he has. Some Indian food that no one in India would recognize. And me not drinking champagne."

"And I bought a big chocolate cake for dessert!" said Chaewon, sliding the cake platter out of its box onto the counter. She then picked four cabin glasses, each a different shape or colour, off the shelf and blew the dust off them. She popped the cork and poured the cider. "I heard Nestor's going to be okay."

"My feelings aren't hurt anymore that he left so early on Christmas morning; he had to blow something up. At least I got to sample the goods before Taiya put a bullet into his man parts," said Artemis, leaning back in her chair. "Do you think I should text him for a second date? I've never had conjugal visit sex."

They gathered around the table and spooned the dishes onto plates that were still cold from the shelves along the wall.

"How is your diesel smuggling story coming along?" asked Chaewon, looking at Winter.

"I'm still kind of foggy. And still don't have a smoking gun."

"Well, you did stop one bad guy."

"Taiya stopped him. And he was the only guy in the Yukon I actually liked. Other than Henry," said Winter flatly. "Meanwhile, the same people just keep getting away with the same shit, year after year. Zach and Amber, for example."

"Do you think she'll win the election if she runs?" asked Taiya.

"Oh fuck, please let's not talk about that!" exclaimed Artemis. "How about Winter telling us what actually happened before you guys got there and saved his ass?"

Winter started the story from when he arrived at Nestor's cabin, wincing occasionally as either hot or spicy food hit one of the cuts inside his mouth.

There were no lights on when he got there. The door was unlocked, so he let himself in. He searched the cabin and garage by headlamp and found nothing, so -- keeping an eye out for headlights on the driveway -- he decided to look for classic hiding spots in Yukon cabins. There was nothing in the outhouse and no interior access to the attic. No hidden storage space under the stairs. So he started crawling along the floor looking for floor screws that looked worn from regularly being taken out and put back in.

Sure enough, he found worn screws by the woodstove. When he removed them, he found a cache of electronics.

What he didn't know, however, was that Nestor ran an illegal trapline in the bush behind his cabin and was out on his snowshoes checking the traps.

"You didn't notice his truck was parked in the driveway?" interrupted Chaewon, a note of incredulity in her voice.

Winter shook his head sheepishly.

"Continue the story, Mr. Bond," said Artemis.

Winter went on. When Nestor returned, there were no headlights or vehicle noises. Just a couple soft footsteps on the kitchen floor.

When he looked up, all he saw was a boot heading for his face. After that, everything was very confused. "Nestor duct taped me to the chair. I have some memory of him apologizing. He said he liked me. It wasn't like what they did to the Russian prisoners."

"But he was still going to dump you in the bush somewhere to freeze to death," said Artemis.

"Yeah," replied Winter with a shudder.

"And why was he attacking the Greens? He was Green himself."

"He said Canadian Greens were too nice. They are losing to the Freedos but don't do anything other than talk about it. They needed to be attacked so they would fight back."

"Mobilize the people, like he said at our Christmas dinner."

"Yep," replied Winter, sitting back in his chair. As he reclined, his sleeve caught a plastic tray of butter chicken, which fell onto the floor beside Taiya. Winter leaned to pick it up, then sat back as a spasm of pain flashed over his brain.

Taiya grabbed a rag and kneeled on the floor to wipe up the mess.

"Hey!" she said, looking up. "Check out these screws. Like you said, this one is almost stripped!" She grabbed her headlamp off the counter and clicked it on. The screws were indeed worn, but they were so old they had slotted heads instead of taking a modern bit. The wood around the screws was also worn, but the screws hadn't been removed in so long that their slots were filled with dust and dirt.

The others stood in a semi-circle around Taiya as she pulled her multitool out of her pocket, opened it and began backing out the screws.

The plywood floor panel was 16 inches wide and two feet long. When the last screw was out, Taiya sat back on her heels. "Time capsule from when Grampa built the cabin?" she asked Winter.

"Maybe. I'd prefer finding his stash of gold coins though."

Taiya jammed her multitool into the crack and pried up the floorboard. Decades of kitchen grime and dog hair came up out of the crack. She pulled the board to one side.

Inside was a very old carton of ammunition, covered with dust. Taiya pulled the ammo carton out of the hole, blew the dust off, and read the label: "6.5 x 55 Swedish."

Winter peered intently over her shoulder. "There's a piece of paper sticking out of the ammo box. What does it say?"

Taiya slid the paper out from under the top of the box, then popped the lid open with her thumb. It was still full of cartridges. She put the box down on the floor and unfolded the slip of paper. It was an old-fashioned receipt form, filled in with neat cursive script: "Anchorage Sporting Goods. Bill of sale. Used Husqvarna M96 Swedish Mauser and two boxes of ammunition."

"Where's the gun?" asked Chaewon.

Taiya ignored her and looked up at Winter with a puzzled look. "That's a weird kind of rifle, Dad. Why does it sound familiar?"

Winter also looked puzzled; a look that, suddenly, changed to horror.

"What?" said Chaewon and Artemis simultaneously.

"This is the same kind of gun…" said Winter, trailing off.

"That someone," continued Taiya, now remembering that old *Yukon Sun* story, "used to kill the guy who deserved to own half of my grampa's mining company."

The room went silent. Winter looked down at Taiya. His father's money paid for the house he lived in. For the child support when he was a kid. For Brett's trust fund. Now, for Taiya's university.

"But, Dad, the *Sun* story said grampa was in Alaska at a fly-in fishing lodge when it happened."

"He also told me one time he almost had enough hours to get his pilot's license. He could have borrowed a plane in Alaska and flown to the lake. There's no radar. No one would know."

"Jesus," said Artemis.

The room went silent, again. Winter let out a long breath and looked out the window at the shadows angling across the dark, frozen lake.

About the author

KEITH HALLIDAY is a born-and-raised Yukon author and award-winning local columnist. He is the author of the MacBride Yukon Kids Series and the Tar Sands Diplomat. After detours in the diplomatic service and management consulting in the big city, he lives in Whitehorse where he enjoys writing, skiing, fat-biking, hiking and kayaking.